THE LOST SAPE

Printed in Australia

Cover and internal design by Shawline Publishing Group Pty Ltd

First printing: July 2024

Shawline Publishing Group Pty Ltd

www.shawlinepublishing.com.au

Paperback ISBN 978-1-9231-0196-8

eBook ISBN 978-1-9231-7107-7

Hardback ISBN 978-1-9231-7119-0

Distributed by Shawline Distribution and Lightning Source Global

Shawline Publishing Group acknowledges the traditional owners of the land and pays respects to the Elders, past, present and future.

A catalogue record for this work is available from the National Library of Australia

DEBBIE HOFSTETTER

This book is dedicated to my grandchildren
who light up my life.
To everyone that reads *The Lost Sape,*
thank you so much.
I want to thank Nick for his enormous patience in guiding me
through plot holes, writers block and proof reading.
And Dex, who watched me type every word.

PROLOGUE

'I bid you adieu,' the little guy said.

Nicole knew he was real. In later years, her parents would say she imagined it, but she was sure they were wrong.

Nicole's parents always said that she had a vivid imagination. Of course, she did. At eighteen months, she'd developed at a fast rate. She walked early, and her vocabulary was extensive. She memorised her times tables and the entire periodic table by heart.

She walked steadily and met the adorable fellow halfway across the lounge room. Her parents sat, each with coffee and cake. The couch was cream with matching lamps on the side tables and a cabinet on the far side was filled with glass and ceramic elephants her mother collected from her travels. The breeze blew in, making the curtains float in the mild summer evening.

He was cute, like a child, with round, blue eyes, and a flat, pale face. He was only the size of a teddy bear. His power buzzed around him in a quiet sound of twinkles, mixing with his chocolate aura. He wore an orange suit with a matching tie and a hat with a tail atop his wispy, straw-coloured hair.

He told her his name was Hamish, a Thisbe from a world called Orra, and that she was special, that she was 'Magic'. He said that he would be back.

But that was nearly eleven years ago, and she waited and looked for him every day.

Was the Thisbe from Orra a liar? Or maybe Nicole's parents were right, and it had always just been in her head.

1

Raisa muttered to herself as she leapt from the balcony of her house in the Frail Realm, in an attempt to become airborne. She was outside the back of her house, in a private garden. She noted the beehives to one side and Dex's shed at the back boundary. No Dellamana would be without a fresh garden. Raisa did these jumps every day, numerous times, to practise her flying. She only managed to prevent an injury at the last moment before her feet crashed hard on the ground. She shuddered and massaged her foot. Raisa realised that even her wings were becoming useless, like the rest of her powers. How awful it was being a Magic living in the Frail Realm.

'You okay?' asked a voice above her.

'Yes, I'm fine.' Her jaw clenched. 'I can't even fly anymore, despite my wing size. I can't run and I have been struggling with a lot more.'

'Talk to me, Raisa. You don't need to go through this alone.'

Raisa pulled herself up to her feet and joined her brother on the balcony. They took a seat in a cushioned lounge. 'I can't meditate anymore. I am catching Frail problems, not just health-wise but mentally.'

'What does that mean?'

'I feel sad and just can't get enough sleep. When we first came here, I didn't feel the cold, but now I do; it's awful. I don't know how Frail ever get used to that feeling.'

'I'm sorry.' Dex tilted his head. 'It means that our baking business should be your main focus. You are a gifted chef. The word is out that our food is amazing and that is why we are doing so well.'

'I know.' She bit her lip. 'You are away so much in the back shed. I feel so alone. Even after all these years of living here, I still hate it. I sit for hours thinking about Orra and how stupid I was to lose my Illuminance. We wouldn't have to live here if I hadn't been so irresponsible.'

'I have noticed you daydreaming. It would be easier if you could get more interested in our other activities. Try and focus away from things you cannot change,' Dex said. 'And you must stay away from the gemstone in the wall. That can't be helping, wallowing over there for hours on end.'

'How can I when the Entrance to the Fire Garden, to my real home, is right across the street? It torments me that it is so close and yet I can't use it.'

'Just try to cut down the time you're over there.' His voice softened. 'Life here is difficult, but we're doing okay. The beehive is full, and the honey is selling fast. I'm building up a good supply of nectar dust.'

Raisa's expression hardened as she shot a look at Dex. 'You're trying to build a Tracer. You need two stones to trace. What would be the point?'

'I'm concentrating on one at present. It keeps me busy, and I love the challenge.'

'Dex, the Tracers in Orra are for Thisbe missions. They are used to pinpoint spots from two different realms. What use would one be? We can't go anywhere. What use is it to have one here in the Frail Realm? The construction would only be held together with your Voltz and won't be as strong as it would have been in Orra.'

'I got supplies delivered from Orra. Zosmine helped me,' Dex said.

Raisa clenched her jaw. 'You what? And why would you keep that from me?'

Dex stared blankly back at her.

'So, you really are serious about building a Tracer. How do you know it will even be able to work?'

'I love that I'm building one. You never know how handy it may be in future. You know how powerful they are, and we may get some benefit from one.'

What a waste of time, Raisa thought.

'I need to be doing Orra work. It makes me happy.'

Raisa had forgotten he had not lost his ability to telemute and could read her thoughts. It was true Dex managed to hold on to most of his powers, and she put it down to his strong saffron colour dose that only elite Dellamana received. He was a Scholar in the Vault, which held Magical texts that controlled curses and revenge spells. A Dellamana had to be very powerful to get such a role.

He loved tending to the generations of written Magic work, safeguarding the ancient powers and tracking the talismanic rings, making sure they were all accounted for. If such things were stolen, it would be catastrophic for all realms. In the wrong hands, it would cause trouble for all Magic and Frail, and the Dellamana would not be as secure as they were. Minding the ancient powers, besides taking care of the Rogue in the Frail Realm, was one of the core jobs Dellamana had.

'I want to focus on my Tracer after we finish the cook each day.'

Raisa sighed. Dex didn't need much sleep, and he needed activities to keep him busy. The large shed on the property was where he did all his Tracer work. Raisa knew he adored being there, doing the work, but she admitted to herself that she was jealous and lonely. But still, it was her fault they were here to begin with. She had lost the colour from her Crystal, her Illuminance; it wasn't his fault.

'There's no use going over it.'

'I take full blame for us being here. If I didn't take my Hallr Crystal on that Frail excursion, we wouldn't be in this mess.' Raisa thought of that fateful day when she took her Crystal to the Frail Realm, something that was gravely forbidden. No other Marnie would be stupid enough to pull such a stunt or even think of doing such a thing, and on top of that, it had been stolen.

Raisa doubled up, clutching her stomach, and let out a cry.

'What's wrong?' Dex asked, as he stood to reach her.

'Something is happening.'

'I can see that, but what? This is just another sickness.'

'I think I am getting a Helix message.'

'No, Raisa, what Magic would use a Helix on you directly? I haven't got one. Unless you were responsible in some way?'

'Don't look at me like that.'

'You either did something or you didn't. Just tell me.' Dex clenched his hands in fists.

'I must have, but I don't remember,' Raisa said.

'You hid it with a silk? I do not believe you would sink that low, Raisa. We are in this together. That you even had the power to silk and hide something from me is appalling. You should have told me, trusted me, Raisa.'

Raisa hung her head. She felt ashamed. It was true. She had covered her tracks with a magical cover called a silk. Dellamana used this talent to form some privacy around their thoughts. Dellamana can mind-read everything. There was an unspoken rule that to use it appropriately was fine. But to use it to deliberately cover a bad action was forbidden. Not that any Marnie would ever contemplate doing that. Raisa felt the enormous weight of a new emotion, remorse, and felt a wave of nausea run up her throat.

'Okay, we had better follow this lead. I will get your shawl. Can you walk?'

Raisa would do it if it killed her. No way would she ignore this.

They walked for twenty minutes past familiar houses, in the suburban, built-up area where they lived. As cars drove past them Dex put a protective arm around his sister. He said, 'I think we should head home; you are too weak.'

'It feels like my muscles are tearing,' Raisa said, with a pained expression. She looked around and saw they were outside the local school.

'There are too many people here. Let's go,' Dex whispered close to her ear.

'Oh my god, Dex, this is a Helix. I am connected to something close by,' Raisa whispered, her eyes wide. 'I can recognise it. Instead of it being in message form, it's pain.'

'Come on, let's get out of here. This will not end well.' Sweat trickled down his face.

A bell rang; they watched children pour out of buildings, the heat of the day etched on their faces, the little ones running with their bags flying behind them. The coil in Raisa's stomach had taken on a life of its own, pulling and pushing, but despite the pain, her eyes sparkled. She felt a rush of energy sweep through her.

At that moment, Dex's eyes nearly popped out of his head. 'It is a Helix, I just got it. That will mean all Magic will receive it. And because you got it first it means it was personal to you.'

'What does yours feel like?'

'No pain, just a heat, nearly scorching. How did you give a Frail a Spark, Raisa?' Dex said.

'Errr, um, I didn't.'

'You gave someone Magic cells and you can't deny this. It's a Spark directly from you, and they have your Magic molecules in them,' he hissed. 'Please don't let this be happening.'

They saw her at the same time. Dex covered his mouth with his palm.

Soon all the Dellamana would know. Not just them, but all Rogue, high and low. Raisa felt her face heat up with shock and fear of the consequences because she did not know how she had this connection with this girl.

The girl looked around, sensing something in her world shift. Her vision passed over them, then back, and she focused on the two individuals standing by the gate. At that moment, Raisa recognised her own power circulating around the girl. She realised why the Helix was in the form of pain, as she could see the girl held pain herself.

Raisa and Dex saw her aura glow at their presence, Magic meeting Magic. They saw her clutch the adult with her hand. The girl's eyes were still on them, wide and glowing.

'She's recognised us!' Raisa was breathing hard. 'She's not afraid, Dex.'

Dex let out a gasp of breath. Raisa felt euphoric as she stared at the face of a Marnie, a child Dellamana, and one of them. Not a full Marnie but close, by the looks of her. Raisa examined the girl's features, her pale skin and upturned nose. Her white-blonde hair was up in a ponytail, falling past her shoulders in curls and a weak, blue aura surrounded her entire body and moved with her. 'Dex, look at that aura. How beautiful is that.'

Dex's mouth was wide open. 'No Frail would be aware of her. Who is she?'

'The adult with her looks familiar,' Rasa said, as another

lovely bolt of energy ran through her. The welcome injection to her weak skills was an unintentional gift from the girl.

'She has Dellamana traits, yet why is she here in the Frail Realm? She has a curse in the form of a Tangle that will be fighting her Magic. I can see the Magic aura particles floating around her are yours. Raisa, what have you done? Why did you hide it from me? I could have helped you.'

Raisa's heart missed a beat at the pain she had caused her brother.

2

Nicole Murphy floated effortlessly, finishing off her dance. She gained such height off the floor. From the corner of her eye, she saw Miss Skoglan's smile before landing silently and finishing with the correct hand position. Nicole knew she was able to perfect her moves because of the Magic, or whatever it was, inside her.

Nicole took a breath and looked away. The girls in the class all curtsied, signaling the end of the dance routine, making sure it was perfect. If it wasn't, they would have to repeat until it was.

Miss Skoglan clapped her hands, a sound that cracked throughout the hall. Nicole covered her ears and watched her teacher's small body float across the floor, her white skirt swishing around her black ballet slippers.

Nicole suppressed a 'yahoo', as everything was up to Miss Skoglan's preposterous standards, and in a couple of seconds, she would be out of here, free for the rest of the weekend.

'Miss Avery and Miss Murphy, stay behind please,' Miss Skoglan announced.

Nicole expelled a breath and rolled her eyes. She gave a small wave to smiling classmates as they silently sashayed from class. Unfortunately for her, her cousin Lena was in the same class and was the ghastliest person on earth. Nicole had drawn the short straw when she got Lena as a cousin.

Through a glass window, Nicole could see her mother, Abby, and aunt waiting outside with the other parents. As usual, they were in deep conversations before the teacher spoke. Nicole and Lena, her stuck-up cousin, exchanged dirty looks before anyone could catch them.

Lena stood in the acceptable first position, although her arms were wrapped around her body, her right ballet slipper tapping. Tap tap tappy. Her signature move, which always irritated the hell out of Nicole.

'Mothers, could you join us?' Miss Skoglan's voice bounced off the white walls in need of a lick of paint, worn down by the passing of years.

Nicole heard the click of her mother's heels behind her, indicating she had been at a work meeting. Normally she worked from home and wore the loungewear she designed and sold online with great success. As her mother stood beside her, Nicole felt her manicured hand gently squeeze her shoulder. Nicole looked up and smiled at her mother's wink. She had brown eyes, and her dark hair was tied up in a ponytail. Despite this, Nicole recognised the constant strain on her face and the constant, deep welt around her neck, which was now red and swollen. Her Aunt Dree was dressed in jeans and a white linen shirt and had short-cropped dark hair, the same shade as her sister. On their feet they wore similar strappy sandals and blue bags crossed over their midsections. They all stood in a row, facing Miss Skoglan.

'I thought it best to discuss this as a group,' Miss Skoglan said, moving to stand in front of them, her eyes darting to each of them. Her lips tightened. 'When you girls came to me at the age of three, I quickly found out how talented you were. While I am very proud of you, teaching you for the past nine years has been fraught with your obvious dislike for one another. This is disturbing, especially since this has not improved over time.' She shook her head and gave them a side-eye.

'What does that mean exactly?' Abby asked.

'I am getting to that, Mrs Murphy.' Miss Skoglan glared at Lena's arms. Lena's response was only a shift of weight from one foot to another, which she immediately began to tap again.

'I believe what you need is a more professional approach to your classes. In order to do this, you are to be separated. The academy has offered one class each a week. This is a great honour.'

'But I love coming here,' Nicole said. She didn't want to pursue a professional career in dancing, unlike Lena. Unfortunately, she excelled in ballet and was pushed by her teacher and her mother. Nicole understood this; she had talent, and they didn't want her to waste it.

'Me too. I can't imagine going anywhere else!' Lena said, losing her cool composure.

Miss Skoglan raised her arched eyebrows. 'This is a fresh start, a new routine, and a place to learn without distraction. You are both too aware of each other; it is starting to affect not only your dancing, but the other members of the class. And that, girls, is not fair.'

'The academy?' Her aunt jumped at this notion, her delight apparent. The academy selected only the top dancers. Its reputation of a no-nonsense, strict work ethic was meant to be adhered to for any student.

Miss Skoglan nodded. 'As you know, the selecting team for the dance academy has been keeping an eye on you girls for a while. The academy only takes a handful of dancers per year and is the most exclusive dancing company in the country.'

'Oh my gosh, that's amazing.' Aunt Dree's mouth widened to a smile.

'I've never heard of anyone being accepted without a full interview,' Nicole's mother said.

'Miss Skoglan, I don't want to go to the academy.' Nicole's eyebrows wrinkled.

'Me either, at least not yet,' Lena said, her voice strong, confident.

'Why?' Miss Skoglan and her aunt said at the same time.

Shaking her head, Miss Skoglan said, 'The only way you two can remain here is to work on your relationship. You have one term to do this, otherwise you will be going to the academy. Fix this nonsense; you are both old enough to take responsibility. This is not a request.' She pointed a finger at them both.

'I'm too young to go to the academy, the minimum age is fourteen.' Nicole ground her teeth. She knew the academy was strict. Dancing there would mean far more work and would be too serious. Up 'til now, dancing came easily for her, and it was the only outlet she enjoyed, despite having to share it with Lena. The pain that was always with her, all over her body, was getting worse when she danced. She didn't think that she would last too much longer. If she didn't have dance, she would have no place to express herself, no outlet.

'The girls are not very nice there – too competitive.'

Miss Skoglan waved a hand in front of Lena. 'That will do you good, Miss Avery. Give you both a taste of what you put everyone else through.'

Miss Skoglan looked at Nicole. 'If you can't fix your issues with one another, you will replace your Wednesday class for the academy, and Lena, you will go Thursday. Classes are at five p.m.' She walked over to her desk and returned with information sheets that she handed to the mothers.

Nicole's face burned. She glanced at Lena; her cousin's eyes were brimming with tears, her face flushed. It would never work, and they both knew it, because they could not stand each other.

3

Nicole threw her backpack into the boot of the car with a little too much force and the zip cracked open. Lena's mother had parked next to them, and she heard the excitement in her aunt's voice. 'This is time for a double celebration. I can't believe the girls are going to the academy.'

'Don't get ahead of yourself. It's next term,' Abby said, as she unlocked the car door by pressing the keys in her hand.

Nicole noticed her mother didn't have a smile on her face, in fact, she looked worried. 'What's the matter, Abby?' her aunt asked, noticing it as well.

'It's nothing, just tired.' Nicole's mother had a terrible time getting to sleep, but that was not the reason for her distant look. Nicole didn't want to be pushed further in dancing and she knew her mother was feeling the same.

Aunt Dree accepted this response and proceeded to leave. 'Alright, we'll see you soon.' Aunt Dree left with a wave. Lena looked the other way.

'Typical,' Nicole said. She opened the car door and immediately fished her phone from the glove box and started tapping on it.

'You are just as bad as your cousin,' Abby said, and her face went from smiling to blank.

Nicole curled her lips; she was filthy. 'What was Aunt Dree talking about?'

'It's Sara's birthday. They're having a barbeque in the park.'

'And you're telling me this now?' Nicole dug her fingernails into her palms.

'Come on, she hardly ever has family birthdays. It's not her fault you don't get along with Lena.'

Nicole ground her teeth, making her mouth twist. She focused on her phone.

'You're going to have to try to get on with Lena better if you're to stay out of the academy,' her mother said, changing the subject.

'The teachers there will be pushing me more. Even these classes hurt me.' Nicole pushed her hand into her left side.

'Is it getting any worse?' Abby put her hand on Nicole's shoulder.

Nicole nodded. 'I don't understand why this pain is happening to me. Maybe I should take a break; it might be the best for everyone.' Nicole shivered at the thought. The pain started out slowly one day, when she was about ten. She had woken to a strange tingling sensation in her arms, and this had quickly led to pain in her fingers. That would last for a day or so and the next morning the pain would be in a different area. She particularly hated it when her ears ached and her eyes were so sore she could hardly keep them open. Her mother had at first taken her to many doctor appointments. It was simply put down to 'growing pains'.

'If you want to do that, you can, Nicole, at any time. Is that really what you want?'

She shook her blonde hair out of the bun and massaged

her head. 'I love the feeling dancing gives me. Despite the stomach pains, it gives me such a feeling of being in control, and I couldn't imagine what it would be like to stop.'

'Look, you did well today, especially after last night,' Abby said. 'After I went to bed, did you get some sleep?'

Nicole thought about last night. They had sat up drinking hot chocolates and discussing the two kids about her age that were at the school yesterday. They weren't exactly strangers, which was clear in the way that they had only focused on Nicole, and, in turn, Nicole had recognised them, even though she hadn't seen them before. Who were they and what did they want? It confused the hell out of her. 'No, I was awake all night. They're connected to me, the girl more than the boy.' Nicole watched her mother pat her leg with a shaking hand. 'But even that boy, there is something about him.'

They both sat in silence until they pulled into their driveway.

'Why don't you have a lie down before Sara's party? And, Nicole, no phone today.'

Nicole got out of the car. She was breathing heavily, trying not to lose it. She did not want to see Lena again.

4

A fist banged on her door, startling her. 'You've got fifteen minutes 'til we leave,' her father, Jack, said, his voice loud. She heard his footsteps fade away. Nicole looked at her watch and was surprised she had slept for two hours, but it was understandable since she had hardly had a wink of sleep the previous night. She got up, yawned and rubbed her eyes. She decided that she better not irritate her dad and upset her mother and just go to Sara's party, but she took her time looking for the right outfit and slipped her phone into her back pocket. As she left her room, the air conditioner started up playing the same dim sound, halfway between a pulsating whooshing and a tune. It was frustrating when the repair man on his numerous visits looked at her straight in the eyes and said that she was being a time-waster. No one else could hear it. Nicole rolled her eyes, stepped over her bag and everything that had burst out from the broken zip and closed the door.

She dawdled downstairs and found her mother packing food for the party in their large, modern kitchen. On the island bench, she spotted her latest school report, which was open on the page proclaiming: 'Nicole works to capacity, but her work is not up to standard. She displays poor concentration and is often moody'. Nicole flicked it across the bench as she walked past.

'You're not to worry about those comments. We know you are more capable than they would ever imagine.'

'It doesn't bother me,' Nicole grumbled. To be honest, it bugged her to no end. She hated the way being misjudged made her chest hurt. There seemed to be an ongoing fight for her real self to emerge, whoever that was.

As she had advanced rapidly through the grades of dancing, her pain increased. It was everywhere – in her head, fingers, even her mouth, but her legs and feet were never affected, allowing her to do jumps and manoeuvers to an extremely high level of skill. It was as if the talent was being threatened by the pain. A thought Nicole pondered all the time these days.

School work seemed basic, yet she could not master it, and because her moods were so uncontrollable, she couldn't focus on anything, let alone the often mindless stuff they taught. This meant she frequently skipped class and hid in the toilet or out on the back field. She knew it was more than being a preteen.

'You're going to brush your hair at least,' her mother said.

Nicole looked at her reflection in the large mirror hanging on the side wall of the kitchen. A girl with large, almond-shaped green eyes and white-blonde wavy hair was staring back, the signs of sleep etched on her pale skin.

'I don't want to go.' Nicole immediately regretted opening her mouth.

'It's been ages since you've seen all your cousins. We can't keep on doing this, Nicole. They are family.'

Nicole groaned loudly, which hurt the back of her throat. The Avery family had three children: Jaya, fourteen; Lena, twelve; and Sara, turning ten today. While she loved

Jaya, she knew that wherever she was, Lena was bound to be. The Avery siblings were close. Nicole was aware of the wave of emotion that would come over her when she arrived at the park; she anticipated the pure jealousy. The other two always made a huge effort to include her, and she did appreciate that.

'How about tomorrow I get you pizza and ice cream for dinner?'

The compromise sounded fair, but Nicole couldn't bring herself to accept it. Instead, her face was red with pent-up anger.

Her father arrived, his hair flying. He kicked the stool hard. 'This discussion is over.' He glared at Nicole. 'Out you go.' Every time her father yelled at her, he would hurt himself. He broke a glass and then stood on it, or he would face plant on the ground for no reason. One time when they were out and he was telling her off, a dog came out of nowhere and deliberately peed on his leg. This only enraged her father and dismayed her mother. Nicole smiled at the memory by mistake.

'You think this is funny?' He marched her to the garage and out to the car with the odd painful poke to her back. She tried jumping away, but he was right behind her.

Behind her, she heard her mother sigh. 'Oh, Jack, stop it.'

'Buckle up. Not another word.' His veins were standing out on his temples. 'I am warning you, Nicole, if you do not behave for Sara and your mother, I will take you out of dancing. I am totally sick of this nonsense and your lack of respect.'

Nicole flinched; she hated arguing with her dad. Their relationship had once been close, but now it bordered on dislike. She didn't want to make him worse, so she shut her mouth.

Her mother approached and got in the front passenger

seat. Her father banged on the steering wheel and made a speedy reverse out of the driveway.

'Please calm down, Jack,' Abby said.

Fine adult role model, Nicole thought. She hoped they wouldn't hit anything and kept her head down.

The rest of the trip was silent, as Nicole avoided the daggers her father's eyes shot her in the rear-view mirror. At the park, she spotted their allocated area decorated with balloons, streamers, and a 'Happy 10th Birthday' sign painted on canvas displayed on a frame. Nicole recognised the flare and handwriting of her cousin Jaya. The painting had a sketched image of Sara. The likeness was astounding. Jaya was the artist, Lena the dancer, and Sara was the acrobatic one, but all of them excelled in school, especially Lena. There was nothing she was not good at.

Nicole stood alone and her muscles tensed as she saw Jaya and Lena together. With a deep sigh, she realised she was part of another wardrobe malfunction. Nicole and Lena wore the same creamy halter-neck top and jean shorts, right down to the white lace on the hem. In the past, they wore the same gear, usually black jeans and red tops. Jaya realised the gaff and shrugged as if to say, 'What are the odds?'

5

Nicole wandered away and settled on a boulder at the side of the park. It was a pretty place with lots of open space. It had swings, basketball hoops and a zip line, which was not too high. Nicole watched Lena zoom across and Sara impatiently waiting her turn.

Nicole was sick of everything spiralling out of control. The Lena thing started when they were babies. Her mother had told her they would scream their lungs out when together. Surely that was not normal behaviour? Both were nearly thirteen and still the nastiness remained, and tensions ran high. Was this to continue for the rest of their lives? Nicole shuddered at the thought. She was different. She could do things no one knew about, even her parents. Her mother suffered from terrible anxiety due to her dad's outbursts and Nicole knew it was all related.

A buzzing noise caught Nicole's attention; she looked from side to side. Then she clearly heard her name being spoken. Alarm registered, her senses alert. A chill ran down her spine.

'I am talking to you, Miss Murphy.'

He said my name. Her scalp constricted.

Nicole jumped and looked for the person speaking.

'Do not be alarmed.'

'I don't talk to strangers.'

'Excellent, we are your friends.'

'Don't panic.'

She couldn't move, not a muscle. She could only breathe; the rest of her was rock-solid. She felt a lump in her throat, and she was internally screaming. She could feel her throat vibrating, her eyes searching for the thing that had done this to her.

Then her gaze landed on who was speaking. It stood behind a low bush a few steps away from where she sat. Where had he come from? She focused on the unfamiliar shape and her blood pulsated in her head. *It was not human.*

'Don't be fooled by my appearance, it is temporary,' he said, tossing his head, throwing back dreadlocked hair in great clumps. Nicole looked at his squashed face, out of proportion body, skinny arms and wrists, and swollen red hands. As he moved, a yellow mist hovered around his body.

'So sorry. I didn't mean to alarm you. I've never talked to a Frail before.' He let out a nervous laugh.

Nicole was immediately freed from the hold he had on her. She flexed her hands and legs and gulped for air.

'I am Rook. I apologise for freezing you. That was a Spark that would not have hurt you.' He cleared his throat.

What was he talking about? Her body screeched at her to run, but she couldn't help but look at the contorted thing.

'I would love the opportunity to start again, without my mistake. We are here to assist you. We are Dellamana from Orra.' Rook grinned, showing perfect teeth.

How can one so sloppy have perfect chompers? Nicole thought, looking at his white teeth.

'Orra?' Her eyes widened in interest. The name sounded familiar to her. She swallowed hard, but it didn't help her feel better. She hoped she wouldn't vomit, but at this stage it was fifty-fifty.

Nicole remembered that her Thisbe, the one she had been waiting for, had mentioned that same word.

Rook's mouth dropped with surprise, after he heard her thought. 'There was a Thisbe visit?'

Nicole took a double take at Rook.

He nodded. 'We can telemute, which means everything you think I can hear verbally. Tell me about this visit. Because there has never been in the history of Thisbe missions one that has gone missing. It just doesn't happen. In fact, it's impossible.'

'He said his name was Hamish.' *He never came back.* Nicole recounted the memory of the little fellow who had been so enthusiastic about finding her and so keen on putting things right within her world. The best thing about it was as she grew up, it gave her an anchor, that there was more to her than an average child.

'Frail are humans, for your information, and you are not one of them,' Rook carried on.

'What did you just do to me?' She bit her lip and looked around. *Didn't he mention a 'we'?* But there was no one else around.

'Oh, that was just a minor mistake due to my nervousness in meeting you. It happens, but do not worry, I have control over it now.'

Nicole eyed him, the edges of his silhouette blurry. Her hands trembled. He had taken away her ability to move. Even though it was only for a couple of seconds, she did not consider this trivial.

'Frail are unaware of us and the work we do.' He took a step closer to her. 'You have skills. We need to evaluate those. If you stay here, they will become weaker.'

Nicole scurried back on the boulder and put her hands up to motion him not to come closer. She wasn't in view of her family now. Trees secluded them. She looked back and forth, considering her options.

'We know about the visit at the school yesterday.' Rook scrunched his eyes.

That did it. How could he possibly know that? *Wait a minute*, she thought. *This is it!* A buzz shivered over her. Rubbing her arms, Nicole weighed up the meeting with the Thisbe when she was a baby. She expected *him* to come back as he had promised, not this dishevelled creature that looked a million miles away from being magic. She took a brief moment to close her eyes and take a deep breath.

'I have to tell you, Nicole, that you also have a Tangle that has grown and interwoven inside you, and it has become mature. The Tangle is a curse, and it is glued to your Magic molecules and is suffocating them. It is the reason we found you, as it was this Tangle that sent out a Helix message, which all Rogue will receive and know where you are. Without Voltz, you are unprotected.'

Nicole's hands shook at the notion. 'What is Rogue?'

'They are the individuals that are not Frail that live in your world. Some have high Magic skills, others are problematic and need monitoring,' Rook said. 'This is done in Orra's head office called Rolte. Rolte is managed by the Prefects who are powerful Dellamana.

'When the Tangle grows, it produces Ripples and draws unsavoury Rogue that do not want to be dragged in. They have very little power to stop this from happening. They have a devastating effect on the Frail that has been infected.' Rook shook his head. 'This Tangle is creating a storm within you. It has damaged your Magic molecules and you do not have any Voltz, which means you can't grow and maintain Magic.'

'What are Voltz?' Nicole stuttered.

'You have not grown any more Magic Voltz since you

were born. The Tangle is taking over them. And since you do not have a Hallr Crystal, you do not have any Illuminance in which to be able to grow more Voltz,' Rook said. 'Voltz are what sets us apart from other magical beings. They are our life force and feed our colours, giving us all different skill sets in order to help Frail and control Rogue. They make us the most powerful magical force there is. Without them we are not really a true Dellamana, you see, Nicole.'

'What happens if I don't grow more?' Nicole walked a few steps closer to him.

'Even if you didn't have the Tangle, this would happen, but with it, it's happening much faster. Your Magic cells would die out, and without those, you will not have enough Frail cells to sustain life.'

Nicole took a moment to accept what he meant.

'This is what you have been wondering about all your life. They are the reason you could do so many things that other Frail could not. The Tangle is the one that is causing all your problems, like the pain you now have in your arms.'

Nicole studied him while rubbing her aching arms. 'Like how I could talk early, walk, dance well and used a laptop to educate myself?'

He smiled. 'All those things.' He nodded. 'You have a responsibility to professionally grow your Magic and work out how to remove the Tangle, and this can only occur with a Magic intervention in Orra. You know you are different, and we can confirm this, if you would trust us.'

Nicole was deep in thought. Could this be an answer to all her aches and pains, her family problems, and her strange abilities? But happening in a totally different way than she expected? She had listened intently to catch him if he was fibbing. She had butterflies racing around her tummy. She felt lightheaded. With a flat tone of voice, she asked, 'I haven't been using my skills in the correct way.'

'Your Magic cannot thrive without care; we have to start this immediately.'

'How?' Nicole couldn't trust the feeling that this was it. At least not yet; it was all happening too fast. And what would her parents have to say about this? She couldn't just leave. She would be in deep trouble if she did that.

'We will do a wedge. This is the way we travel from realm to realm. Not far from here is a rock wall. Implanted in this wall is a tiny, quartz gem, the Entrance to Orra.'

With a fake smile, Nicole asked, 'How big is this gem in the wall?'

'It is smaller than your fingernail.'

Nicole's eyes widened and she stepped back, shaking her head.

'I know you are overwhelmed at the moment. You are about to take charge of your skills instead of them taking over you.'

Nicole's skin flushed, and her gaze bounced all over the place.

Rook smiled. 'It is grand that you met Thisbe. That is all the proof you need.'

She never forgot the name; it had given her the beginning of an explanation of her strange talents. She knew he had been real.

6

Nicole jumped as a mangy cat appeared next to Rook. He had bald patches and other strands of hair standing on end, and his tail had no hair whatsoever.

'This is Dinkletons. He is a Stoneycraft who lives on a planet called Vail, close to Orra,' Rook said.

Nicole thought the cat smiled. His right eye was gross and in dire need of a vet; it was wonky and gooey.

'This eye opening and closing is about the number of facts I am receiving. This sickly appearance is a side effect of wedging. Your gravity is harsh.'

She nearly fell over backwards as the cat spoke.

'There is a whole race of cats?' Nicole touched her throat.

'We are not cats,' he said, trying to keep a straight face and failing.

'You look like a cat to me.' Nicole rubbed her chin. Not a healthy one, with his missing clumps of hair, dripping nose, and exposed sharp, brown claws. His ears were deflated and flopped on his head. And the eye looked infected, with weepy green muck.

'We hear your thoughts. It is natural to us,' Rook said.

'Telemuting is the formal name,' Dinkletons said.

'Are you going to do something to my brain?' *Are they aliens?*

'Course not. We are not aliens, not in the sense you are thinking about,' Dinkletons said. 'Just because we don't come from the Frail Realm does not automatically make us aliens. We operate on Voltz, and they don't. There are Magic worlds and there are non-Magic worlds. Voltz make us Magic – they are like light electricity bolts that fire up our Magic.'

They don't look Magical in any way. Nicole looked from one to the other.

'Ha, you would not know a Magic creature, even if you fell over one,' the cat scoffed.

Nicole's cheeks reddened; they heard her thoughts.

'If you knew how many types of Magical creatures are living in your world, you would be staggered,' Dinkletons said.

'The Frail Realm is always full of Rogue. Prefects work on a place in Orra called Rolte and they make sure there are not too many Rogue in your realm at any one time as this can cause an imbalance with Frail, causing allergies or sickness. Rolte ensures that rules are obeyed, and they stay in control,' Rook said.

Nicole felt unbalanced on her feet. 'I have been uncontrolled as well.'

'That is why we are here, to give you the opportunity to put things right,' Dinkletons said.

'Our Magic is made up of particles called Voltz. These are developed from our environment, and we are able to absorb them into our bodies to link us to our powers. Voltz are embedded in every Magical molecule inside us and also create our aura.' He indicated the yellow mist circulating all around him. 'This keeps our Magic growing,' Rook said.

'I can see the yellow. Is that your aura?'

He nodded.

'What do the Voltz look like? I can't see them.' Nicole peered at the colour moving around Rook.

'There is a special place in Orra called the Moon Garden where you can see them. They are like purple arrows that join together,' Rook said. 'Once your Magic is under control, you will be permitted to see them anytime. Voltz allow Dellamana to manufacture Magic continually. With this Magic, they are able to do their jobs and assist your world.'

Nicole felt like her eyes were going to pop. It would take a while for all of this to sink in. She wiped her wet palms on her shorts.

Dinkletons asked Rook, 'Is Thisbe on the ground? I want him to go check the family, keep an eye on them.' He pointed a paw in the direction of Nicole's family through the trees.

She remembered how small he was, with a perfectly formed body, blue shiny eyes, and matching lashes. She even remembered the sound of his voice. 'How many Thisbes are there?'

'Thousands. It's rare to find out their specific names. Hamish must have liked you.'

'Can you tell us more about the Thisbe visit?' Rook asked.

'My parents were sure I was going crazy and convinced me it had been all in my mind.'

'That Thisbe did not put in a report that he had spoken to you,' Dinkletons said and looked at Rook.

'What does that mean?'

'Hamish went missing after meeting you. We knew he was lost, but now we know when he went off the grid,' Rook said.

'Wonder what happened to him...' Nicole frowned.

'It has been decades since a Thisbe went missing.

Prefects have been trying to locate him without success. They are not easy to kill but can suffer – that is the worry.'

A familiar, soft music caught Nicole's attention, but at this moment, it was the least of her problems.

'We have to go,' Dinkletons said.

'My parents will freak out. Why didn't anyone come over when they saw you talking to me?'

'Frail are not able to see any Magic unless they are sanctioned to be visible,' Rook said in a soft voice.

'There is no time left. You will come to Orra with us,' Rook said. 'You can come back and explain to your parents what is going on, but for now, we have run out of time.'

'We promise if at any time you want to come back, we will return you without hesitation. You are in charge. You must get your Magic cells under a prescription.' Dinkletons spoke fast. 'You will be able to organise your skill set to work properly for you once you have your Illuminance.'

Nicole tried to calm herself; she put her hand on her head to stop herself from thinking about the consequences this would lead to. She leaned away from the cat. It was so creepy watching him say the words, his mouth moving, his whiskers pulsing wide from his face.

'You haven't seen anything; a talking cat will be nothing.'

'Tell me again.' The anticipation made her swallow hard. She looked over to where her parents were having fun – they didn't look at all worried about her. But still, to drop off the face of the earth was cruel. They would be beside themselves and her dad would crack it.

'You come to Orra with us, where we will investigate your origins and Magical position, among the other things we mentioned,' Rook said.

'I believe you. It's freaky though.' Nicole's hands covered her face. She had to make things better for herself and her parents. 'I find it really hard to go with you. It goes against everything my parents have told me to do.'

'We understand, but we do have proof. You remember Thisbe, and you know there is something more about you that you need to understand. The Tangle has grown into Ripples – you must fix these as soon as you can. Staying here is not an option.'

'Let me go over and talk to my mother.' Nicole was uneasy.

'She won't let you go, Nicole, and you know it,' Rook said, shaking his head. 'They will understand later, I promise you.'

7

Raisa and Dex had arrived home from the school. Inside, Raisa shrugged off her shawl and sat down on the grey lounge. Across one wall were books and the journals that Dex had written before they got their computers up and running. He had collated a collection of information about Rustic activity.

Raisa gasped; the pain in her back was terrible, the feathers of her wings were digging into her skin. As her magic Voltz, the building blocks of all Dellamana power, had lessened she had grown wings, which symbolized her magical weakness.

Dex approached her. 'What can I get you?'

Raisa was hyperventilating but managed a broken, 'I can't catch my breath.'

Dex raced out to the kitchen door and returned with her puffer. She took two deep inhales and let the medicine seep into her lungs. 'Thanks. I need to think about what I'm going to do.' Raisa flinched.

'Get some rest. You can't do anything in this state.'

Raisa got up and walked slowly down the tiled corridor and into her room. Her bed was a double with a brown quilt cover and matching pillows. She had a walk-in closet and row upon row of different coloured kaftans and scarves. Beside that, she had her own bathroom. The windows overlooked the back garden and the fan above her bed just moved the hot air around. The sun filled the room with stifling heat. Sweat covered her body, her wings gently laying on her back. Raisa was anxious as she had slept far into the Saturday just gone. That was another problem with her weakening power: she slept, sometimes for days. Not today – there was too much to think about.

Because of the Helix message that was sent to everyone, Nicole Murphy was out in the open and in danger from Rogue wanting to take parts of her aura. Raisa knew that without a Crystal and her colours, the Illuminance, Nicole would not be able to hang on to the tiny aura she had, and her Magic cells were in serious danger of being wiped out by the Tangle. Without her Magic molecules, she wouldn't have enough Frail cells to live. It wasn't that easy just to go and get more blood. Because she was part Dellamana, it didn't work like that. No more Frail cells could be made, but Raisa thought they could be made stronger. The girl had to maintain what Magic cells she had.

Raisa thought, somehow, she had transferred enough power to make Nicole Magic. She racked her brain to remember when this could have happened. When they first arrived in the Frail Realm, there were only a few times she ventured out on her own. Raisa was sure she had silked all this information to prevent her brother from knowing what she did. With her dwindling skills, she had forgotten as well. Not a very clever thing to do.

***

Raisa sat up and rubbed her eyes. She looked out the window at the sun rising in the early morning.

The door opened. Dex leaned on the door frame. 'She

has Marnie characteristics, caused by a Spark, and also a Tangle from who knows where,' Dex snapped. She could tell by the clothes that he still wore from the day before that he hadn't slept either. 'A gift and a Tangle are not a good combination. That poor girl, she will have a combination of talents. Abilities no Frail would be able to understand, if they knew. Not to forget the many doses of trauma that will never leave her. That is no way for a young girl to live.'

'I'm in the dark as much as you are.' Raisa sat up, balancing, waiting for her wings to shift into place.

'Don't even try to lie. I can't believe that you would hide this from me and use a silk on your own brother.' He raised his voice, startling her. Dex never yelled.

Raisa dropped her head, unable to look at him. She knew she was going to have to deal with this silking mistake with Dex, admit she had done it, and, even worse, he would learn what she had done. When she was in Orra, she used this skill all the time in order to obstruct the telemuting abilities of the Dellamana and keep her thoughts private. But to have done this to her brother, her only ally, was just the worst thing. Despite the fear, she felt a rush of excitement.

'This might not be all bad,' she said and followed him into the kitchen where he had made honey and banana smoothies. They had four commercial ovens for their baking business and a large working space with two island benches.

Dex sat down at the kitchen table. Raisa joined him and took a sip of her drink. 'That girl is Magic and living in the wrong world. Raisa, tell me you had nothing to do with that Tangle.'

'The Spark is mine, obviously. I could see that. How can a Spark make a Tangle unless something was added to it at the time?'

'I know the Spark is yours! Everyone would know that now the Helix message has been sent.' He stood up and banged his fist on the table. Raisa flinched. 'There is definitely a toxin there. Most Tangles consist of half to full toxins. I didn't have enough time to study her, but it will be poisoning her and those around her if the Tangle has advanced into Ripples.'

'I'm sorry, Dex. I don't know. I wish I could tell you more,' she whispered.

'Something happened the first month we were here. Remember at the Hale farm?' he said, accusation in his voice.

'Yes, we went there for avocados.' Raisa remembered.

'You came home upset one day; you were flustered.' Dex jabbed a finger at her. 'I knew something was up.'

'The adult at the school with the girl is her mother. Her name is Abby, I remember that,' Raisa mumbled.

'You know them?' His body froze on the spot. 'You know they saw us and the girl recognised us as Magic? I heard her.'

'Abby is Lily Hale's daughter.' She looked up at Dex. 'That is all I remember. I had no Illuminance; I didn't think I had enough power to cause a Frail to have Dellamana cells.'

Dex's voice cracked. 'Yet you did manage it very well, because she is here.'

8

Dex handed his Crystal to Raisa. 'Tell me what happened. I will bring down the silk. We need to get to the bottom of this.'

Raisa fiddled with his Hallr Crystal, admiring the beauty of it, the light and colour; his Illuminance still shone bright. 'We hadn't been here long, maybe just a few weeks. I was out getting avocados from the Hale orchard. I knew there was only one person that lived there and that was Lily because I had been there many times. I was behind a tree when a car drove in. Lily came out of the house, and they all left together.'

He sat down now, with a sigh of relief.

'I went inside. I know – I am sorry.' Raisa knew they had made a pact never to go inside Frail houses.

Dex covered his eyes.

Raisa continued, her eyes closed and her mind focused. 'Cupcakes sat on the bench. I was hungry, so I had one or three. Then I got rid of two Puck – they were so gross and sticky. They were sliding all over the floors in the lounge. Dirty, little Rogue, but they did clean up the carpet like a vacuum but left welts all over the place. Frail would never see those marks. It was interesting being inside a Frail dwelling. I never realised how untidy they are.'

'Your skills were stronger than we thought if you were able to get rid of Rogue Puck. I know myself how hard they are to remove, even outside.'

'In a bedroom, I picked up a man's ring. It belonged to Lily's husband who had died years before. It had memories inside; vibrations of history invaded my mind and gave me a spike of strength to my Magic.'

'Tell me you didn't take the ring!' Dex groaned.

'I wasn't going to do anything with it. I was just enjoying the feelings. They were raw and made me feel wonderful. Then I heard a noise. I still had the ring in my hand when I went into the lounge.'

Raisa then remembered clearly.

'Lily had come back into the house, and we came face-to-face in the living room. We were both paralysed for a moment. Lily shouted to give her the ring. I said to her that I would leave, but I called her by her name.

'I reached out to try and calm her and to let her know I would not hurt her, because not in a million years would I want to harm a Frail. But I was so overwhelmed by the situation that a Spark came through me, and Lily was knocked off her feet and looked injured. It was a matter of seconds, and I was shocked, confused about how it happened. Sparks never have that effect. To make matters worse, then Abby and her sister arrived.'

'So, the adult at the school is Lily's daughter, Abby,' Dex said. 'Lily is the grandmother.'

Raisa felt chills run down her back. She nodded.

'Ah, Abby was pregnant with the Magic girl when you entered the Hale house. The power pulled to the baby. The child is pure force. The energy would attach there. That's who the girl is. You made her unborn child develop Magic molecules.'

Raisa moved carefully and sat in a chair. She felt lightheaded. 'I barely touched Lily.'

'It doesn't change what happened. Frail babies are extremely susceptible to taking on Magic currents – there's a whole section in Orra Vault to make sure this doesn't happen.' He sat upright.

'But you saw her! She is unharmed and gifted.' Raisa felt attacked, but deep down she knew she shouldn't. She deserved all of this. She had it coming.

'I have studied this in Orra's Vault. When Frail are exposed to Dellamana power, their cells can't process it. Nicole as a small, growing baby in the womb could have been killed or propelled to another realm.'

'She has my power; I grew it, nurtured it, and gave it to her by mistake. I would never let any Frail have it otherwise. You know that, Dex. We could work together, if the Prefects allow us to.'

'They won't let you near her.' Dex shook his head in dismay.

'Oh, lighten up. A few particles will rejuvenate me.' Raisa had to take this opportunity regardless of how Dex felt.

Dex looked around tentatively. 'Raisa, you have broken one of the biggest Laws: "Do not touch a Frail".'

'But I didn't.'

'You did with the Spark. It is the same thing. They will come for her.' Dex stood up and stretched.

She shook her head. 'It was *not* my Spark.'

'There was no one else there.'

Raisa felt awful but wondered where the Tangle came from. 'There had to be, and you know it.'

9

'What happened to Lily Hale when she fell over?' Dex was pacing the room.

'I'm not sure. I got out fast.'

'At best, her sanity would have been removed, and at worst, you could have killed her,' Dex said.

'A Spark cannot kill a Frail, Dex. Stop that.'

'Well, you are to blame because even if a Spark didn't do it, it has played a part. If you weren't there, this would not have happened.'

'I tried to go back to help later, but I was too scared. Can we hide?' Raisa's hands shook violently.

'Are you serious right now? No one can hide from Thisbe.'

'Orra would have got the Helix at the same time you did.'

Raisa spluttered and trying the find the right words said, 'Let me talk to her, or at least try?'

'It is not something I can control, so why ask me?'

'Can we try to be positive? It may be a way for us to get back to Orra if I fix this.'

'We don't need more heat, Raisa. We have enough trouble just getting by.'

'With a Tangle wrapped around her molecules, she would have been suppressing her Magic for a long time. Probably all her life,' Raisa said, tightening her fists.

The tug in Raisa's tummy was starting up again. She jumped up, grabbed her shawl, and ran out the door with Dex close behind, rolling his eyes.

They took a few wrong turns before Raisa stopped at a park.

'She's here.' Through the trees, Raisa saw the girl from the school and two distorted figures. They were in deep conversation.

'I told you, Raisa, we can't interfere when Orra is in charge.'

Raisa started to cry. Just seeing them, despite their distortions – they were splendid. She recognised Dinkletons, the Stoneycraft from Vail and designer of stars. And Rook, whose talents in Orra were renowned in the Vault. It made perfect sense that once they received the Helix message, they would be the ones that were sent to help her.

Without warning, Raisa swept off her shawl and flew into the air, her wings wide in the sunlight, leaving Dex in the shade. Raisa was surprised at her abrupt surge of energy. She hadn't been airborne for a long time. If this was a taste of what the girl could offer her, she couldn't imagine what more was to come. Being so close to her pure Magic caused a flash through her body. She fanned her wings to the widest girth and soared through the trees. She felt amazing.

Who knew adrenaline was that wonderful?

***

'We have company, Rook,' Dinkletons said.

Hovering six feet above them was a girl with huge red

wings. She looked to be Nicole's age. A wingless boy stood beneath her. Nicole locked eyes with the girl. A feeling of recognition swept through her: they were the same two that were outside her school yesterday. Nicole squinted. She hadn't noticed the wings yesterday, but how could she miss them? They were wide of girth and red. They were so close. She got dizzy and fell. Rook leapt to her safety, protecting her with his short arms. It was the first time he had even touched a Frail, and he tried not to harm her with a messy spell, this time with success.

'Nicole, we have to go right now,' Rook said, and all at once she was thrown high in the sky up to the clouds, both Rook and Dinkletons next to her. She screamed. Below her was the park. The people were a long way off.

'We are about to wedge to Orra. Hold our hands. Or in my case, take a paw.' Dinkletons' whiskers quivered.

Nicole closed her eyes, unable to look down. The breath was taken from her as she plummeted down towards the ground. She needed to look even though she was terrified. Great balls of light engulfed them, falling all over their bodies. She took a careful look at Rook and Dinkletons, scared to make any big moves as the direction changed abruptly with horizontal twist and turns, the light racing with them, making circles that made her dizzy. Water engulfed them, as if they were in the middle of a breaking wave. Feeling utterly present in the moment, Nicole took a second to stare at her surroundings.

Trees had separated Nicole's parents from where she sat, but they had known where she'd walked off to. If they came looking for her, they would discover she wasn't there and panic. Nicole counted thirty seconds before she finally came to a stop.

'You did well,' Rook said, his eyes bright. 'There are two Thisbe with your family group. They will make sure your parents don't notice you're gone.'

Nicole didn't care how they were going to do this, just as long as they did. Filled with relief, she gasped for breath.

'Where are we? Did we go through the gem in the wall?' She got up off the soft grass where she had been ejected from the light passageway.

'Yes, we did. That was the big drop. The gem is a long hall that connects the Frail Realm to the Entrance,' Rook said.

'I saw those two yesterday at my school. I didn't see the wings, though, on the girl. They were covered.'

'Raisa and her brother, Dex. They have lived in the Frail Realm for many years,' Rook said.

Nicole wrinkled her nose. 'They kind of looked like me.'

'We are called Dellamana, and we all have similar traits, but at the same time we are unique.'

'Are you telling me I am one of you?' Nicole's eyes widened.

'Nicole, you are Magic, but we will get a better idea once you get checked. The Tangle attached to you goes directly against your own power. It decreases and confuses it and causes the Ripples,' Rook said.

'Would it cause my mother to have nightmares?' Nicole asked. 'My father is getting out of control with his anger.'

'Ripples drag bad Rogue in. Your mother has a Night Hag attached to her; they cause night terrors and rashes on her skin. Your father has a Knocker, which is a type of Goblin in snake form. They connect to anger, and when it starts, the Knocker turns the tension in the house up.'

Nicole's lips curled back in disgust. 'Yes, that sounds exactly like what they are experiencing. How do you know this?'

'The Prefects are monitoring their actions. This will calm them down knowing they are being identified,'

Rook said. 'It was reported that the Rogue are trapped in the Ripple and want out. Your mother being frightened and your dad being angry are boring to them. Prefects are trying to get them to settle with the promise of freedom.'

'If these Ripples come from the Tangle, then it is coming from me? Am I doing this to them?' Nicole looked hard at Rook.

'Not on purpose. We believe the Tangle started causing Ripples around four years ago; they started small but now have gained momentum. This is because you have not grown your Magic, your aura or your colour Illuminance. Had we left it any longer, the Tangle would have taken over.'

'What would happen?' Nicole was scared to hear the answer.

'When a Tangle is strong and let loose in Frail Realm it can make transfers to Frail around you and infect them in many ways,' Rook said.

Nicole drew her lips tight. 'I get that, but specifically how?'

'By dragging Rogue that do not want to be there and attaching to individuals and the environment around them. This can make them sick, especially little Frail. In your case, the Tangle has taken over the Magic side of you and it must not develop anymore.'

'What would happen then?' Nicole asked.

'There would be a lot of lazy, impatient and aggressive Frail,' Rook said softly.

'That is awful.' Nicole covered her face with one hand. There was no way she would be responsible for that mayhem!

'We hope to have prevented it. But yes, Frail would catch a Tangle like a cold, and then the Ripples would cause mayhem. The Frail Realm would not be the same; Rolte would not be able to control the Rogue and their movements.'

Dinkletons tilted his head. 'Raisa, the girl with wings,

is responsible for making you Magic. She did this with a Spark, which is an uncontrolled spell.'

'A bit like when I froze you but far worse,' Rook said.

Nicole was intrigued by this news, shocked that one so young could fly, or even have wings. Dozens of questions overran her brain. She looked to Rook for further explanation.

'Raisa is old in comparison to Frail. Dellamana live much longer.'

Nicole's mouth gaped. 'They didn't look much older than me. How do they live in my world looking like twelve-year-olds?'

'They were industrious. They used their skills. They became bakers and ran their own café business,' Rook said proudly. 'Dex was once a Dellamana who had the highest colour, which is saffron. He worked in our Vault, with me, actually.'

'You know that she definitely did this? Caused a Spark to turn me Magic?'

'The only way for Frail to become Dellamana is by receiving molecules from one of us,' Rook said. 'She and her brother have been living in your realm for thirteen years. We must work out where and when this occurred. If we want to take control of the Tangle you have, we must catch it at its birth.'

'But that could have happened at any time. It will be impossible to find that out,' Nicole said.

'The good news is that the Tangle could not have started without being in contact with your Magic molecules. So that narrows things down,' Rook said.

'A storm has built up; this is where your Magic and the Tangle are fighting inside you. The Tangle is making things difficult with your skills, putting them off course and continually making you frustrated. Only one can win, and it must not be the Tangle, and it is winning at the moment.

We have to be thankful because without the storm we would not have found you,' Dinkletons said in a serious tone. 'The storm caused the Helix message to be sent.'

'The issues the Tangle has caused with your family cannot grow now that you are here. However, we must fix the damage it already has done,' Rook said.

It is not all good being Magic, Nicole thought with a shiver.

'The Hag and Knocker came from the force of the Ripple. They were sucked in,' Rook said. 'The Rogue would have felt imprisoned, and that is why your mother had nightmares and your father was irritated and this situation got worse over the years. The longer the Ripple stays the more damage it does. But in the case of your parents, we would estimate they have been there for roughly three years. Ripples develop extremely quickly once started.'

Nicole surveyed where they had landed. She was in a garden, with dozens of multi-coloured flowers, the air bursting with their fragrance. Flames swayed all over the area and interacted with the flowers, stretching them and making them sway. Thin streams of orange and red fire darted around. Full, leaping fire strands reached in circles and high in the air, making a swishing sound. It was the most gorgeous garden she had ever seen.

'This is the Entrance to Orra, the Fire Garden,' Dinkletons said as he waved his paw and stood on two legs. He strolled through a halo of flames. Nicole thought it looked like a tunnel. He emerged, showing her his paws. 'See, no damage.'

Rook pressed a transparent rock into her palm and made her curl her fingers closed. When she opened them, she found a chain with a Crystal in a magnificent setting. 'This is your Hallr Crystal. Every Dellamana has a birthright to own one, and you are well overdue. Your Magic molecules are crying out for the colour gifts called the Illuminance.'

'And once you start to get your colours, the Voltz will grow,' Dinkletons said.

Nicole allowed Rook to put the necklace on her. She found it hard to concentrate being in such an amazing place and receiving such a gift. But the lingering thought of her mother being terrorised by a Night Hag upset her. She wanted to know more about it and her father's Rogue that got him so out of character. *What do they look like?*

'You don't want to know what they look like, Nicole,' Dinkletons said. 'Focus on your Crystal right now.'

Nicole looked at the Crystal. It was a big gem, transparent and held within a gold frame. The light sparkling off it was unreal.

'The Hallr Crystal is formed according to the Magic it serves. No two are the same. This Crystal has been waiting for you,' Rook said.

'Raisa lost her Illuminance, the colours inside. This caused no more Voltz to be made and so grey colours came into her Crystal,' Dinkletons said. 'That is why she had to leave Orra.'

'With the greys come Sparks. The same one I gave to you, remember?' Rook asked.

How could I forget? 'But does that mean I will have Sparks as well?'

'You will not be able to Spark in Orra. Rather, you will get blocks.'

'The Entrance is open,' Dinkletons announced, as the fire cleared to frame a passageway. Nicole peered into its borders and could see a jumble of flames exploding into each other, and strong winds blew everything together.

'We will all go through together,' Rook said.

Nicole stepped back. She could feel the heat swim around her body. Her hair fluttered around her face from its breeze.

Rook took her hand and, with a crooked smile,

motioned her forward. Dinkletons meowed. They all laughed, but she was nervous. They walked into the flames. The fire skimmed and danced, moving her hair, touching her face and body. Nicole watched an intense halo form with great strength. She put one foot in front of the other, concentrating on getting through. Her companions were by her side, Rook's hand in hers, Dinkletons' tail next to her ankle. Time slowed and she tried to stand up straight and not hunch over. Finally, the flames faded away. She was now through the fire tunnel, with not a burn on her.

'This is Orra,' Rook announced.

10

Stepping out of the Fire Garden, Nicole knew that Raisa would play an important role in her life. They would have no choice; they would be drawn to each other from their common Magic.

They stopped to gaze ahead. Nicole saw what she could only describe as buildings, but they looked so different to the ones in her world. They had some structure to them but seemed incomplete. The sky was pink with yellow and red sparkles, and the planets in the background were so clear. Nicole rubbed her eyes.

'The impossible colours,' Dinkletons said. 'They are made up of Voltz.'

They walked over a wide bridge, where the water pounded underneath with great turbulence and barreled over a waterfall. The edge of the rapids had a framing of lush moss in loads of different greens.

As Nicole skipped to keep up with Rook, she noticed flowers the shape of tiny girls, their dresses cream and red, perfectly shaped and smelling like perfume. Black dots clouded Nicole's vision as her head grew heavy, causing her to stumble.

'Whoa, are you alright?' Rook steadied her. 'You can

rub the Crystal and then rub your eyes with your fingers, and it will give you relief. The Crystal will heal you.'

Nicole nodded and did what he said. 'Wow, that's amazing! The sting has gone.'

They walked the length of the bridge and came to a gate. Nicole had to tip her head right back to view the whole thing. A haze hovered, and as they moved closer, a monstrous arm pushed the gate up. Despite the load, it moved silently, and when it reached the top, a bell rang out. The doorbell, which sounded like a musical car horn, didn't match the radiance of what she had seen and made her giggle.

'We changed the bell to add a little fun,' Dinkletons teased, as he raced ahead.

On her right, a swimming pool swept through the arches and disappeared into the trees. Its water was black, and Nicole could see her reflection in the mirror-like surface. She wondered what it would be like to jump in and swim for hours.

They walked into a carpeted entry of the nearest building, a cavernous space. Nicole breathed, deeply impressed by the enormity of the space. 'So awesome,' Nicole mumbled. Everything managed to look cosy, with lots of cushions on large furniture scattered with flair. Nicole's eyes fixated on one picture ahead of her. The lines and angles were similar to how her cousin Jaya drew. Nicole scratched her head. It was uncanny. Jaya had her own unique technique, yet this picture looked almost as if her cousin had drawn it.

Rook said, 'Unseen Voltz provide the light here and promote the impossible colours.'

'Is this the same Voltz that you have in your aura?'

'Yours as well. We are all connected by Voltz; they make us who we are and separate us from other Magics. Because we can manufacture our own, we are more powerful than any other Magical realm.'

'Ahem.' Dinkletons flicked his tail.

'Sorry, the second most powerful,' Rook said, smiling at Dinkletons.

'The impossible colours come about by wavelengths and a different spectrum Orra creates. They are colours that do not occur in your light range,' Dinkletons said.

'I can't believe this is happening,' Nicole said with a sigh.

Blonde-haired Dellamana were everywhere, standing on the stairs, on the balcony above and in front of her. They didn't look at all like Rook. They were fascinating. Their faces looked human, and they all had distinct differences. Their skin, the shape of their faces and the green, almond-contoured eyes and, more importantly, their individual auras, separated them from other worlds. Nicole could tell they were magic.

They looked at Nicole, and she made eye contact with many. None of them had wings.

'Why did Raisa have wings?'

'That is because she could not produce Voltz anymore. They keep us in this state. Once removed, it can cause things to happen, like wings. Rolte reported that she started to grow them after six years in the Frail Realm,' Dinkletons said.

'And Dex?'

'Yes, he still had the colour in his Crystal and Raisa did not,' Rook said.

Rook and Dinkletons walked in front of her in the middle of a hall that changed from blue to green. They stopped and looked around at her. They looked nothing like the distorted individuals Nicole had just met.

In Dinkletons' place stood what resembled a lion. He was huge, as tall as her and wide. His eyes were saucer size and the light streaming from them was so intense she couldn't look into them. His mangy coat was replaced by a glorious mane, radiant with gold and silver flecks. A pulsation of steam spilt from him, and she realised Magic and uniqueness were essentially who he was. She watched as the puff of smoke faded away.

The yellow aura that surrounded Rook in the park was now the only thing recognisable – it drifted around his body. He was tall and had muscular arms and legs. His hair was short and flopped thickly onto his forehead and was so blonde it effervesced.

She looked all around her. Their hair styles varied, and all the females had elaborate braids. Matching deep-green eyes brought them together as a race. The skin was varying in paleness, and all had upturned noses. As a group, they looked the same, but when Nicole looked closely, they were all different in their own way.

'When we wedge shift, distortions take place. We are back to normal now as we are back in the Magic Realm,' Dinkletons said.

'You look so different. Did it hurt?' Nicole asked.

'Not for us Stoneycraft. We don't feel pain.' Dinkletons shook his mane, the long hair settling in slow motion. A pixie-looking guy came forward from behind the Dellamana and drifted his hands around Rook and Dinkletons. Long red hair reached his waist. He had a round face, big dark eyes, and fat cheeks. His lips were nearly the same shade as his hair. He was very short, only reaching Nicole's waist, and was smartly dressed in beige shorts and a matching shirt. Nicole watched him in a trance, her eyes fixed. She silently questioned, *When do I begin to accept this as real?*

'This is Zosmine and is not a pixie; he is one of many House Belba, a Magic, which we could not function without,' Rook said. 'Their main job is to clear Thisbe blocks caused by gravity in the different realms we visit.'

Zosmine smiled at her, and she smiled back. 'And

anyone who wedges. I make sure they are fully back to their old selves. Wedge residue can get caught in the molecules, so we must make sure they are cleared.'

Nicole didn't know what to make of that and said nothing.

The Dellamana were looking at her in a way that let her know they wanted to talk to her, like Raisa and Dex had done at her school meeting. Their gazes told her they were mind reading, or telemuting as they called it. Invading her brain and pulling at her thoughts without her permission. It felt unnerving with so many doing it.

'Forgive their staring. This is the first time they have seen a Frail in Orra.' Dinkletons sauntered over to her.

Nicole could not wait to find out more. This was the best day of her life. Finding out she was Magic, with skills, even if they were mismanaged – well, she didn't care. This meant the awful frustration she had experienced all her life would be a thing of the past. She had a Hallr Crystal, one that would provide her with protection and build her Magic through colours and things called Voltz, Magic on the outside that blended with her very own aura.

As they made their way through the huge space, Nicole looked around. Some areas had low ceilings, others had high ones, and then the place they walked into now had no roof at all. Nicole stopped in her tracks and gazed upwards again at the yellow and red sprinkles among the pink sky.

'We will take a seat here before you go to have tests, and do not worry, they are not intrusive.' Rook motioned for them all to sit. Nicole wandered over to look in the water, where large fish came scrambling to the surface and blew bubbles at her. Their bodies were yellow with blue eyes, and they could float on the surface of the clear pond like ducks.

'Let us explain to you what is going to happen now.' Rook sat back and crossed his long legs.

Nicole turned and sat in the nearest high-back multi-coloured seat.

'Once the Helix message was sent, it was confirmed that you and Raisa are connected by the same Magic,' Dinkletons said.

Nicole nodded as she listened carefully.

'The Tangle would have thrived without you building Voltz to take it down. This creates power for the Tangle and then it is able to produce stronger and more terrible Ripples.'

Nicole couldn't wait to feel normal again. She remembered getting better at ballet, but then the pain would be there all the time, an example of the good power against the Tangle.

Rook rotated his hands. 'So, picture the Spark and the Tangle moving around and interacting with each other inside you. When the good Magic is growing so is the bad Magic. They both grow with you in their own ways, causing conflict in all areas of your life,' Rook continued.

'First, we will have to minimise the damage as fast as we can,' Dinkletons said.

'What is happening with my parents now?'

'The Night Hag and the Knocker have had time to take a firm hold,' Rook said gently. 'Once they are removed, they will leave a wound that will require your Magic to heal.'

Nicole stood and walked around the room. Her throat closed over and she bent down to calm herself. 'At least the Prefects can remove them.'

'Ah, that's the issue. They can't. They can only communicate with them to go easy on your parents.' Rook shook his head.

Nicole widened her eyes. 'Err, are you are saying I have to remove them?'

'That's just for starters. We need to find out when this Tangle first attached to you,' Dinkletons said.

'If Raisa started this, couldn't she help remove it since it is her power that I have?'

'She would, but she can't do anything without her Illuminance. So, that makes her useless in this situation. We have to find other solutions,' Rook said.

Nicole's stomach flipped, as a thought came into her head. *This is about me.*

Dinkletons and Rook stared at her, 'til something clicked for Nicole. 'Okay, I have to go sort these Ripples out.' But how? The idea was daunting.

They nodded. 'You will also experience blocks,' Dinkletons said. 'Probably worse than Marnie due to the Tangle and the damage it will have done to your Magic cells.'

'I want to know all about the Marnie.'

'Young Magic have to deal with blocks – it is a part of the growth of their Voltz. They come from a loss of control over their emerging colours and weaken Magic cells. Frustrations come from this and manifest in steam, flashes, small explosions, and fires. This causes Marnie to be moody and sleep a lot. This does more damage, as Magic cells do not require much sleep,' Rook said. 'And, as time goes by, neither will you.'

'Too much is not ideal.' Dinkletons shook his mane, and it smelled of lilies.

Nicole scratched her head. 'And I will be in this situation?'

'Afraid so. All Magic go through it,' Rook said.

Blimey, Nicole thought. She wasn't looking forward to explosions from her body or fire on her hands.

'All Marnie have to find their own solutions to their blocks. It will start as a tingle then grow to flashes, hot fingers, lips that burn – so be on the lookout,' Dinkletons said.

Nicole looked at her Crystal, warm on her skin and bright orange, and so far, her hands looked normal. 'I will go back and help my parents get rid of these horrible Rogue that are attached to them. And soon, so they don't notice that I have gone. I need to explain what is happening.'

11

'We will do a short jump now. Orra is just too big to walk everywhere. I will show you this time, and then after this, you can practise,' Dinkletons said. 'When you are with the Marnie, remember, they are not allowed to jump anytime they like. They have to get clearance from a Savant, their teachers.'

'How do Marnie get around if they are unable to jump?'

'They use a Zizis, which is a large room that transports on a stable floor. You will go in one soon. They are operated by Belba. The Belba you just met does not operate the Zizis, he has other roles. There are Zizis stations all around Orra. But let's do the jump.'

'So, how do you do this?' Nicole stared at him.

'Hold your Crystal and tell it where you want to go,' Dinkletons said. 'Focus on the kitchens. I will be right behind you. Don't be worried.'

She held her Crystal away from her body. Nicole found herself moving upward. She watched her feet leave the ground below her and rise. Dinkletons was well below her, staring up at her, his whiskers waving up and down. The sensation was like being underwater but with strong flippers that propelled her movement. She looked around and saw many Dellamana also jumping; they waved and called out 'Hi' and 'Well done, Nicole' to her.

She floated through rooms. The confines of the roof, walls and even furniture didn't hinder the movement. They swayed and swerved like characters in a video game. Each Dellamana was in charge of their own destination and could change direction anytime. They waved and yelled greetings. A normal Dellamana process, that now, she guessed, she was expected to do.

Darting sideways, she found herself in a space with pink sky and red and yellow glitter. G-force hit her hard. Her stomach dropped, but at the same time, it was kind of exciting.

They arrived on solid ground, Dinkletons leading the way with such elegance for the size of him. In the park, he was a small, runty cat; here he was as big as a lion. It was glorious to cast eyes on him because he was beautiful, and the magic he exuded was intoxicating. He had a strong effect on all her senses. Her eyes grew wide and sharp, her nervousness left her, she felt happy and safe in his company. Her Crystal glowed bright yellow, when before it had been merely a smudge. He gifted her the courage to continue.

One side of the room was open to stretches of a garden, framed by yellow tulips. There was no roof, just the pink space filled with glitter that she had just been a part of.

Dozens of kitchens spanned the area. She was busy looking around when she saw two airborne individuals coming from the other side of the kitchen. They moved so fast; all she could see were masses of red hair flying. They landed steps away from her.

'Hello, Miss Nicole, I am Zosmine, and this is Shanazz. We are Belba.' Nicole noticed both had red floppy hair and exaggerated, puffed-out cheeks.

'I saw you before.' Nicole pointed to Zosmine, who puffed out his chest in glee.

Dinkletons arrived next to Nicole. 'You did well with that jump. Your orange colour helped,' he said.

'Sir.' Shanazz bowed politely to Dinkletons. 'Delighted to meet you, Miss Nicole. We have a gift.'

Nicole watched Shanazz take a small bottle out of her pocket and hand it to her. The little Belba only came up to her waist. Her hair was wild and haloed her cute face and half her body. She had puffy cheeks, and a large nose that nearly touched her thick, red lips. She wore a pinafore, light-green arms on show. Her legs, while short, were in proportion to her size.

'This is a mood scent,' Shanazz said, handing her a small bottle. A breeze came from the other side of the huge space and blew her thick hair.

Nicole turned the bottle in her hand. There wasn't much liquid in there. She held it up and peered inside. 'But what does it do?' She lifted the bottle.

'This will make you curious. It will change your Frail inner voice. You know the one that tells you negative things, like you can't do something?' Shanazz leaned in close.

'It will rewire your thinking, Nicole.' Dinkletons smiled.

'That's impossible,' Nicole said with a shake of her head.

'Oh, don't you worry, it will work. Negative thinking will get in the way of you being able to bond with your Crystal,' Shanazz said and reached up and touched Nicole's hand. 'A bothersome Frail trait that doesn't do you any favours.'

'And once I do that, I can start to heal Ripples?'

'Well, it will assist. Get you started and all that,' Shanazz said. 'Let's not jump ahead of ourselves.'

The beaming faced Belbas bounced from foot to foot.

'How are you finding Orra so far?' Zosmine asked, his face beaming.

'I feel lightheaded.'

'We can fix that, just a minor block.' Shanazz squeezed Nicole's hand.

'We clear the Thisbe blocks. They are always collecting blocks that attach to them while on their jobs,' Zosmine said, nearly breathless.

With a pained expression, Nicole said, 'You mean they get them while wedging?'

'Yes. Such activity requires great use of the Voltz, the power within. Thisbe need regular tune ups.' Shanazz's joke failed to impress Nicole.

'I am not looking forward to doing it again. It is not for the faint hearted.' Nicole closed her eyes for a moment. The idea was chilling. 'I have to get home somehow.'

'What is this faint heart?' Zosmine asked, poking his tongue into his already full cheeks.

'It means not brave.' Nicole's hands felt clammy at the thought.

'Well, never fear, we can help with this affliction. Mood scents are an area we deal with, especially with Thisbe and their daily work. Sometimes they get fuzzy brains and can become unfocused. We can help with these,' Zosmine said. 'We heal their sore feet and anything else that has been affected by wedging.'

'It must have been a shock to come here and find out about your second family.' Shanazz's mouth took up half of her face.

Nicole smiled. 'Am I really part of the family?'

'Why, yes, of course.' Shanazz snorted as if this was a ludicrous statement for Nicole to make.

Nicole smiled. They were so lovely, these Belba. She felt comfortable in their company. Dinkletons sat nearby with a goofy grin. He seemed happy she was making friends.

'Now that you are here, you won't have to hold your abilities back. In fact, I would advise you not to,' Shanazz said. 'Don't be scared of your skills. Once you start to get the colours in your Crystal, you will grow your aura and then your Voltz, which will make you stronger as each hour passes. Do not focus on the Tangle right now.'

'But one goes with the other,' Nicole said.

'You have not been working on your Magical base. Now you can. Things will be different,' Shanazz said.

'How do you think your parents will cope once you return?' Zosmine asked. 'Your family is in for the biggest ride of their lives.'

'They have been surviving with me all my life. I have been difficult to manage.'

They all laughed.

Nicole thought about the situations she had got her parents into. Things they had to explain but couldn't find the words to. Building gardens in their friend's yards. Talking with a big vocabulary for her age and knowing the alphabet by the time she was nine months old. She would hear the comments like, 'She walks well for her age,' and 'Wow, she uses two syllables. Amazing'.

'The constrained magic that you have would have kept that fairly well under control, as magic does not show itself to Frail just for fun,' Zosmine said, a slow smile building. 'It would be fascinating to see how you went in normal life, seeing the pulsating magic fighting with the Tangle.'

'Yes, it's been hard going and confusing, but at least now I am learning why I am different from others.' Nicole ran her hand through her hair.

'Getting back to business.' Shanazz threw Zosmine a sharp frown. 'You will be fine to wedge after you get the Prefects' okay.' Shanazz nodded. 'We made all your clothes. Something we whipped up in half an hour. Most Belba insisted on making one piece of clothing to be fair.' Shanazz scrunched her nose. 'Good luck and come see us soon.'

'Yes please, and I would especially love to hear of your childhood.'

Dinkletons displayed a wide grin. 'I don't think you're the only one, Zosmine.'

The Belbas backflipped in the air and then they were gone.

12

'Ah, this is Jinn and Strom. They are Marnie, children of Orra,' Dinkletons said once the Belba had left, gesturing to two Marnie standing nearby 'They will take you to 1320, the Lab you have been assigned to. And then after that, you will attend a class where you can learn about the colours that will be gifted into your Crystal.'

Nicole looked at the approaching Marnie and quickly whispered to Dinkletons, 'Why can't you take me?' She noticed colours flicking through her Crystal. But the Marnie had arrived. Nicole made a face, pleading with Dinkletons not to leave.

Strom had a wide grin plastered on his mouth and when he got closer it was suddenly wiped from his face. Strom's powerful presence filled the space, and she felt an unnatural stillness. Nicole had the desire to run. She cleared her throat and dragged her focus away from him.

The other Marnie, Jinn, acted confident but had steam running up one side of her body. Nicole noticed the girl had curly hair, the same as hers. Nicole took in Strom's mop of hair, jeans and black T-shirt and Jinn's spaghetti-strap brown dress. They wore clothes that any other kids would wear at home.

'You're not Frail,' Strom said, raising his white eyebrows, still not smiling.

'I have Magic skills.' Nicole nodded.

'Well, that's obvious.' Jinn said, hands on her hips. 'Wowzers, look at your Crystal.'

'Yes, the colours are coming in,' Nicole said. She looked at the colours as they changed as if they were lights turning on and off. She couldn't stop looking at it.

'Is that the way to welcome our guest?' Dinkletons pressed his lips together.

'Just initial reaction, I guess.' Jinn smiled.

'Well, based on those colours, you have a lot to do before they settle,' Strom said as a red spark pinged off his nose and up into the air.

Jinn erupted in giggles. 'Strom, could you be less obvious?'

'Stop it, Jinn,' he said as he elbowed her.

Nicole thought that Strom had a strong charisma about him, something lovely she couldn't put her finger on. She was shocked when her face burnt. The Marnie looked at each other. *Damn, they can telemute.*

Nicole knew she was here to help herself, to save her infected cells and grow more Magic to make sure she didn't get sick. To deal with these Ripples was daunting, and she was shaken just thinking about it. The Belba mood elevator was amazing – it gave her confidence and whisked away her negative thoughts. As they popped up, they disappeared. Nicole thought if she could bottle it for people, it would help so many.

Strom was pointing to her Crystal. 'Ha-ha, there's a grey.'

Nicole looked and saw a light beige colour sitting in the middle of her Crystal. 'How do I get rid of it?'

'Oh, that's an easy one,' Jinn said as she looked into it.

Strom rolled his lips together and moved his head

from side to side. 'Meditation is the best way for larger problems. We can tune out and mindfully move the Voltz to the grey colours and remove them.'

'Voltz melt greys in a jiffy,' Jinn said. 'But you have to have them to be able to do this.'

'Whenever we go past the fountain, we bathe the Crystal and that removes dots, which are the beginning of greys,' Jinn said.

'I've never meditated before.'

'That is appalling,' Jinn said. Her face was a picture of shock. 'We go to meditation every day with a Savant; we love it, very therapeutic for the irritating greys.'

'Hey, it's gone,' Nicole said, referring to the grey. Nicole's Crystal was now a green colour, no beige in sight.

'You're welcome. Those are so easy to remove, you don't need to rush off to meditation once you get the hang of it,' Strom said.

Jinn noticed the vial in Nicole's hand and her jaw clenched. 'You have a mood elevator?' Sparks, steam, then little fires erupted on Jinn's fingers.

Nicole jumped back. *Wow, that was intense.*

'Jinn, stop that. Of course she has a mood elevator,' Dinkletons said in a sharp tone that stilled Jinn.

'Sorry,' Jinn said to Nicole as she shook the flames out. 'It's just we only get those on our birthdays, and they are every twenty years, and you stroll in and get one without having to earn it.'

'Yeah, I agree. It seems we have been ripped off,' Strom grumbled.

'What? Really? That is a long time – we have birthdays every year.'

Steam rose from the feet of the Marnie, inching its way up to their waists.

'I will leave you three to get acquainted,' Dinkletons said.

Nicole swallowed rapidly as she watched Dinkletons go. But not before giving him a moody eye.

'You're stuck with us now,' Jinn teased.

She was willing to try new things and embrace the challenges even if inside she was second-guessing herself. She looked again at the vial. The mood elevator had tiny instructions that read, 'Apply when required, created by Shanazz and Zosmine Belba'.

She felt her hands go clammy. She popped the tiny cork off the bottle and applied one dab to each wrist, immediately feeling self-assured. The feeling of panic vanished.

Jinn and Strom both sighed, crossing their arms in unison.

'Sorry, but it's the other way around. You are both stuck with me.' Nicole smiled and they walked for a long time in silence, with Jinn and Strom giving her sneaky looks.

'You know that using the mood elevator in front of others is rude,' Jinn said.

'Really, how so?' Nicole asked. They were in a laboratory area with rows of glass doors with numbers on them.

'Put it this way: it's like eating candy in front of someone that hasn't got any,' Strom grumbled.

Nicole laughed; they were so easily rattled. 'Sorry, guys.'

They stopped outside a sliding door, similar to the one she had seen when visiting the hospital when her dad had his appendix out. 'This is 1320, only the best Lab in Orra. We'll come with you,' Strom said.

'We all have assigned Labs, but I only know of a few Marnie that go to 1320, and they are the brain boxes,' Jinn said. 'You will only have Nava to deal with. She can be quite...' Jinn said.

'A hard case.' Strom softly pushed Jinn.

'Oh no, I will be okay.' She didn't know what tests they

would do so she wasn't going to take any chances having them in the room with her. She put the mood elevator vial inside her pocket.

Jinn folded her arms and sat down heavily on the couch opposite. Nicole forced a smile and in return got a glare and rolling eyes from Jinn and a laugh from Strom.

13

Nicole pulled the door and entered 1320. It was like walking into another world separate from Orra. Nicole noticed the oval-shaped room was over two stories high. There was no floor, but somehow, she didn't fall. She felt her feet go numb as she looked down at the gorge below. The room was made of thin wood and had large gaps that opened out to the outside and as Nicole stood close, she could see the deep, harsh ravine.

'Come in, don't linger over there.'

She wondered if she should have brought Strom and Jinn in after all. Looking around she saw no needles or scary machines; in fact, it was plain, with just a few screens on the walls and one desk with balls as seats. The red from outside pulsated inside and once in disappeared. *It is freaky*, Nicole thought.

'I'm Nava and I will be doing your tests.' Nava walked past her swiftly, not waiting for an answer. 'Follow me.'

Nicole followed. Nava was elegant and formal, wearing a white suit and no shoes. What was it with shoes? None of them wore any. They approached a desk with two sitting balls in the middle of the room.

Nava held up her hand, showing Nicole a small

black rectangle in the centre of her palm. 'This is a palm computer; you will be getting one once I have uploaded the files. So be ready for it. It will arrive soon, and you will get a notification sign. It will store information about Rogue in the Frail Realm as well. You will need to familiarise yourself with its functions. Any questions, send me a message here.' Nava pointed to her hand near her pinky finger. 'You will also be able to send messages – we call them Rebo7 – anywhere here and in the Frail Realm.'

Nicole's eyes widened. 'Blimey, I'm getting one of those? How will I use it?'

'You have a portable phone, correct?'

Nicole handed it to Nava, who played around with it for a minute.

'Your palm computer will replace this but feel free to continue using this.' Nava handed it back and lifted her palm.

At first, Nicole was taken aback at the blue list written on Nava's hand. She read it out loud. 'Full body scan, frail percentage, Dellamana percentage, establish level of damage to cells, full bloods, hair assessment, full dental, anxiety levels, pain levels. How are you going to do that?' Nicole looked around.

Before Nicole looked back at Nava, a tiny bubble flew off her table and began to circle, hovering at different points around her body, and then returned to Nava's long fingers. She raised her eyebrows in surprise that it did not pop; it looked so delicate.

'This device is called a Gloine. It is both investigative and performs treatment. It is a Magic tonic transfer device that will start to heal your Magical molecules. Unfortunately, all have been infected.'

Nicole could not take her eyes off the perfect little transparent bubble.

'Have you ever had a blood test?' Nava motioned her to sit on one of the balls. Nicole bounced on it for a bit.

'Yes, when I was born.'

'Tell me about this?'

Nicole frowned. 'How would I know? I was a premature baby.'

'Oh, I am sure you do. Just think. After all, it would have been a rudimentary, painful examination.'

Nicole thought. She actually did remember it, remembered the blood seeping out of her arm into a tube. She could hear her mother's voice soothing her. 'I didn't cry.'

Nava smiled. Her hands flew over a glass surface – she rolled back and forth as she typed and swiped, highlighting complex equations. The numbers and symbols moved fast, vanished, and then reappeared.

'This is a form of mathematics. Based on the Gloine initial exam, you arrived with over two hundred blocks from the misuse of your Magic, which has been reduced to less than one hundred and seven already. This is a good start. We will administer a healing prescription to the Gloine. This will continue to work to rebuild the Magic molecules that are deflated and put some energy back into them. Once you grow your Magic, you will have fewer blocks. You must consolidate those racing colours in your Crystal. That, in turn, will settle and reignite your skills, but only to a certain point, as the Tangle is well attached.'

'But how do I stop the colours coming in so fast?'

'The Gloine will help, and as you become more aware from a Magic perspective, so, too, will your molecules be free to grow within this new, safe environment. In the Frail Realm, you have not been using them properly because of the Tangle. Wedging, jumping around Orra, using the fountain to get rid of small grey colours will help.' Nava turned to face her, and Nicole was stunned by her bright green eyes, similar to Strom's. 'Plus, not only do you have to deal with the Tangle, now that you are here, you will have to focus on your Crystal, learn to keep the solid colours and remove greys.'

'Like the Marnie do?'

Nava nodded. 'Similar, but you have more to deal with. They are accustomed to managing their greys. All they have are small blocks, like fire and steam, and Marnie do not do Ripples. They learn about them and the possibility of getting them if they are not concentrating on their colours, dealing with issues as they arise. And this, Nicole, is what you must do.'

'I want to be able to do it.'

'I am sure you will find a way. Now, your dental is complete. You have perfect teeth.'

Nicole thought, *That is why the dentist always raved about my teeth.* Now she knew why.

'Now, for your information, your hair follicles are pale purple, an indication of your Dellamana side. You have never been sick in your life?'

'That is true. My mother said I have a strong immune system.' Nicole was thinking about having purple roots. She tugged at her hair.

'She is right; however, it is more complicated than that. You will have this Gloine follow you for now, to continue to disperse the medication to heal where it needs to. As it heals, you will get better with your Magic skills. It is so small you won't even notice that it is there.'

'So this will follow me?'

'Everywhere.'

Nicole watched Nava fiddle with the Gloine, type more on her screen and release it back towards Nicole. 'There. We are done for the time being.'

Nicole stood and the tiny Gloine followed her across

the room. 'And, Nicole, use that mood elevator soon – you're going to need it.'

Nicole turned and there was the little bubble, at shoulder height. It wasn't too bad. In fact, it was a comfort to know it was healing her.

14

Nicole found Jinn and Strom still sitting where she left them outside 1320. Her eyes squinted as the light was less bright in the hall compared to the strong colours of the lab.

'How did it go?' Strom asked her, jumping up when he saw her.

'I have purple hair.' She was met with open mouths. She also heard a little bit of inner dialogue. Was this telemuting? 'Also, do you have palm computers?' Nicole asked them as they moved through the long hallway that changed colours.

Both held their hands up. 'When you get yours, we can teach you how to play the nugget game. We all play. It's the best game ever,' Jinn said.

'That's if she will be allowed,' Strom said, frowning.

'Errr, she has purple hair, for goodness' sake, of course she can play.'

As they walked, they explained the game the Marnie play. 'You start with three nuggets; the purpose of the game is to earn more of these. As you gain more you can get a blade of grass, a leaf on a tree and as you build them up you can then get your own flower in the Frail Realm,' Jinn said.

To Nicole that sounded amazing. 'Wow, for real?'

'As you earn your nuggets you go through the levels in the game. Those just mentioned are the lower levels. A snowflake and the four-leaf clovers are highly sought after.'

'You missed one, Jinn. Don't forget the starfish.'

Jinn folded her arms. 'It was general coverage, Strom, if you don't mind.' Steam and what looked like fragments of glass escaped from her fingernails and out into the air.

Nicole hoped that would never happen to her. *Did it hurt?*

Jinn shook her head. 'Nah, it doesn't hurt, but it's not a good thing to be creating. It's not glass either.'

'Just a nasty grey presenting itself, right, Jinn?' Strom teased.

'Anyhoo, we were talking about the nugget.' Jinn pushed Strom away. 'It's a living game where the prizes are actually pieces of nature. We love it,' Jinn gushed.

'It sounds like fun.'

She made eye contact with Strom; the intensity of his glare caused a rush of excitement to run through her. She looked away, suddenly shy. She felt her heart skip a beat.

'So, what is the plan?' Jinn asked and linked her arm through Nicole's.

'I want to help my parents and cousin with the Ripples that have come from my Tangle.'

'Nasty. Fancy getting to the stage of being able to send Ripples.' Jinn shook her head.

'Tangles and Ripples,' Strom said as he shook his head. 'No Magic should ever have to deal with them.'

'Well, my parents are getting the brunt of them, so I have to do something. What does a Ripple look like?' Nicole asked as she waved away the steam that was pouring from the two Marnie – a sign of a block.

'I have seen them in the Lab. Under controlled conditions, of course, they are quite lovely,' Jinn said.

'They look like a zigzag with a long tail that flicks from side to side, hence the name,' Strom said.

'How long are they?' Nicole asked.

'They range in size, the smaller the deadlier,' Jinn said. 'The smaller the tail, the faster it wags and the more cells it can latch onto in Rogue and Frail.'

'Thank goodness none of us have ever had to deal with those,' Jinn said, and they both stared at Nicole. 'Must be horrible to not have control.'

Nicole shrugged her shoulders.

'Okay, we have to get to class,' Strom said.

'Oh, good, I will practise my jumps.' Nicole smiled.

'You're allowed to jump? Why, that's outrageous!' Strom yelled. 'Can you honestly believe this, Jinn?'

'Certainly not fair at all,' Jinn grumbled.

'We have to travel in the Zizis. Marnie are hardly ever allowed to jump. Not 'til we get our blocks under control,' Strom said, and he made a left into a wide corridor. They walked through a gate and then a small platform and onto the large, flat surface of the Zizis. The walls were the yellow and red glitter of the sky, just sitting there, moving slightly. She didn't know if it was the space or a wall.

'It's the outside of Orra, not a wall,' Jinn said.

On one side of the Zizis was a lounge area. Bean bags lined the spare spaces and Nicole saw a kitchen where the smell of fresh baking filled the air.

'I have refreshments and smoothies.' A Belba walked over to Nicole, grinning. Another Belba stood with her and asked, 'Just the three of you?' All Belba wore the same thing but in different colours: red, blue and green dungarees with no shirt and, sure enough, no shoes.

'Just us,' Strom said and raced towards the lounge and dove headfirst onto it. Jinn followed and Nicole walked over and sat opposite the two Marnie. She sank deep into the cushions. Then a group of noisy Marnie came exploding in and they squeezed onto the furniture, making Strom and Jinn move over to share.

This way of getting around was far better. Nicole made herself comfortable in the soft cushions and took the smoothie the Belba held towards her. She looked around as the room moved away from the door through which she had come in. She couldn't tell how fast they were going, there were no windows, but the red and yellow glitter all fell away to the wide openness of the pink space, leaving them on a platform.

The Zizis was fascinating to Nicole; to her, it was like a magical carpet. The Marnie that had joined them spoke to Nicole all at once, and the steam was too much. Luckily, she didn't have to cope for too long as they came to a stop. She happily waved to the Belba as she got off and found herself in a school setting, with many doors leading off to a large circular area.

'I have to go to a different class than you two,' Strom said as the group that had been on the Zizis ran past, their auras floating in their wake.

She actually heard him say, *I'm bummed*. A definite telemute. She felt lightheaded and used her Crystal to prevent any embarrassment.

'Oh, okay, thanks.' Nicole took a good look at Strom. His green eyes, framed with thick, white lashes, pierced hers and his face went pink. Strom ran off and entered the third door along with other Marnie boys, who were all craning their necks to look at her. Nicole could hear their voices. 'Who is she? She has Magic molecules, and, wow, we have to talk to her later.'

'Right, that's a first,' Jinn grumbled and shook out the little fires on her fingers, like it was as normal as blinking. 'Damn blocks.'

'What do you mean?' Nicole asked. But her face was burning; she nibbled on her bottom lip.

'Can't you see? Strom is behaving like a lovesick idiot.'

15

In the class, Nicole listened with interest to the teacher they called their Savant. Fascinating facts about where and how Marnie received their colours and how to prevent the blocks that materialised as steam and fire. How their eyes could light up rooms with their strength and, in doing so, could weaken them. All through the class, it seemed she was the only enthusiastic student. All her other classmates stared at her and shot her question after question. After, they were given ice blocks on chocolate sticks that they called nectar bars. Nicole took big bites; it was so delicious, creamy, and melted in her mouth. Outside in the corridor, Marnie were everywhere. Green eyes hit her with their full force, and she took a breath in. Nicole guessed they looked – in Frail years – from seven to thirteen years old.

The girls were dressed in sleeveless dresses in all colours. The boys had the same fine-spun silk in long shorts and tops. Their auras lit up the hallway – the depth of colour and the swirling cloud was dreamlike.

Nicole was trying to think about what she had to do. It was hard to with all the Marnie noise going on around her. Even their auras felt loud as they blended from one

Marnie to the next. Colour lit up the corridor. Since all had different colours, the rainbow effect was astonishing.

'They have been warned by Prefects to stay away from you. They are too much energy all at once. We are the privileged two,' Jinn said.

'I wondered why they're not bombarding me.' Nicole looked at the groups of Marnie who still stared unashamedly at her. Nicole turned away; she felt uncomfortable under their blatant gazes.

'You have got to come to the Depaysement with us. The yellow house is where we do all our prep, rainbow work and games.'

'What is rainbow work?'

'We make them, and once we are good at it, the Savant lets us send it to the Frail Realm.' Strom said as he emerged from the crowd and joined them again. 'I have sent a few.'

Nicole noticed the look on Jinn's face. Something had touched a nerve.

'So, word has got around. Everyone knows you're here,' Strom said, pointing to the crowds that were talking and looking at her.

'Hi, where did you come from?' Nicole asked, avoiding his eyes.

'He's been to the Moon Garden.' Jinn pouted. *It's the best excursion.*

Nicole was going to have to get used to reading thoughts. She felt nausea sweep over her.

'Anyhoo, before I was so rudely interrupted, I was discussing with Nicole the Depaysement.' Jinn turned to Nicole and pulled her along. It was hard for Nicole to concentrate as there were so many Marnie watching her. They stood in groups and were all over the hallway, staring and talking about her. She could feel Strom's presence behind her.

Strom was not having any of it, and he caught up and

linked his arm with Nicole's free elbow. Nicole went red again and her shoulders slumped.

'Oh, Strom, you are so annoying!' Jinn flared her nostrils.

Nicole laughed at Jinn's sullen look and Strom's fast-paced stride.

'All these doors lead to classrooms that all have their own name. See, I just came from the Moon Garden, like all those Marnie over there with the orange hats,' Strom said.

'We came from the class H & C, Hallr and Colour.' Jinn squeezed her arm.

Nicole saw bright titles over the doors along the hallway. She spied Electromagnetic Fields, Quantum Physics, Magic Scale, and Dissection of Auras, among others. 'Those classes look hard.'

'Easy peasy,' Jinn said in a sharp tone. 'The best time, of course, is prep. Anyway, enough talk of boring school classes, we don't have you long enough to waste our time on drivel.'

'Do you like fast rides? There are many at the Depaysement. The one I love is being shot out of a cannon underwater. We go for miles,' Strom said after a moment of hesitation.

'I don't do thrill rides.' Nicole's eyes bulged at the thought.

'I'm sorry for your boring life,' Jinn said. 'Look, if it's not action-packed, we are not interested. Marnie don't do boring, just so you know. If you think we are mad, the activities of the Belba would horrify you.'

'I heard Frail parachute out of planes. That is pretty cool,' Strom said, pushing his nose into the conversation.

'Not children.' Nicole turned to look at him.

'Why on Frail not?' Strom voiced his objection.

'You have to be a certain age. Children can't just go

around doing everything they want.' Nicole felt his arm through hers. She must stop blushing.

'Once we get control of our grey colours, we are not Marnie anymore. I'm nearly at that point,' Strom said, puffing his chest out.

Jinn groaned loudly, making other Marnie look at her. Belba walked amongst them. The contrast between the white and red hair was dramatic.

'Strom, you are full of it,' Jinn said, as she pushed her chin up.

'I have no idea what you are on about,' Strom snapped back.

'Anyway, Marnie aren't allowed to do anything of real importance,' Jinn grumbled.

'You make rainbows and send them to the Frail Realm, I think that's important,' Nicole said. 'You have lots of time to yourself in the Depaysement and that nugget game sounds fantastic.'

'When Marnie do anything remotely bad, all Orra knows it and it is documented in Rolte, which, for your information, is the place where the Prefects work on monitoring Rogue in your realm.'

'Well, I guess that is for your own good.' Nicole was scolded by their flinching faces. 'If a kid was shot off in a cannon underwater, they would drown.'

'How do you live like that? Sounds ghastly!' Jinn pressed her head back. 'We can hold our breath for ages if we want to.'

'How long can you hold it?'

'Oh, I have never timed it. Have you, Strom?'

'No, me either. Why would you?' He shook his head.

'So, guys, I'm going home to try to sort out the Ripples. All I can think of now is to use what Magic I have built up and use my Crystal. It can heal, right?'

'It will be powerful in the Frail Realm,' Jinn said.

'Of course, I will have to take Dinkletons to wedge to the right spot.'

Strom and Jinn abruptly stopped in their tracks. They exchanged a knowing look and gestured to Nicole's Crystal.

'What?' Nicole asked.

'You, me and Strom have the same colour pink in our Crystals,' Jinn said.

'It's not very often three Dellamana have exactly the same colours, like we do. The pink Crystals together will increase healing,' Strom said.

'How do they do that?'

'Because the pink has a touch of saffron colour, which is powerful,' Strom said.

'The Prefects have a full dose of saffron,' Jinn said.

'Only Dellamana that get saffron in a whole dose can be a Prefect. So, our pink colours together are really useful,' Strom said.

'All the colours mean something, from providing health, strength, and protection from blocks turning into bigger issues. They all have different roles. They can work on the emotional or physical requirements of a Magic,' Jinn said.

'For Dellamana, our specialty magic is the purple coloured Voltz. All the other colours give us our skills. Like the Prefects, they are a little different. They have strong purple Voltz, plus their red colour in their Crystal is of the highest shade. Some Dellamana who are good at creating colour in the Frail Realm have really strong greens. These matching with their Voltz gives them very high skills in that area. Other Dellamana who are scientists like Nava have strong silver colour. Dellamana would not be very special without our purple building blocks of purple colour.'

Nicole gave a hesitant nod.

Strom sighed. 'It really takes a long time for humans to catch on! No Marnie has the same shade of any colour, which makes us individuals, see? But we all have purple Voltz. The magic force that makes us Dellamana.'

'We all have our different colour sets. Orange can come in thousands of different presentations.'

'I don't get it? Why is it good for us three to have the same pink?'

'Because, dummy, Strom and I are the only Marnie to receive the same shade of pink. And now you have it also. So the three of us are linked by that colour and are able to put them together, of course for the greater good,' Jinn said as a relaxed smile crossed her face.

'Jinn and I have used them in pranks on other Marnie. We have never used them in the way a pair should be used,' Strom said.

When Nicole did not answer, Jinn said, 'All the colours together are called the Illuminance.'

'Yeah, I can see that.' Nicole nodded.

'Give the girl a pat on the back and a medal.' Strom tossed back his hair. 'Still, I can't for the life of me work out why you have that shade of pink. You are, after all, part human.'

Jinn nodded in agreement, steam pouring from her mouth. 'It's totally grossness, in my opinion.'

Nicole ignored them and the steam that now surrounded them. She thought about what they had said. Jinn had her pink colour and that contained a slice of saffron. How was it that she was not able to send rainbows yet?

'Ahh, excuse me, that is my only weakness. Damn rainbows.'

'We could be your WingMarnie,' Strom added.

Nicole folded her arms. What on earth were they talking about?

16

'Okay, so what does that mean?' They were still in the corridor filled with Savants coming out of classrooms. The teachers were dressed in black robes with red trim. As they walked, they chatted with others, waved, and took a good look at Nicole as they passed by.

'Think of us if you need help. We are your Marnie – there's a reason we are allowed to show you around,' Jinn said with a serious face.

Nicole shrugged her shoulders.

'Look, see how we have the same shade of pink,' Strom said. 'Up 'til now, it was only Jinn and I who had that.' They all looked at their Crystals. Both Marnie had their pink highlighted and watched Nicole's go through the rapid changing. 'There!' they yelled. 'We both saw it the first time we met you. We couldn't believe it.'

'Back in the day, Marnie who had identical colours were allowed to help with curses that needed extra healing. Marnie that had good control were allowed to join short missions. But we are not allowed to do that anymore.'

'Certain Marnie have too many blocks to do the job, and these actually remove the protective ring around the Crystal, making it exposed and vulnerable to theft,' Strom said.

'So, that could have been Raisa's problem? Not just because she took her Crystal unprotected to my world.'

They nodded solemnly. 'Stinking bad luck.' Strom pressed his lips together.

'Her blocks caused her to make the decision to take her Crystal to my world. And because of the amount of blocks, her colours were not protected by theft?' Nicole looked for confirmation.

The Marnie nodded. Jinn was no longer puffing steam.

'So the inside colours of the Crystal could be pulled out?'

They nodded again. Strom sighed with satisfaction.

'All she had left was her Crystal.' Nicole's eyes widened.

'A useless yet beautiful artifact,' Strom added.

'We don't know if the entire colour file was taken. She may have been left with the dregg colours,' Jinn added.

Nicole changed the subject. 'Talk to me about Dinkletons.'

'Look, we can get into big trouble,' Jinn said.

Nicole assumed the spoilt Marnie rarely got into trouble. 'Okay, so when was the last time you saw a Stoneycraft?' Nicole threw her arms up past her head.

'Oh, they come for celebrations from time to time. I have seen about ten Stoneycraft all up. They don't speak to the likes of us though. They interact with Prefects normally,' Jinn whispered.

Nicole saw Dinkletons at the end of the corridor; even though he was far away he seemed close. His power consumed the area.

'What is with the eye?' Nicole shuddered as she remembered the first time she saw Dinkletons' gross eye closed with a sticky green substance that had made a line down his face.

'They don't rely on their eyes for sight. Their Magic projects all around like a satellite, and they can take in more than a mere eye would. So they have access to everything,' Strom said, looking around. Other Marnie were making faces at them, at hearing the conversation.

'Like a living computer?' Nicole asked.

Strom shook his head. 'Dinkletons' race can multitask, they can do heaps of things all at once. For this, they need more time alone than your average high-achieving Magic.'

'So they can think better alone?'

'Not really, but they like their alone time.'

'For Pete's sake, you will confuse the girl,' Jinn interrupted. 'They must divide their thoughts into logic, as Stoneycraft call it. They don't have a brain like you and I.'

Strom laughed. 'Way to go not confusing her.'

Jinn grabbed Nicole by the shoulders and looked straight into her eyes. 'Their "logic" is an immense power. Power that exceeds *all* the magic that exists.'

'That ever has and ever was.' Strom dramatically waved his arms around.

17

'Hello, Jinn, Strom. You been taking good care of Nicole?' asked a voice, causing all three to jump. Jinn flushed red in the face. Strom yelped, sparks flying, and Nicole realised they had been caught gossiping, but how had he got there that fast?

'What an interesting conversation.' Dinkletons stood eye to eye with the three. Nicole admired his lush coat, his saucer eyes and beautiful aura that bounced off him. She thought about what Jinn had said. That his race was the strongest of all the Magical beings. It was hard to comprehend that this was the same mangy small cat who she first met at the park. Now he was large; in height he came eye to eye with her. The power in those eyes of his made it impossible to look into them for too long. She had to tear her face away.

Jinn gushed heartily. 'I have a lab class.'

'Wait a minute.' Nicole hugged Jinn. 'Thanks for everything.'

'What about my hug?' Strom asked smiling.

Dinkletons laughed. 'Off with you, Strom. Stop teasing.'

After this hurried goodbye, they were both gone down the hallway, which burst into music.

'The music is for their blocks,' Dinkletons said as they watched them disappear.

'The steam is harmless enough?' Nicole asked.

'Try keeping control of hundreds of them.'

'I guess. They are so...'

'Like you?'

'When I go home, do I have music to help my blocks?'

'That is already installed on the television, in the music section.'

'Magic music will be interesting.'

They were walking in the opposite direction of all the Marnie, who were all excited about the Stoneycraft and the girl with the Magical molecules just steps away from them. Soon it was just Dinkletons and Nicole.

'Did you enjoy the class?'

Nicole nodded. 'It was cool. I hate school; it is so frustrating being there.'

'Of course you don't.'

'I am at the bottom of the class.'

'You should excel; everything in the Frail Realm should come easy for you.'

Nicole thought about her cousin and their toxic relationship.

'What happens when you are around her?' He intercepted the thought.

'I never want to be in the same room as her.'

'Is it like a dragging feeling?'

She shook her head. 'No, it is raw, like I can't protect myself from her.'

'That is not good for everyone involved. Lena will be feeling the same.'

I never once thought about how this affected Lena.

'Not your fault or Lena's.'

Nicole stopped. 'A Tangle is the bad one, right?'

'How long have you felt this way about your cousin?'

'My mother told me that when I was a baby I would cry only when Lena was around. I never cried any other time. We would both be screaming 'til one of us was taken away. As kids, we ignored each other and still do. I find being in her presence awful.'

'You spend a lot of time together when you go to dance class? What about school?'

'How did you know about that?' Nicole did a double take. She had told no one about her dancing or Lena yet.

Dinkletons' whiskers straightened like long, hard spikes and stuck out about two hand lengths. 'We did a full background check on you when the Helix message reached Rolte.'

'I suppose it would not have taken long.' Nicole laughed weakly.

'A true relationship curse has the potential to ripple through families. You can see how it has affected both your family and Lena's. How are you with your other cousins?'

'We get on well.'

'In time, those ties would be included in the curse. A growing Tangle sets off more and more Ripples, causing maximum grief and it was just a matter of time before they would have caught the Tangle.'

'I don't like the sound of that. So, my Ripples have not harmed them?'

'Only your parents and Lena so far, but as we have said, that would not have lasted.'

'Do they get affected by my blocks?'

'Blocks and Tangle harm you. The Ripples harm others,' Dinkletons said. 'Remember your blocks are from repressed Magic.'

She looked down as she walked. She was thinking she was starting to get the terminology now but, man, it was confusing.

'Wonder why Lena was caught in all of this?'

'I am sure you will find out.'

I will find out?

'Tell me about your dad.'

'To be honest, he's mean. My mother is nervy around him. And he always hurts himself physically. At first it was only minor things, but they are getting more serious. He hasn't got any friends and the ones my mother had won't come around anymore.'

'Yes, we uncovered a few accidents: the broken finger and several wounds that needed attention. Are you aware that your father suffers blinding headaches?'

She wasn't.

'Marnie never cry, by the way. Even when they are born, they are quiet. Crying damages Magic cells.'

'So, if I cry it causes pain?'

'Oh yes, that and other blocks. The Tangle and its Ripples projected themselves into all areas of your life. Split off to different issues – your dad and mother, Lena, school and your physical pains and moods are all connected.'

Nicole nodded, deep in thought.

'Lena will be jealous of you.'

Nicole shook her head. 'She hasn't anything to be jealous about. I suck at school; she doesn't. She is at the top of all the year's classes in every subject.' Nicole thought about her cousin's confident personality and how she felt invisible around her strong character. She pictured her standing in a group with her friends, the way she stood out and took the attention. The faces of others told it all: admiration mixed with envy. Nicole saw it every day, but from a distance. 'I am jealous of her.'

'It should be the other way around.' Dinkletons right eye was shut.

'We are both good at dancing. Neither of us is better than the other. Doesn't matter how much I try to be better, I can't.'

They made their way outside on a tiled walkway. Nicole could see herself in the shiny surface. She noticed Dinkletons' eye was still closed, and now understood she needed to allow him his Magic alone time.

They came to the bottom of a staircase. On the landing was an impressive fountain. It had three tiers. The water was a beautiful shade of aqua and the fountain was made of white marble. Nicole heard a slight hum coming from the water as it fell. 'The Marnie did not mention how big it is.'

'This spring has cleansing elements. Marnie need to do this often because your Crystals capture muddled thoughts. This helps minimise their greys in a controlled environment.'

Nicole popped her chain into the clear water. Soon, faint dots came to the surface of her Crystal.

'You have a few muddled thoughts that will now be cleared. These are the beginning of blocks you will start to get from now on.'

'What are things that Marnie can do to harm themselves?' They stood at the bottom of the three, tiered levels leading to the fountain.

'Full-blown blocks can cause jumps to go haywire, which is why they are not allowed to do this activity. They can physically hurt themselves. They can also project other Marnie to places in Orra, which is not a pleasant experience for the one on the receiving end.'

'Oh wow, that's intense. How come I am allowed to jump?' Nicole asked as they walked slowly ahead.

'You have a Prefect watching you whenever you do it. Don't worry; you will only do a few short jumps this trip and your blocks are not yet established, but they will come, by the look of those colours racing in your Crystal.'

Nicole breathed a sigh of relief about the jumping. She thought about what he said about managing her Magic.

Now she knew what was expected of her, and she had to start putting it all into practice. *Watch out for greys.*

Dinkletons ran ahead up another set of stairs and out of sight while she struggled to attach her necklace. She found herself in an opening with faint music. It sounded familiar. Her thoughts were starting to organise themselves in her brain in better order.

Her mind wandered to Strom and his deeply expressive eyes and the way he looked at her. He could read her thoughts – a great advantage over her. All Dellamana had a spectacular glow from their faces; something about Strom's stood out, like Nava's green eyes.

Why did she keep thinking about Strom? Anyway, she wasn't here for a boy's attention. She had more important things to do. But his noticing her felt good in a terrifying way. She would not think about him again. Well, at least she could try.

She drew a deep breath. She had to focus on what she was going to do back home. How was she going to get rid of the Night Hag and Knocker that were clinging onto her parents? A shiver ran down her spine at the thought of it. Would her Crystal be enough? She had Dinkletons there to help her. All she knew was that she had to act fast to get her parents relief.

Dinkletons was around the next bend, leaning on a door frame. 'What took you so long?'

'You don't have to run off.' But she felt good at having that time alone.

'Ah, but you enjoyed that five minutes, didn't you?' When she didn't answer, he said, 'You need to find your own feet. I am giving you that space. You just had your first prescribed fountain and music therapy. If we smothered you, it would throttle your growth. Magic requires room to settle.'

'I am not a Marnie, so why do I get those treatments?'

'You're pretty close.' He blinked.

She followed him through double doors. 'This is your private space; it will be for all future trips.'

Everything was big and luxurious. The bed was covered with cotton multicoloured pillows that sat atop a puffy quilt with a giant 'N' printed on what Nicole thought looked like golden beads. Nicole noticed lamps on each side of the bed, hovering without a bedside table. They moved with ease in a figure eight, their colour changing every few seconds and filling the room with light so extraordinary it made her room back home seem dull.

'This light is so different.' Nicole looked around. *Future trips?*

'The impossible colours originate here in Orra. The reason that your light is not as vibrant at home is because that is has no magical components.'

She pushed open a door to two bathrooms. One inside and one outside, which was filled with the yellow and red glitter. Nicole thought she would feel uncomfortable having a bath among the glitter but today had been a day of accepting the unacceptable.

A voice startled her.

'Good day, Miss Nicole, can I interest you in a bath? Perhaps a treatment, as it is twelve years overdue. Your poor hair is in desperate need of attention.' The voice came in stereo from all around. She heard Dinkletons laugh from the other room. Nicole went back into the bedroom. 'A talking bathroom?'

'That will only be in place when you need Magical pampering. This is also something you have to keep up. It is all keeping you in good condition for your Magic to settle.'

Nicole moved to the closet, which was jam-packed with everything she could possibly need. Her clothes all had a golden tag saying Belba. She noticed off-hand that some of the clothes she already had similar to back at home, like jean shorts, big tees, sports caps and designer sneakers, exactly as her cousin Lena had. Was that a coincidence?

Instead, she turned and said, 'Everything is lovely. Thank you.'

'By the way, all of those clothes have been replicated for you in your new wardrobe at home.'

'How did that happen?' Nicole bounced on her toes.

'You are Magic, and because of this, you are entitled to these perks. Belba have already set it up.'

Nicole realised her parents had to be told about all of this. She stopped pacing. 'I need to go see my parents. They deserve to know what is going on. And I've got to do something about the Knocker and Night Hag.'

18

'Will you come with me?' She looked into the saucer-size eyes.

Dinkletons put his paw onto her arm. 'Of course I will. You have the Gloine and your Crystal colours. Even though they are racing they can still help you.'

'I feel physically stronger. I used to always feel tired.'

'And how are you doing mentally? Are you able to focus better?'

'I think so. I can telemute a bit and can get rid of dots that come to my Crystal.'

'And what do you think that will be doing?'

'It is making me stronger in my Magic.'

'If you can telemute, it means your Magic is being reignited, which is wonderful, Nicole.'

'I think I should take Jinn and Strom as our Crystals will work together and make the healing stronger to get rid of the Hag and Knocker.'

Dinkletons was wide-eyed, both eyes beaming at her. 'You know about the Marnie Crystals working together? I thought those rascals would tell you as soon as they saw that pink.'

She nodded. 'I need all the help that I can get.'

'It will be best to just take one on this trip.'

'They told me two is better.'

Dinkletons grinned. 'Just one for this trip. Strom is a better choice Crystal colour wise, as he has passed his rainbow test so has more control. That is when he puts his mind to it.'

'I know about them building rainbows, but what is the test?'

'When they feel they are ready for the test, they have to prepare the colours and make sure they are stable and stick together. They would make three rainbows to pass the test. Strom has done this; Jinn has only sent one rainbow so far. But to be fair, it is a difficult test.'

Now Nicole knew why Jinn had made that face before.

'If saffron is the colour only given to potential Prefects, then Jinn and Strom both have a slice of that colour already?'

'Yes, Jinn will be able to do her rainbows soon, though sometimes she rushes them and knows she needs to slow down. She is tipped to be a strong Dellamana in the future. It will be good for her to stay back this trip. She needs to overcome the block of irritation. Come on, don't worry about her. You need to meet the Prefects.'

Nicole sighed. At least that would put off telling Jinn she was not coming with her to the Frail Realm. But the thought of meeting the Prefects was scary. She wrapped her arms around her waist to try and calm the nerves.

***

'The Arx is where the Prefects have meetings away from Rolte,' Dinkletons said as they jumped from her bedroom to the top of a flight of stairs.

'That was a fast jump,' Nicole said, feeling dizzy.

'That is because you came with me. I move in fast forward. Sorry about that.'

Dinkletons went ahead, his great paws taking each step with such grace that he seemed to glide. His coat smelled like coconut; the mist coming from his aura was filled with gold and silver flecks. Nicole reached out to touch it. As her hand moved through the floating glitter, it settled on her palm. She felt a jolt then heat.

Nicole was thinking about how awkward it was going to be talking to her parents about all of this. Would her dad blow up and leave, or worse send her into her room, and not listen to a word?

Dinkletons hurried Nicole along. They walked towards a glass door that opened as they got closer. In the room sat two old Dellamana. As Nicole walked closer to them, the door closed behind her. The room was as big as her school hall and filled with not the expected modern, out-of-this-world furniture, but plain, basic, solid antique pieces. Large tables made from wood and gold, chairs that were intricately carved, rugs that looked new, but Nicole knew otherwise.

'This room houses rare artifacts from all over the worlds, not just yours. See that table?' He gestured his head. 'That is made from prehistoric trees from your world.'

'What about those?' Nicole pointed to a row of strange sculptures.

'Nah, those are from the Old Masters. They live in a planet very far from here.'

As they walked the long distance from the door, Nicole could not help being distracted by the strange museum of treasures.

'They are Prefects from Rolte,' Dinkletons said. 'We don't refer to them as Dellamana. Don't be shy,' Dinkletons teased and flicked his tail at her.

They were dressed casually, which surprised Nicole. The lady wore a simple dress and the man a T-shirt and brown pants. Their hands were splayed on the seat arms, the Hallr Crystals they wore as rings drawing Nicole's attention. She could see colours moving from where she stood. Their auras were the same: thick red and blended together. Looking at it made her face ache.

She came to a stop a few feet away from where they sat. Dinkletons whispered in her ear, 'Those chairs they are sitting on are the oldest known in all the centuries of any planet that exists.'

The female averted her eyes to Dinkletons. 'It is wonderful to see you Dinkletons and thank you for your help with this.' She looked to Nicole. 'Welcome to Orra, Nicole. I am Mahala and this is Jivan.'

Nicole noted the ease of Dinkletons' body language. He sat and was relaxed. She realised that it was he, rather than these two Prefects, who was the most important one present.

'Not every day we see what is standing right in front of us,' Jivan said, peering at her. 'You are Sape.'

Nicole had a sudden weakness in her legs. Sape? *What does that mean?*

'We will get to that,' Jivan said as he waved his hand about. 'Prefects are old, as you can see. We don't act like old Frail people, mind you; we can run and think clearly. This is due to our saffron dose from the Crystal. Not all Dellamana receive this colour. If we get it, we can choose if we want to go into service on Rolte and become old or stay within Orra.'

'Yes, Strom and Jinn told me about the saffron. Rook has the saffron?'

'Yes, he and Dex, the one you saw in the Frail Realm, have saffron. But there are many Dellamana who receive saffron and stay within Orra,' Jivan said.

'Why do you have to look old?' Nicole thought it didn't make sense if they were that powerful.

'It is an honour to receive the full dose of saffron and be admitted to Rolte. Looking old does not concern us.'

'Some Prefects don't, but most do.'

'You work in the head office. Where is that?' Nicole tilted her head. This old stuff was too complicated, Nicole thought. There were young looking Dellamana and now these old Prefects; she couldn't get her head around it.

'Rolte is on the rim of Orra. It rotates continually around the edge of Orra, but slowly.' Jivan laughed. 'To give you an idea on how slow. It would take over four Frail years for Rolte to rotate once.'

Mahala spoke softly and Nicole could only just hear her. 'Please use your Crystal to help soothe your eyes. Our auras are strong and can sting. Even Dellamana are not invincible to it.'

Nicole did as she was told. She rubbed her Crystal with her hand and then held it to her eyes. It helped a little, but the ache was still there in her temples.

'Auras are our Magic on the inside coming into form on the outside. Our auras create Voltz that are returned into the body. This maintains who we are and our Magical abilities.'

Before she knew it, Nicole was speaking. 'So, the aura's role is to make Voltz? I wondered what its purpose was.'

Nicole thought about this. She pictured everyone and their auras, the different colours and the way they moved, cloud-like, around their owners.

'So, what they are, Nicole, is an example of Magic in the making. When Magic is first designed in the body it appears as an aura on the outside of us. Within this aura are our very special Voltz.'

'How do I start to make Magic?'

Jivan grinned. 'You are doing it already. Once you

have colour building up in your Crystal, it happens by itself. Voltz are developed. A complicated process, but Voltz make us very powerful and set us apart from other Magical races, because we can grow more Magic, while other Magic are born with what they have. And you, dear, have a blue aura. Auras come in many impossible colours, and no two are the same shade; it is as original as you. Yours will slowly come into view. Just give it time.'

It was the best information. Up 'til now, she didn't really understand what auras were other than light.

'Now, do you know that Raisa is responsible for your Magic abilities and that she has lost her Illuminance, the colour out of her Crystal?' Jivan asked.

'Yes, and because of this she is not able to grow anymore Voltz,' Nicole answered.

'That is right: if you have no Illuminance, which is the combination of all the colours in your Crystal, you cannot grow Voltz. Just like you were not able to grow Voltz in the Frail Realm. You survived on your base Magic, like Raisa has been doing,' Jivan said. 'You understand?'

Nicole focused on listening and nodded.

'Raisa's Illuminance is in the Rustic Realm. When she lost it on the Marnie excursion to the Frail Realm, we were able to track it.' Mahala stood up and walked towards her. 'It was found in a toxic world, which is poisonous to our Magic cells. It was what we call a Kyacin atmosphere, and the elements that make it up are arsenic, lead, and polonium and are on our caution list.'

'Meaning we can't go anywhere near there,' Jivan said.

'What about Frail?' Nicole asked.

'Frail are resistant to Kyacin.' Jivan smiled at Mahala. Nicole had said the right thing.

'First, you want to go see your parents and we understand that. Remember you are on a Magical trip as Sape and not Frail. This requires a different mindset from what you once had. It will give you a taste of the Magic side of your realm.'

'I am a Sape?'

'Yes, Sape is where you stand within the Dellamana Magic scale. Nava sent the results a few moments ago. They will be sent to everyone's palm computers now. A Sape is when you have more Magic cells than Frail cells,' Mahala said.

'And not enough Magical molecules to be a full Marnie or, in time, Dellamana,' Jivan said.

Nicole's mind was reeling; goose bumps ran down her spine. *A Sape, like one of a kind.*

'You will be safe with Dinkletons, and I hear that you wanted to take Strom?'

She nodded. They smiled. A blush crossed her face and she had to look down.

'You are doing well in receiving colours,' Jivan said.

'I am noticing I can telemute some things, but the colour is racing. I can't work out the individual colours. Will this be a problem?'

Jivan leaned forwards in his seat. 'There is a good side to those colours coming in fast; it means you have been gifted them. They will all be yours to use once you are ready.'

Nicole wanted to ask them how she could slow the thoughts that raced through her mind, thoughts that chattered endlessly.

Jivan surprised her with a smile. 'Just think of it as a process to get to where you need your Magic to be. All Marnie go through this process; it's a growing pain type thing.'

She shook her head. 'But what does that mean?'

'You need to be attentive to the messages delivered by your Crystal; they will be almost audible as your skills increase. With your rapid new growth taking place, you will never stay the same. Your Crystal will advance as you do,' Jivan said. 'You will be told many times you must manage the greys as they are the root of blocks. You went many years without tuning into your Magic, and now you are making up for lost time.'

'I have seen Marnie with torch-glowing eyes as well.' Nicole thought back to the halls of the school and the Marnie with eyes that beamed all sorts of different colours.

'Yes, that as well,' Jivan said. 'We have made a note of those Marnie.'

'The flames do not burn them, do they?' Now she was worried she got the Marnie into trouble.

'When you have fire on your body you must try to understand where it comes from. It might be jealousy, frustration, or tiredness.'

'Know that whenever you're not in Orra, Prefects on Rolte will be monitoring and taking care of you whenever you need them.'

Nicole thought, *Will I ever be alone, or will I forever have Dellamana telemuting my every thought?*

The Prefects got to their feet. Nicole noticed the ease of the motion.

Mahala came over and took her hands. 'Of course it doesn't work that way. We have Magic respect for you and your privacy will be paramount to all of us. This just means we are not far away if you ever need us.'

She passed her a pair of white stockings. 'These are cloud-stepping boots. You need to use one per trip to safeguard your Illuminance. They will protect it by keeping Rogue at a safe distance. They are a warning from the Prefects to keep away.'

Nicole sat down on a nearby chair and slipped them on. She watched them adjust themselves to fit, stretching and shrinking to the outline of her shoe.

19

The wedge felt the same as swimming through water, framed by light shining towards an unseen path. Dinkletons was beside her, and he looked like he was enjoying the ride. Both his eyes were closed, and his whiskers vibrated. He sat with his long front legs elegantly crossed over at the paws. Strom was opposite her and still held the thrilled expression that he had taken on when he knew he was coming with her. Nicole didn't want to remember Jinn's reaction. She had thrown her hands up and stomped away, leaving little fires in her wake.

Five turns and three long drops took her breath away, and they arrived in the park, hidden from her family. She knew that Dinkletons could navigate with pinpoint accuracy to any spot in the realms. This made the whole thing less traumatic, even with the long drops. She leaned against him the whole trip and felt happy he was coming with her. When she looked at him, he winked his good eye. He was always calm, and it rubbed off on Nicole.

Strom stood, eyes darting all around. 'This is awesome.'

Nicole noticed he had only slight distortion. His hair was dirty blonde, not his normal white. His hands were double the normal size. 'Are you okay, Strom?'

'Oh, it hurts, but it is worth it to be able to come to the Frail Realm,' Strom said. But Nicole could tell by his hunched shoulders and the fact that he was turning away from her that there was no way he would complain to her. 'This is my first experience of pain. I have an improved respect for Frail.'

Dinkletons looked wet and thin. Instead of the beautiful gentle giant he actually was, he was now an untidy mess. Nicole felt heaviness in her chest for them. At the same time, the aches hit her as well. She sat on the grass, holding her head that felt it would explode.

'Why do you distort?' she gasped.

'It is your gravity. I might look awful, but I feel no pain.'

Nicole staggered over to a nearby pond and looked at her reflection.

The person looking back was not her. Staring back was something hideous with a lopsided face and body to match. When she moved, it moved. Everything was twisted.

'It is only temporary,' Strom said. She looked up and he smiled, making her stomach turn upside down. Her face burned. 'First wedges are the worst, apparently.' He guided her away from the water. 'Better not to look.'

Panic threatened to take over. 'Why didn't you warn me it would be this bad? I am from this world.'

'The Frail Realm's gravity is very strong. Put that with a wedge, and it happens to all wedgers,' Strom said.

'You both need to hold on for a minute. Never again will it be this long,' Dinkletons said.

'You promise?'

'I have relief,' Dinkletons said.

'Tell us fast.' Nicole's eyes glowed with tears.

'I have a dart wave that will take the pain and distortions away sooner.'

'So how come you and Rook didn't use it the last time when you collected me?' The tips of her fingers were stinging. She shook them, but they still hurt.

'I have only just developed it. As you have Frail in you, you are more at risk of pain because your cells are not familiar with the gravity of moving from one realm to another.'

'As your future will be here and in Orra, we need to make it less traumatic for you.'

'Dinkletons, you are a life saver,' Nicole said.

'Look, they are leaving,' Strom said, pointing to the party in the distance. They were gathering their things and making their way back to their cars.

'I've been gone the whole party? Dad is going to be filthy.' Nicole watched some of the group get into cars and drive away. Sara was waving at her. She waved back.

'Look, someone is coming,' Strom said.

'That's my dad. What do I do?' She looked at Dinkletons and Strom for a quick answer. Her hands began to shake.

But he had already arrived. Nicole, wide-eyed, watched her dad look at Dinkletons and Strom. She didn't know if she looked normal. Her legs pulsated and she found it hard to stand up straight.

'You look like you've been dragged through a hedge backwards. What have you been doing?' Her dad's face was strained, his neck was red, and his posture stiff. He didn't move his arms, instead leaving them resting at his sides.

Strom leaned in towards her dad with a grin on his face. Dinkletons was looking at her with a penetrating focus. 'You know your onions, Pops.'

Nicole cleared her throat. What on earth was she going to say?

Behind her Strom laughed, he had thought the phrase 'What on earth' funny and the level of anger was something Strom had never seen before.

Her dad shot a look of fury to Strom, who was still trying to contain his laughing. 'Nicole we are leaving. Alone.' He shot Strom yet another angry look, which started Strom off again.

'Get a hold of yourself Strom,' Dinkletons said, but he knew what the Marnie thought was funny. He couldn't really blame him. It was, after all, the first time he had witnessed such a loss of control; it had the same result but different delivery in Marnie. They did not call it anger but 'mislead' blocks.

The voice that came from her dad now scared her. He boomed. Everyone in the park could hear and looked into their direction.

'Right now, you little shit, or you will regret it.' He pointed to the ground next to him. 'All you ever do is cause your mother and I problems. It's got to stop and right now.'

'Brutal,' Strom said, suddenly serious.

At this moment, Nicole did not know how to handle her dad. This was the worst she had ever seen him. How could she reason with such a mood? Tears filled her eyes and she felt a panic build in her tummy and move up into her throat.

Nicole felt a scratchy tail on her leg and turned to see Dinkletons right beside her. Rook also had moved forward in support. The one eye that was opened seemed to give her strength, the tail tightly wound around her ankle.

Her dad was breathing hard, his lower jaw jutted out. He watched the two beside his daughter and his eyes nearly popping out of his head. His nostrils flared while he tried to catch his breath, seemingly incredulous at what the cat was doing.

It was such a small gesture having them beside her, but had great results. Nicole found a response.

'Dad, you have to calm down. This is not a suggestion;

you have to stop and listen,' Nicole said. 'These two are going to tell me, and you and mum, what we have been waiting all my life to learn.'

'Ahh, you are going to go on about the mumbo jumbo again.' That was what her dad had always referred to her 'differences'. Always in a negative impatient way.

'Whether you like it or not, I am going to take a chance and see if any of what these guys have told me is true. I have to find out.'

Nicole waited for her dad to explode. He always did when she questioned him, but instead he said in a tone softer than a yell, 'You've missed Sara's birthday. You are a selfish little girl, Nicole.'

'Well, that's a shocker,' Strom said.

'You shut the hell up!' His face contorted with rage as he pointed a finger close to Strom's nose.

Strom closed his mouth tight and pretended to zip his lips shut.

Nicole watched her dad double take when Strom pretended to throw away the key to his hips, his face feigning stupidity.

Her dad's face went bright red.

'I didn't mean to be away for the whole thing.'

'You tell that to poor Sara. We are ashamed of you.'

'Ouch, that hurt,' Strom said.

'I thought I told you to be quiet?' His jaw was clenched, his finger close to Strom's face. 'I don't like you, son, and I don't want you hanging around my daughter.'

Strom took a step backwards, holding up two hands. 'Chill, dude.' He whispered to Dinkletons, 'As if he has a choice.'

'Look, this is my Hallr Crystal, given to me this morning. It is Magical and links to my colours that make me strong. This is Dinkletons. He took me to Orra, my other home.'

Her dad's eyes blazed at her. 'You're unbelievable. Walk home, Nicole. I want you out of my sight.' He stormed off.

'Well, that went well. I thought your parents knew about your gifts,' Strom whispered.

Nicole's shoulders slumped. 'They know a little. The rest will blow their minds.'

20

'How far away is your house?' Strom broke the silence after ten minutes of walking.

'Not far. Another five minutes and we will be there.' Nicole walked ahead of them on the narrow footpath. 'But I'm still not sure what I'll do when I get there. They've never made me walk home before. I'm in big trouble.'

'Your father is hilarious.' Strom giggled.

Nicole looked away from Strom. 'He wasn't trying to be funny.'

'You could've fooled me.'

Dinkletons and Strom laughed.

Nicole looked back at her companions. Both bounced along like this was another normal day. She glared at them, and Strom shot back, 'Come on, Nicole, this is so much fun. Can't you just relax? You can't blame me; I've never been here. It's fascinating. I love Frail. Everything looks much smaller than I remember from the Rolte screens.'

The pain was now gone and Dinkletons had told her the distortions had disappeared after he used the dart wave on her and Strom. But not one of them was giving her any advice on what to do when they got to her house. What was she going to say?

'If anyone has a plan, now would be a good time to share it,' Nicole tried.

'Oh, stop, Nicole! There are Sylph Rogue over there,' Strom said. 'Wow, they are busy.'

A few metres down the road, a group of creatures flew into view. Nicole stopped in her tracks, too stunned to move. Dinkletons whispered, 'They haven't seen us yet.'

Nicole watched in fascination. They were the size of a small dog. They looked like a cross between a peacock and a pigeon, apart from their wings, which cascaded and floated in different lengths. Their tails were balls of transparent fire and appeared to be like feathers. Before she could take in the detail of their coats, shape, and colour, they disappeared as quickly as they'd arrived.

'Where did they go?' Nicole asked with frustration.

'They knew we're here. They recognised our higher Magic.' Strom scoffed. 'What a pack of killjoys.'

'I was still watching them. They were lovely,' Nicole said, looking around for more. 'It's hard to imagine such things here, and hard to believe no one can see them.'

'No one can see Sylph but other Magic folk,' Strom said with a satisfied smile.

'So, I couldn't see them before today because of my tangle?' Nicole was puzzled. 'But I managed to see the Thisbe when I was a baby.'

'Thisbe can be seen by everyone if they allow it. They are a different category of Magic from the Rogue you will see here,' Strom said.

'What do they do here?' Nicole asked, referring to the Sylph.

'You can answer that in a minute, Strom.' Dinkletons flicked his tail around Nicole's ankle. It felt creepy and scratchy. 'When you are alone here, all you have to do is speak up and they will listen to you. Just get their attention before they freak out and disappear.'

'So, how come I can see them now and not when I was growing up?'

'Now you have your Crystal, your Magic is able to grow and you are building your first Voltz,' Dinkletons answered. 'Back then, the Tangle was in charge. You are now able to gain control.'

Dinkletons nodded to Strom, signaling he could speak. 'Sylph glide around and gain energy from pollens in the air. They are productive and keep the Frail bee numbers up and assist in the pollination of flowers.'

Before the intriguing creatures left, Nicole watched them fly to the ground, scrambling to get up and banging into each other, squealing as they good-naturedly shoved and pushed one another.

'They are so silly. Do they stay here or go back to another world?'

'Sylph are one of the many Rogue who live here. They have a close affection with some Frail dogs; they go sleep with them after they finish work.'

Nicole realised that there was more to learn about the Sylph.

21

They arrived at the flat driveway of Nicole's family home, a pretty, white, two-storey home.

'Good job, Nicole, best garden I've seen yet,' Strom said, his arms folded and taking in the rockery and the roses.

'How did you know I did the garden...?' Nicole stopped when she saw them shake their heads at her.

'We can tell it has Dellamana energy,' Strom said. 'I stand corrected: Sape.'

'So, everyone knows about me being a Sape?' She remembered the Prefects telling her they would send the message.

Strom held his palm up and after a few taps she could read:

```
Nicole is Sape, high-level Magic.
```

Nicole felt a headache pulsing above her eye. What was she going to do and say? She didn't have time to prepare. To be flung into this situation this fast was mind-blowing.

The front door was yanked open, and her parents stood in the entrance to the house. Her father's eyes were intense, and his mouth was set in an unimpressed line. Her mother had a 'please explain' expression on her face.

'Who the hell is this kid?' her dad yelled, loud enough for the whole neighbourhood to hear. Nicole flinched and swallowed a lump in her throat.

It didn't help that behind her Strom laughed. Clearly, he found what her dad said funny again. Nicole turned and saw Dinkletons give him a stern look. Strom pulled his face into a blank expression.

The surreal situation, combined with the fear that her dad would snap, made her erupt into a fit of nervous giggles. It seemed Strom felt the same and she heard his nose snort, which made her laugh even more.

Her dad looked at Strom and pointed. 'Get lost and don't come back.' He grabbed Nicole's arm and dragged her inside. 'This is no laughing matter.'

'Let Nicole tell her story,' Dinkletons said.

Nicole's parents stood rock-solid still. Her dad's grip on her arm loosened, and her parents' faces drained.

'What's the matter? Cat got your tongue?' Strom said.

'You are aware Nicole is different. Yet you choose not to listen because you think she ruined her cousin's birthday. Well, I can tell you, Nicole has her own problems to sort out.' Dinkletons spoke calmly.

Nicole realised by the looks on her parents' faces that they were aware they were about to find out whatever was wrong with their daughter. She could hear their thoughts, clearly, spewing questions. She looked at her Crystal, surprised to see it had stopped on pink. Strom lifted his ring finger. To Nicole's relief, it was pink as well.

'Ditto,' Strom said.

Inside the house, her parents' eyes, and the eyes of the Night Hag and Knocker, pierced hers in expectation. Both the Night Hag and Knocker had been pulled into this situation without their agreement by Nicole's working Tangle. The Rogue looked at her with black looks.

This complicated and split her good magic, making it malfunction, and all because she did not have enough magic Voltz to maintain and build her good quality magic. Her mother had a Night Hag firmly attached to her. It gnashed its long sharp teeth at them and hissed in the hope that she could be freed. Her dad had a Knocker, a snake-like Rouge that spiraled around him, giving his body sharp pokes as it slithered over him. It did not hurt her father but made him mad, irritable and irrational. Nicole could see how the Knocker was affecting him in the short couple of minutes she had observed them. She should have known there was a correlation between her issues and her parents. Her father had his arms folded defensively, but at this minute he was quiet, which was most uncharacteristic of him. How could he complain when the cat had spoken? Her mother closed the front door, and her hand was pressed against her throat, her eyes thick with panic.

Nicole's eyes watered as she got the first glimpse of the Night Hag and Knocker. They were behind her parents, and they were terrifying. Nicole saw that the Night Hag had her long, skinny arms wrapped around her mother's shoulders and neck, which had a mean, red welt on it, running from her ear to her throat. Nicole shivered.

The Hag gnashed its teeth and rested its head on her mother's shoulder, hair sprawling down her mother's arms. It was leaning its whole body weight on her. Nicole looked at her mother's feet; the Hag had entwined its leg around one ankle. No wonder she always had a sore back and was constantly tired and headachy, dragging that thing around with her all day.

Nicole dragged her eyes to her father's situation. The Knocker took the form of a snake that had his body wrapped around her father's neck. The Knocker's head hovered away from her father's body and moved around. Its body was brown and had sharp horns on either side of its head, which kept poking her dad. It lifted its head high and low. No wonder her dad was always mad.

Why do I get to see them now? she thought.

Because your Magic is growing, Dinkletons replied. *Your parents will not see the results of the Knocker and Hag when they look in the mirror. No scratches, welts, or bruises.*

Holy moly, they are brutal, Strom telemuted.

I can't do this, it's too horrible. But Nicole knew she had to help them.

'The Thisbe that visited me when I was eighteen months old was real.' Nicole looked at them through her eyelashes and hair that had fallen halfway across her face. 'Hamish was supposed to come back but he never did. That is why all of this has been going on for so long.'

Nicole heard her parents exhale.

'We all know I am different, but we didn't know why, right?' Nicole said as she pushed her hair away.

'Has it got to do with those two at the school?' her mother asked, and her dad groaned.

Nicole could tell her parents were upset, but to their credit, they managed a small nod.

So far so good. But despite this, the constant prodding of the Knocker on her dad's body resulted in the change of his mood right in front of her. He looked flushed, his veins stood out on his neck, and he seemed disoriented. Nicole felt so sorry for him at that moment. How long had this been going on for? She would hate to think. Her parents were being tormented and even though she experienced the brunt of it, she was the cause.

Nicole watched as Strom wandered into the connecting lounge and became engrossed in the pictures on the wall, touching everything. Nicole thought he looked silly going from one thing to another with his arms clasped behind his back.

'Kid, you knock that off,' her father said to him. Strom giggled under his breath and went into the next room.

'At the park, two people came to speak to me. I had to go back to their world for us to be safe and for me to learn what I am all about.'

'The same two we saw?' her mother asked, wide-eyed.

'No, but they are part of all of this. I'm learning about what I am. I'm called a Sape, which is a Dellamana with human blood. While Strom here' – she pointed to where he had been – 'is a child of Orra. They call them Marnie.' Nicole decided then and there not to tell them about the Night Hag and Knocker they had been infected with. It was too much.

'You went away?' Abby asked.

'Yes, to my Magical home, called Orra.'

Her mother went a sickly shade of green. Her father pursed his lips. Abby reached out to Jack and rubbed his shoulder in order to keep him calm.

They were interrupted by Strom, in the other room. 'Hey, Nicole, you better come check this out.'

Nothing was more important to Nicole than this discussion with her parents. Strom could wait. But before she could continue speaking, she caught Dinkletons' eye (the good one). His smile was twisted, showing his missing teeth. He crooked his neck and said, 'Go ahead.'

22

She led the way. Her parents and Dinkletons followed her into the modern kitchen, fitted with cream countertops and wood. Fresh flowers from their own garden sat in the middle of an island opposite the sink. Strom stood a few steps into the room and off to the side and flung his arm to show the pandemonium unfolding before her eyes.

They were crammed in all over the kitchen. Packets of food were ripped open. Rice, chips, sugar, flour were spread all over the kitchen floors and surfaces. The culprits were cheeky, as they had seen her and continued.

Nicole couldn't believe what she was seeing. The creatures that filled her family's kitchen had big backsides that wobbled as they moved. Bottom heavy would be an understatement. It would be funny if they weren't trashing her kitchen. All had black hair and narrow, mean, red eyes. They all had two teeth that overlapped thick lips. The small bodies were nicely dressed in shorts and matching tops in all different colours. It seemed they were stocking up on takeaways as well, as each held a hessian sack over their shoulders.

However, a few seconds later, when they saw Dinkletons, they froze. 'Stay where you are, Absonsams.'

They obeyed immediately: hands stopped in jars, fingers holding or jamming contents into their small mouths. Some were about to throw things and stopped as if in slow motion. Nicole heard the crackling of the food under their feet; a glass smashed narrowly in front of her, spilling strawberry jam. The thick substance was filled with shattered shards.

Nicole saw her parents standing behind Dinkletons. They too were looking around. It was obvious to Nicole they could not see the Absonsams, but they could see the mess.

'We've had a break-in?' her dad asked.

'Over to you, Nicole,' Dinkletons said.

Nicole widened her eyes at him. *You're joking, right?*

'You must deal with them,' Strom whispered, now serious.

Nicole cleared her throat and fumbled a step closer. Every single Absonsams took a step back from her. She did it again and again; they all moved back. Behind her Strom exploded in laughter, and so did she for a minute. She closed her eyes for a second to get control of her giggles. 'Stop it, Strom.'

The Absonsams moving in time with her steps had caught her off guard. Were they playing with her or what? She took a step, then they did, then stood perfectly still like statues. Even their faces froze. Not one of them took their eyes off Nicole. Through this banter, they looked naughty. Their eyes flicked side to side, telling her they wanted to or were getting ready to flee.

Beside her Strom stifled a laugh. 'Are these guys for real? Surely you can't take this mob seriously?'

Nicole tended to agree, apart from the shambles they had made of the kitchen. 'What are you doing in my house?'

Some of the Absonsams choked on their food and spat

it out. Nicole cringed. Strom poked his tongue out and wrinkled his nose. One of them came from the shadows of the others and spoke in a very loud voice. 'Why, it never bothered you before?'

'Things have changed. You will not mess my house up again,' Nicole said. She looked at her parents who were muttering to each other in confusion and heard Dinkletons shush them.

'It's almost impossible to be part of a conversation where you can't see what is going on,' Jack said.

Nicole turned to face her parents. 'I know it's crazy stuff, but I will explain. I just need to deal with this.'

'You humans can't talk, you are always messy,' the Absonsam said. Then, seeing Nicole move again, the Absonsams stepped back once more. The one that spoke was about two feet tall. 'We have been helping ourselves in here for years. We have seen you grow up, oblivious to your Magic.'

Nicole crossed her arms, took another step, and shook her head. 'From now on, you will do what I tell you to do.'

'Tough chance of that happening.' The Absonsam stood hunched over and meek, not at all the picture of a fearless leader. 'It is what we do, how we live.'

'Really?' Nicole placed her hands on her hips. 'We will have to sort that out. We can't have you going into Frail homes and trashing it.'

'It's only the kitchen, besides they don't see it. There are the Chars that come through and tidy. If we stopped, we would be doing them a disservice. Chars love to clean.'

Nicole walked forward, closer to the Absonsam leader, and held up her hands for him to stop talking.

'Hang on. We will leave,' said the Absonsam, sensing there was no reasoning with this girl, this Sape.

'You will leave when you tidy this kitchen!' Nicole was firm. 'And you will never come back here again.'

The Absonsams rushed around on their short legs and cleaned up faster than Nicole thought possible. In the end, their noses were all red. 'Satisfied?'

Nicole nodded, and they wasted no time getting out through the open windows they had come in by.

'Will they listen to me when you're not here?' Nicole asked Dinkletons.

'Absonsams are part of the Goblin family and are big gossipers. They would not dream of doing that now they know you are aware of your Magic,' Dinkletons said.

Nicole looked around the sparkling kitchen. 'They should make better use of their cleaning skills and do something positive rather than wreck places. I didn't see any of these inside the house before or even felt the mess they made.'

'The Tangle hid them. You, as Magic, would have prevented many from entering your house, but not all. They would have taken advantage of you not seeing them. They would have had fun with it,' Dinkletons said.

'So, what happens to the mess in other houses?'

'Prefects send in the cleaners, normally after the mess is made. Everyone knows Chars are the cleaning Rogue,' Strom said.

'Did you see or hear anything at all?' she asked her parents. They now looked out of place in their own home.

'A mess, but then it went, just like that,' Abby said. Nicole noticed her parents were holding hands for the first time in years.

'It's hard to think that Frail never see these creatures. What other sorts of Rogue will I encounter?'

'Frail, Rogue – what are they?' Her dad coughed.

'Frail are humans. Rogue live here with us; they are all around,' Nicole said.

'And you see them, Nicole?' her mother asked.

'Yes, I will now.'

Her mother started to cry. Nicole held her hand. She would have hugged her, but the Hag glared at her. 'It's a good thing.' She hoped.

'We better sit down and talk,' Dad said. 'Nicole, this is crazy stuff.'

They each sat on one of the kitchen island's comfortable stools.

'All my life I had Magic cells, from the time before I was born. All those strange things that happened – being born early, doing things other children could not do – were due to this. There is one thing, though: along with this, I have a curse. It's called a Tangle, and it caused me to behave the way I did.' She looked at her father, who was staring at her intently for the first time in years. 'This Tangle is still with me. It has grown over the years into Ripples and these harm others. It has caused all sorts of problems, from relationship breakdowns to poor schoolwork. I have to work out how to decrease its power. I have to start with the Ripples that are affecting you guys.'

'What is affecting us? How?' her father asked impatiently.

'Really? You don't know?' Strom questioned.

Nicole looked at her mother. 'Your nightmares and anxiety are from a Ripple. Dad, your issues with me are also connected. The way you feel and react is not your fault.' Nicole wouldn't scare them to death by telling them about the Night Hag and Knocker.

'Lena! That explains all that drama,' her mother said.

'How do you fix these things?' Dad asked.

'So, this is my Crystal, given to me when I got to Orra.' She showed them her Crystal. She could see the brightness of the stone reflected in their eyes.

'It's exquisite.' Her mother gasped.

The colours started moving 'What are the colours doing?' Her dad tensed, his temple pulsating.

Her parents stared at the stone in wonderment, but her dad took a wary step back.

'I know, Dad. It's overwhelming when you first see it,' Nicole soothed.

'The colours are not of this world,' Dinkletons said. 'They are from Orra.'

'It looks dangerous with all that swirling of colour,' her mother said. 'It looks hot?'

'We have to move on to Lena. So, let's get started,' Dinkletons prompted.

'What will you do?' Her father scowled and clenched his fists. Nicole knew most of it was from a hard dig in the ribs from the Knocker.

'I'm going to use what Magic is available to me. Which means putting Strom's and my pink colour together, and since you have made the healing dart, Dinkletons, I thought I could use that as well. In class we learnt all about the colours and how to use them on blocks, so I am going to try this.'

'Nicole, we could try using our inner Magic and Voltz together,' Strom said.

'How do you project that?'

'We can put our Crystals together and draw both of our Illuminance energy. It theoretically can double the zap,' Strom said.

'It's a good idea. It will project it farther into the ripple. Good thinking, Strom.' Dinkletons applauded.

'You with me, Strom, let's do it. Okay?' She looked at her parents.

They said nothing but looked uncomfortable. Her mother's hands were shaking, and her dad's face showed that he was far out of his depth.

Nicole placed the Crystals in their hands. 'Now, hold hands and cover them with your palms.'

Her parents closed their hands around the Crystals

and an eruption of light shone between their fingers. Her dad was about to let go, but Nicole intervened and held his hand tightly over her mother's.

'Relax. This won't hurt,' Nicole said.

Strom's green aura and her blue aura become visible. Her dad's mouth fell open and his eyes glistened with fear. Everyone in the room flinched as a screech came from the Knocker. It untied itself from around her dad, gave him one more poke to the throat and slithered out of an open window.

'What was that?' Her father jumped and ran his hands over his neck. His eyes were big as he said, 'I could feel that thing on me.'

'I heard it,' Nicole's mother said. 'It's terrifying.'

Strom broke the silence with a loud, 'Wow, how fantastic was that!'

Nicole looked behind her parents. The Knocker was gone, but the Night Hag remained. It threw its head around in anger. Dinkletons telemuted, *Boy, she is stuck hard. We need to let her settle for a day at least and give it another go.*

We need Jinn, Nicole replied.

'So, what now?' her mother asked. 'Did you get rid of the Ripple?'

Nicole's eyes filled. 'Most of it.'

'What do you mean most of it? I still have something on me?' her dad asked.

'Err, yeah, only large residuals of temper, and it's not you who needs to be worried,' Strom said, looking at the Hag.

'Now, don't worry about me, I am in good hands with Dinkletons and the Dellamana. This was the first thing I had to fix but there is more I have to do. So, I will be coming and going.'

'You can't be doing that. You're only twelve years old,' her mother said, her hands flying up in the air.

'What more do you have to do? I'm not happy about this, Nicole.' Her father stared at Strom. 'And exactly what did you mean by a temper?'

Strom pointed at her dad, now not happy with him. 'It will not come as a surprise to you, Pops.'

Nicole looked at her mother. 'I have to find out when I became Magic and when the Tangle infected me so I can remove it and stop the Ripples from continuing.'

'We already know that it was from a banished Dellamana called Raisa. She didn't mean to make Nicole Magic,' Strom said.

Her mother had her hands in fists and two big blotches of red stained her cheeks.

'There must be something we can do to stay connected,' Nicole said.

Dinkletons flicked his tail; it felt scratchy on her leg. Strom rocked back and forth on his feet. Both were silent, offering not one solution.

Nicole was thinking. Surely they could be in touch in some form. Then it came to her. Her hand computer could link to her mother's phone. *Could that work?*

Strom telemuted, *I have no idea how Frail technology operates. It looks so unnecessarily complicated yet so basic. I skipped that class.*

Dinkletons telemuted to Nicole, *Give it a go. It may work. Sending messages to a Frail mobile from a palm computer has never been attempted, if that's what you are talking about.*

Her parents turned their heads from one to another while this telemuting was going on.

'What's going on here?' her dad said, his voice loud.

'Just a private discussion, Pops, no need to worry,' Strom said.

'Look, kid, do you want me to knock your block off?' Her dad took a step towards Strom.

In the end, it was too much for Strom to resist. Nicole

was horrified when he said, 'It's you that's getting your head knocked off.'

'That's enough, Strom. Be quiet.' Dinkletons encouraged Strom to move away from Nicole's dad. 'Come over here and sit down.'

Nicole led the way. Strom wandered over to the elephants in the two cabinets on the side wall, taking his time to examine them. 'These are fascinating. I didn't know Frail collected things. What is the point of having more than one?'

Strom was ignored.

'I'm going to try something. Do you have your phones?'

Her father took his out of his pocket. Her mother went into the kitchen and retrieved hers off the charger. Back in the lounge, they sat like school kids, close together, their mobiles on their laps. Her dad's fresh scepticism showed with an eye roll. Her mother was jumpy.

'Come on, Nicole, what are you doing?' her dad asked. She knew he would feel out of control with this situation and would hate the whole thing.

Nicole held her hand up. She pressed the top of the thumb to activate her palm computer. The purple screen came to life. She'd played around on it but had never done something specific like send a message.

'I'll be able to send messages in Orra and to you in Vail, Dinkletons. So, I must be able to ring or message their phones.' She pushed another button. A nugget came across her palm. It said:

```
Welcome to the game, Nicole. Push any button
to start your adventure.
```

'Yay, that's the game we were talking about. You have it,' Strom said from across the room. He marched to her side and reached up to give her a high-five. Nicole ignored him.

Closing that off with a push to the end of her pinky, the home screen came on.

'Swipe up, there are about ten pages in that screen,' Strom said as he peered over her shoulder.

Nicole looked for the message icon. *It won't appear as a telephone,* she thought. *It will appear as something else entirely.* She swiped through the home screen and saw the word `Drift`. That seemed like it! She tapped the icon and quickly typed:

```
Send Strom: Hi.
```

Strom's palm tinkled in music form. He typed on his palm quickly in response. Nicole's palm received a message back.

```
Hi yourself.
```

She sent messages to her parents' phones. They glanced expectantly at their phones, but nothing appeared.

Nicole frowned. She pushed the `Drift` button again, and saw that there was another option, `Rebo7`. She clicked the icon. Immediately another icon appeared: `Outport`. She pressed it.

```
Have you clearance for this?
```

'Swipe your Crystal over that; it will get you in,' Strom said.

She collected her Crystal from her father.

Once that was done, she sat back down. `Outport available` came up on her screen in red.

Her parents sat and fiddled with their phones.

Nicole typed a message and hit send. `Sending` appeared on her screen, followed by `Sent`. Her parents' phones beeped a shorter, harsher tone than what came for her and Strom's palm. Nicole typed `Sending` and then it came up with `Sent`. She had sent two different messages to her parents. She smiled when their phones beeped, but it was a different tone to Strom's and her palm computer.

While her parents read their messages she waited. After reading, they both looked up and smiled.

'Okay?'

Her parents nodded shakily.

'We can message anytime, okay?' Nicole asked. She went over and kissed her mother on her cheek, avoiding the Hag. When she turned to her dad, he held out his hand and they did something in between a hand squeeze and a shake. Their guards were still up with one another. Nicole guessed it would take more time for him to get back to normal, to adjust to life without the Knocker.

'Now, we better go see Lena,' Strom said.

'I'll drive you. Can't have you three wandering the streets,' her dad said.

'Thank you.' Nicole gave Strom back his Crystal. Nicole and Strom looked at each other a little too long. Dinkletons flicked his tail and her parents had pained expressions.

23

'They won't know what's going on, Nicole. You've never been to Lena's house on your own, ever,' her dad said. Dinkletons sat up front, and Strom and Nicole sat in the backseat of their car, their hands almost touching.

Strom's little finger touched the back of her hand, sending a shiver up her arm.

'Did you use some of the mood elevator?' Dinkletons asked.

'I did. It's so incredible the way it turns nerves into calm, and negative thoughts are turned in a better direction.'

Strom grinned at her and took full hold of her hand. Nicole could only look ahead.

'That is adorable,' Dinkletons said.

The car pulled up to the driveway of Lena's family home. Nicole took a deep breath.

'See you later, Pops,' Strom said as he bolted out of the car and slammed the door shut, making her father jump.

When everyone was out of the car, her dad responded by screeching away.

'He's one crazy dude,' Strom added as they made their way to the Avery's house.

'Did you feel the atmosphere in the house was less tense when the Knocker left?' Nicole asked.

'The air was lighter for sure, but it will still take time to resolve. It will get even better when the Hag is gone,' Dinkletons said.

'How did the Ripples affect the air?' Nicole said.

'The Knocker and Night Hag polluted the air with gases that opened the house up to Rogue and bad karma, like fighting, poor concentration, and food going off. Visitors wouldn't have enjoyed being in that space,' Dinkletons said.

'That's true. Over the past six months or so nobody wanted to come over,' Nicole said. 'These Ripples are dangerous. I have to be able to stop creating them.'

Before making their way up the path to the Avery's front door, Nicole went into her palm computer and brought up the same screen as before. She sent a message to her parents' phones again.

Immediately she got one back from her mother.

```
I am okay now, as long as we do this. I love
you, be careful.
```

She then sent a `Rebo7` message to Rook.

```
Hi, Rook. I've been with my parents. So far,
so good. Just testing this out.
```

They were now outside Lena's house. Nicole's palm computer pinged with the reply from Rook.

```
I am so pleased.
```

Then she sent a message to Jinn, telling her she would be more involved with the Hag. Jinn responded.

Sure thing, dude.

Her message ended with a heart emoji.

Nicole smiled and sent back a thumbs up icon. *How incredible is this? Being able to message from my hand to another realm?* She daydreamed for a minute, taking it all in.

'Are you going to Rebo everyone in Orra?' Strom asked. He was standing by the front door of the two-storey house. One side of the garden was her aunt's roses; the other side was grass. It was a brick house with a red-tiled roof.

Nicole ran up to where he stood. She didn't want Strom meeting her aunt first. 'Wait for me next time.'

Nicole felt nervous. She had no idea how she was going to deal with this. But it had gone well with her father, so hopefully it would be the same with Dinkletons' help.

Her Aunt Dree opened the door and the look she gave was expected. Her bottom lip jutted out like it always did when she was angry. Nicole didn't blame her. Dree shot an uneasy look at Strom and Dinkletons.

'Nicole, what a surprise. Do your parents know that you're here?'

'Hi, Aunt Dree. They do.'

Dree nodded. 'Are you here to apologise to Sara? You know she was disappointed you sat the party out. Although, for the life of me, I don't understand why she has already forgiven you.'

'Maybe it's due to her charismatic personality,' Strom said.

With so much going on, Nicole had forgotten about Sara. 'I'm sorry. I promise it will never happen again.' She shot Strom a 'shut up' look.

'Well, we will see.' Dree folded her arms and stared at Strom. Nicole could tell that Dree thought it odd she was here but felt that maybe there was hope. The corners of Dree's eyes shone when she was happy. She could hear her thoughts. *This is the first time Nicole has made any effort. Let's see where this goes.*

'I'm here to talk to Lena, if that's okay with you.' The urge to run was overwhelming; instead, Nicole shuffled her feet back and forth.

Hang in there, Dinkletons soothed.

'I'm not sure what you want, but you can go in once I ask if she wants to see you. Just you; your friends can stay out here.' She was sure Dree saw the cat smile by the tilt of her head. Nicole shot Dinkletons a warning look.

Nicole noticed Dree staring at Dinkletons. He had told her it was difficult to act like a normal cat. His intelligence was evident on his face.

Jaya pushed through the door, breaking the moment. 'No way. You're here?' Her eyes were big, and her hands splayed out in front of her. Then she saw Strom and stopped.

Nicole had not been prepared for the impact of this moment. She knew herself the way Strom made her feel. Nicole could hear Jaya's inner dialogue and could sense her feeling caught completely off guard by the sensation that was Strom.

By telemuting Jaya, not only could Nicole hear her words, she also felt her emotions. Jaya was taken by surprise by Strom's looks and his eyes, and of the confidence he easily carried. *Whoa, where did this guy come from? His eyes are a weird shape, but how could they be so green?* She heard Jaya think as she slumped on the door frame trying to look cool.

'I'll go talk to Lena, but I can't promise anything. You wait here,' Dree said and slipped behind the door, giving Jaya a push to come inside. But Jaya wasn't going anywhere.

'Nicole, what are you doing? You want to see Lena? Why? What is going on?' Jaya's face was full of expression and showed surprise at her cousin being on her doorstep.

'I need to discuss something with her.' Just then Nicole's palm sounded. She couldn't look at it in front of Lena.

'What was that sound? That doesn't sound like your phone.' Jaya leaned in towards Nicole.

'It's mine,' Strom said.

'Oh, okay.' Jaya smiled at him. That seemed to be enough to satisfy her, because it was the gorgeous boy who had spoken to her.

Jaya's head popped forward. 'That cat just smiled at me. And who are you?'

'Hi, I'm Strom, Nicole's friend.'

'I know all Nicole's friends. They happen to amount to a grand total of zero, and I have never seen you before in my life.' Jaya studied him. 'You do look familiar.' Jaya twisted her mouth to one side. Nicole heard Jaya's thoughts. *I would definitely remember you.*

'How nice of you,' Strom said.

Jaya will work out that they look similar any second now, judging by her blatant staring at Strom. Nicole was keen to get the attention off him.

'You guys, please, just behave for five minutes,' Nicole said.

Luckily the moment passed as Dree returned to the door and everybody's attention was drawn to her.

'It's no surprise. Lena doesn't want to see you,' Dree said.

'You look like Nicole apart from the hair.' Jaya pointed a finger at Strom.

'You actually look very alike,' Dree added, frowning.

'Aunt Dree, I need to speak to Lena. I have a way to fix our problem.'

'And what might that be?' Jaya said, still staring at

Strom. Nicole could see that Jaya was drawn to him. She shot a look at Strom who was unaffected by Jaya's interest. It was the first time she had ever seen her cousin blush. She was usually the one that made the boys nervous.

Nicole considered. *Well, it's not every day you get to meet a Marnie from Orra.* She should have expected Strom would cause a commotion.

Strom winked at Nicole. She half smiled back, then the pain hit. It raced along her arms and into her hands. This happened whenever...

Lena stood at the door, already tap-tapping her foot. 'It's okay. I decided I wanted to hear what she has to say. Whatever that is.'

Nicole rolled her head back in relief. 'Thank you, Lena.' She looked over at Dinkletons, who looked pleased with himself. He had obviously done something to bring her out here. But right now, she didn't care.

With the relationship curse still thriving, this was a huge moment for them both. They were coming together on their own terms, for the first time in their lives.

Dree squeezed Lena's shoulder, and both she and Jaya went inside and closed the door. The group moved away onto the front lawn. Nicole could see Jaya in the living room, peering out a gap in the curtains.

Nicole glanced at her palm and read the message from her dad as she walked.

```
That's what I am here for. Anytime.
```

He seemed to be feeling better already because that was the nicest thing he had said to her in years. Nicole felt her heart jump. *This is going to work.*

'I don't know where to start. So I will just say it. The faster we can get this fixed the better we will feel,' Nicole said. They were all sitting on the grass in a circle. 'Our relationship has a curse. This is going to seem strange to you. But you know how bad we feel when together?'

Lena widened her eyes and tilted her head waiting to hear more.

'I have abilities and skills, but also because of this, I have a curse that has affected us. Makes us hate each other and gives us physical pain.'

'A curse? You have got to be joking.' Lena looked from Nicole to Strom. She could hear Lena's inner voice talking about Strom. *My gosh, he's gorgeous. Those eyes are gorgeous.*

Nicole saw Dinkletons' deliberate nod.

'Ah, what is going on here?' Lena narrowed her eyes.

Nicole knew that she had to get her to hold both Strom's and her Crystal, but by the look on Lena's face, she was just about done with this conversation. She had to do something quick.

Dinkletons telemuted, *Don't worry, Lena is enjoying herself. She doesn't want to leave Strom.*

Strom laughed out loud.

'Stop it! Can't you be serious at all?' Nicole shot at him. But she couldn't stay mad at him.

'Obviously not.' Strom grabbed some grass and looked at it intently.

'Why did you laugh just then?' Lena said, touching her face.

'Because you like me, but that is okay with me as all girls do,' Strom said.

Lena had a tremor in her voice. 'Oh, really! And how would you know?'

'That would be telling.' Strom smiled at Lena and it seemed like she nearly dissolved in front of them out of embarrassment. He handed Nicole his Crystal, which was a ring he wore on his middle finger.

'I need you to hold these.' Nicole handed Lena the two Crystals.

Lena's eyes nearly popped out of their sockets as she held the two Hallr Crystals in her hand, Nicole's necklace and Strom's ring. 'They're so beautiful. Oh, they have little lights in them! How adorable.'

Lena told Nicole, 'You're going to tell me what is going on. I've had to put up with this curse, so you say?' *It makes some sense, and I could never work out why we were never friends.*

Nicole stared at her cousin and saw the confusion etched on her face. In that moment she was so overwhelmed by what she saw she had to close her eyes. It was the damage that had been done by her Ripples that stared back at her. *She* had done this. It was her fault and not Lena's.

'Are you okay?' Strom asked her and put his hand on hers.

She looked at his lovely hand, with its soft white skin and well-shaped nails. The touch meant a lot in this moment.

She looked across into his green eyes that were shades deeper than her own and nodded with a small smile. She realised that this was her first crush. He was annoying and lovely at the same time. Well, after all, he was a Marnie, with an unfair advantage.

24

Lena and Dinkletons were watching them.

Strom and the cat laughed. Lena shot her head over to the cat. 'Whoops,' Strom said.

Nicole felt so embarrassed that her eyes watered.

Strom was still holding her hand. 'It's okay. Keep going.'

'Lena, I have Magic skills, but other bad things are happening as well. You know how my mother has nightmares and my dad and I don't get on?'

Lena nodded. 'And you're saying we don't like each other due to this? Wouldn't being Magic allow good things to happen, not bad?'

'It does, but the way I became me, something happened, and some bad stuff attached to me.'

'Do you really expect me to believe this?' Lena looked down at the Crystals that were warm in her hand.

'After we leave, you'll start to feel better about Nicole. You might even be able to think about her in a good way. Have you ever done that?' Strom asked.

Lena and Nicole made eye contact. Both shook their heads.

'I don't need you to believe me. Just let the stones do the work. You have nothing to lose.'

'You'll gain a cousin and a friend, and be able to wear clothes that are different,' Strom said grandly.

'How do you know about that?' Lena shot at Strom, eyebrows creased in alarm.

'Oh, Nicole told us that you turn up in the same threads.' Strom laughed.

'Okay, do what you have to do. But this doesn't mean I believe you. Sounds like balderdash to me, just an excuse to let you off the hook for being a horrible witch.'

Despite the harsh comment, Nicole laughed.

'Hey, you can't call Nicole that. She is part Dellamana, which is the opposite of low-level Magic.' Strom stood up, casting a shadow over the group.

Lena became very still. 'Low level – what do you mean by that?'

Nicole caught Dinkletons focusing his good eye on her. She tried to telemute, but she got nothing; he had done a good job at silking his thoughts so she could not hear them.

The light in the Crystals once again ignited. Tiny flames of yellow poured through the gaps in between Lena's fingers.

'Don't drop them,' Strom said, placing his hands under Lena's.

'Wow, look at those sparkly bits!' she exclaimed.

Nicole got up off the grass. 'Lena, it's all done. We have to go now, but I will talk to you again soon about all of this.'

'Hold on,' Lena said and got up onto her unsteady feet. 'What is done? Nicole Murphy, you will not go 'til you tell me what you just did.' She handed Nicole the Crystals back, which were now searing her skin. 'Ouch, what is that?'

Everyone was surprised when they saw one tiny purple arrow dissolve into Lena's palm. 'Where did that go?' she screamed and frantically shook her hands, jumping up and down.

'That is an over-exaggeration if I have ever seen one,' Strom said. 'But amusing.'

'It's fine, Lena.' Nicole took her hand; it was the first time she had ever touched her. An electric shock spread through them, and Lena flung her hand away from Nicole's.

'What was that purple arrow?' Lena asked. 'What's wrong?'

'It was just part of the spell to help us,' Nicole said, not really knowing what to say. The dart should not have been there, even she knew that. Darts were parts of Voltz and only Dellamana had them. Maybe she and Strom somehow set one off between them, in the form of a messy spell. *Well, the Prefects will know all about it now.*

'I want to know more.' Lena moved closer.

'Not yet.' Nicole moved away from Lena and started walking to the footpath.

'That's it? That is how you are going to leave me?' Lena yelled.

Nicole saw Dree and Jaya open the curtains in the lounge room and look out at the lawn, not even trying to hide their stares. In the next minute, they were both outside and had reached Lena. Dree put her arm around her, and Jaya stood beside them, her face blank.

25

The three of them wedged straight back to Orra after talking to Lena. Strom had wanted to hang around and go to a takeaway restaurant to try Frail food, but Dinkletons had said no.

In the grand foyer of Orra, there were many Dellamana there to greet them. Jinn made sure she was up front and Zosmine gave her the job of giving out the nectar bars that only wedgers received and helped herself to one. Although that was not allowed, but Rook let it go, as he knew how hard Jinn had taken it when she was not allowed to go to Orra with Strom, Dinkletons and Nicole.

'Thanks for the Rebo; it was great to hear from you.'

'I think it's amazing I can do that outside my world.' Nicole took bites from the yummy bar. This time she had a white chocolate one. 'Why could Lena see the purple thing? Was it a Voltz?' Nicole asked.

'It wasn't a true Voltz; rather, something happened with Dinkletons' healing dart that interacted with your Magic and created the arrow,' Rook said.

'My Magic – I made it?'

'I think so. It didn't come from Lena,' Rook said.

'Have you ever seen it before?' Nicole asked, taking the last bite of her nectar bar.

Rook shook his head.

'Dinkletons, what does it mean?'

'We are not sure. Nava is looking into it.' He turned away, which puzzled Nicole.

'What happened?' Jinn asked, her eyes wide.

'There was an arrow that appeared when we were removing the curse,' Strom said. 'It was pretty cool to see.'

'An arrow? As in a Voltz? Nah, that can't be,' Jinn said, shaking her head.

'But the thing is Lena saw it. You don't see Voltz like that, right?' Nicole asked loudly.

'No way,' Jinn said.

'She must have some Magical molecules to do that?' Nicole felt hot. 'It wouldn't have hurt her in any way, would it?'

'Not with that colour in it,' Dinkletons said, turning back. 'It is a strong Magical current, even though it was only teeny.'

She turned to Jinn. 'The Night Hag is still attached to my mum and that's why we need to take you back. The colour therapy and Dinkletons' dart weren't enough,' Nicole said and thought about the other dart, the smaller one that Lena had clearly in her palm. Where had that come from?

Jinn squealed and danced around. 'I know that's going to be so good.'

'The Hag has a strong hold on your mother. It might take a few goes and then healing from you, Nicole, once you get home,' Rook said.

Nicole heaved a sigh and sat down on the closest couch. 'That was so intense.'

All of a sudden, heaviness overwhelmed her, and she couldn't move her head or speak. Nicole opened her mouth but no words came out. She breathed hard, her eyes wide to alert the others about what she was going through.

'We need a dose of Moonagic therapy,' Rook said hurriedly. He looked at Jinn and Strom. 'You two better come.'

The Marnie didn't have to be asked twice. Jinn whispered to Nicole, 'It's only the best place to visit.'

'So you said.' Nicole managed a small smile. She didn't feel like going anywhere but her room. Seeing the Hag and Knocker was terrible, and to know the Hag was still there was unbelievably hard. Plus, how was she supposed to heal the wounds they left? Strom had mentioned the 'temper' in her father. How would she deal with that?

They jumped quickly. They landed in a market garden – the colours of the vegetables were stunning. An enormous, pink moon sat so close that Nicole thought she could reach out and put her hand on the surface. She squinted her eyes in response to the bright light. Rook held one of her arms and Jinn held the other.

'That was out of this world. I wish we could jump all the time,' Strom said.

'Are you alright?' Rook asked Nicole.

Nicole was flabbergasted at the beauty of the moon; it was made up of every contrast of pink, so much so that it was confronting. She opened her mouth to reply, but nothing came out.

'Give the moon a moment to link to your Magic and help you recover,' Rook soothed. 'Being in the illumination of the moon will awaken your Magic further. It has a different energy than our colours and can purify your Magic cells and help the prescription do its work.'

Nicole felt like she was going to faint. For a minute, everything was blurry. Jinn rubbed her shoulder. Nicole gushed out, breathing hard and coughed. 'What happened? That was awful.'

'That was a buildup of the Tangle trying to stop your Magic from expanding, a physical Magical storm,' Rook said.

In a moment, warmth covered her, and she could see and feel the energy. Her blue aura enveloped her once again, more vibrant than the last time she'd seen it. She looked down at her body with its blue sheen in wonder.

'Your aura is highlighting your Magical self.' Rook was in wonder at seeing the Sape light up.

Jinn smiled. 'You are connecting with your Dellamana side, your Voltz. Can you see them?'

Nicole looked at the blueness around her hands and she could see the Voltz. Tiny, purple dots flickered as they made their way around her aura. 'Wow, this is awesome.' Nicole considered the arrow that she had seen with Lena; these arrows were the same colour but different in shape.

'Everything will be magnified here. This is how the moon zone functions. Your Voltz are only visible here, but this confirms that they are now working on the rejuvenation of your Magic cells. This is enormous because it means that you are making your own Magic now and this is wonderful,' Rook said.

'We come here to receive Moonagic rehabilitation,' Jinn said, dancing in one place. Nicole thought Jinn had a really good flare for dancing. The way she moved – she was so flexible and coordinated, much like herself.

'This place looks similar to the kitchen garden.' Nicole noticed, looking around.

'The two areas join up, but it's too far to walk,' Strom said.

'Over there is Yatsala.' Jinn pointed into the distance.

Nicole looked where she pointed, past the moon to a yellow mist that swirled around in circles.

'The colour is called palos. It doesn't exist in the Frail Realm,' Strom said proudly. 'It is one of my most favourite impossible colours.'

'What is Yatsala? More of Orra?' To Nicole, it looked like outer space, framed in a yellow mist. 'It's unbelievable.'

'It's the gateway into the Stoneycraft worlds, where Dinkletons comes from,' Rook said.

'To go through there, you require Stoneycraft clearance, which will open a portal called a Propylaeum,' Rook said. 'Propylaeum are doors; they exist on every planet. They link each world together. But they must be monitored. Prefects are in charge of the Propylaeum here in Orra and in the Frail Realm. It is how Rogue get into the Frail Realm legitimately.'

'When we wedge, do we go through these?' Nicole asked.

'Wedging is skipping the line,' Rook said, shaking his head. 'A short-cut.'

Nicole turned to Rook, eyebrows raised. 'So, there are ways to travel to different Magic worlds?'

'Only for Magic folk. A Propylaeum is a secure barrier only opened after applications have been approved to travel.'

'Like tickets to go on a plane to another country.' Nicole looked to Rook for confirmation. 'Would I be able to travel through these things?'

'You will have no need to travel as ordinary Magic do. You will continue to wedge.'

'I wouldn't mind trying it once.'

Strom leaned down to the garden and pulled out a potato that had the proportions of a basketball. Then Jinn pointed to a lettuce that looked too large to be lifted with two hands. It was then Nicole saw the Dellamana. They were in groups around the Moon Garden, collecting food in great bins. Some waved at her. She smiled and waved back.

'Everything is far bigger compared to what you are used to,' Rook said. 'I've seen Frail food from the screens of Rolte. Carrots especially are very small.'

Nicole looked at the array of growing things. Some items were familiar, like carrots and pumpkin, but most were strange-looking, and she had no idea what they were.

'We have different types of food that wouldn't be able to grow in your world. You'll taste some of them tonight at dinner.' Rook showed her a blue, leafy plant with bulbs at the end, similar to a beetroot.

'Besides being a place of rejuvenation, another role of Moonagic is to grow our food quickly and in abundance with the highest level of nutrients we need for our Magic cells. Look! You can see the growth unfold.'

Nicole looked around and could see in fast forward things growing from small to ginormous.

'Dellamana and Belba that work here have an interest in horticulture and harvesting. See all the properties? 'Rook said.

The structures Rook pointed to were unassuming, round, and clear, the size of an air balloon that hovered and collected the food with a beam. Once full, they hovered over to a huge building where the contents then disappeared from the balloon-like structures. She turned back to where the crops were, and they were nearly replaced with new growth. It was incredible to watch.

Rook pointed to one unusual-looking plant nearby. 'This is croze, which grows in minutes, and is a delicacy here. We all love it and eat it in most meals.'

Nicole wrinkled her nose. To her, it didn't look tasty, but prickly and had a strong smell. She watched the croze grow. Their swaying movement unnerved her as there was no wind; they looked alive. 'What does it taste like?'

'The best way I can describe croze is that it infuses an

entire meal with an addictive juice. Like someone who loves chocolate in your world,' Rook said.

26

Back from the Moon Garden, Rook walked ahead of Nicole, Jinn, Strom, and Dinkletons towards the glass doors of the Arx. 'We can now safely let you go on your next trip.'

Nicole was trying to work out a plan. Her priority was her parents. Her shoulders slumped as she felt she hadn't had time to process what she was going to do.

She planned to go to her parents and use Jinn and Strom's Crystals together with hers to attack the ripple and put some healing colour into it. She might well use Dinkletons' dart for good measure, as it was strong in healing their distortions faster. She detested that she had to see the Night Hag again, but she had to do it for her mother. She had to work out how she developed the purple arrow, but for now, no one knew where it came from. Nava was the only one to hazard a guess. She said that it was made up of the new molecules that Nicole was growing at a fast rate. But that didn't explain why the purple arrow that was essentially a precious Voltz was transferred to Lena.

She saw that Jinn and Strom had their cloud slippers on. Jinn was jumping side to side and getting a decent lift like she was on a trampoline. Sweat ran from Nicole's temples, her hands were clammy, and for once the Crystal was not helping her, as she felt nerves in her stomach start hammering her. She looked at Dinkletons for help.

'You two just go over there for a minute,' Dinkletons said to Strom and Jinn who moodily complied, sparks filling the air. 'And try to calm down.'

Nicole sat down. Dinkletons came close, both eyes open. She was able to take the radiation from his eyes now without getting blinded. 'Are you alright?'

'I guess. I wanted a break,' Nicole said, feeling drained. Nicole realised she wasn't afraid of the wedging but was afraid of what dark things her mother might say. 'I feel I need to prepare for the Hag.'

'It's a good idea.' Dinkletons' giant face touched hers in a kiss. 'Your Crystal agrees.'

Relief washed over her. She closed her eyes.

'Take all the time you need. The Prefects are monitoring the Hag. She is aware now that her freedom is coming to an end, as she saw the Knocker leave,' Dinkletons said.

'Will it go easy on my mother?'

He shook his head. 'Once in the Ripple, they are bound to its confines and within those she will naturally give your mother nightmares and sit on her at night.'

'And hang over her all day, giving her rashes.' Nicole felt guilty. 'It's just not affecting her at night – it's all the time and for years.'

'You were successful with the Knocker.'

'I want to learn more about Rogue, so I won't be in the dark. I need to learn to put my colours together on my own and use them. Especially if I can't get Raisa's Illuminance to wipe it out. I will need some defence.'

'Give that new purple arrow a try. It has been gifted to you because you have come a long way with building your Illuminance. Remember, you must have colour in your Hallr Crystal to build Voltz.'

Nicole remembered the little Volt fly from her Crystal and settle into Lena's palm and disappear. *What did that mean for Lena?*

She saw steam forming around Jinn and Strom and heard the loud voices of the Marnie being told the wedge had been postponed.

27

Back in her room, Nicole changed into soft, blue pyjamas after a shower. The shower water had come from all directions and had nearly knocked her over. Her hair smelled like a mixture of perfume and had golden highlights that hadn't been there before. For the first time, there was no one in her room, including Dinkletons, which is how she wanted it tonight. Orra was a place of hustle and bustle. There was never a dull moment, whether it was Marnie running all over the place causing fires and strange lights, or Belba going off to do their chemist work and Dellamana on their way to their areas of expertise, moving from the Vault to the Moon Garden, kitchens or Laboratories. They all had a place where they fit in, and they were all either jumping or in the corridors. While Orra was a peaceful place, due to its continual development of Voltz, it was a busy world.

She wandered out into her spacious lounge and looked outside at the red and yellow sparkles of Orra space. It looked beautiful. She could see the odd Dellamana jumping through space on their way to an unknown destination in Orra. Nicole drew the purple curtains. She didn't want any distractions.

She messaged her mother saying where she was and what her room looked like. Her mother replied.

```
Send pictures.
```

So she did. She sent photos of her bedroom and her in it.

```
Your father seems better, more chilled.
What's he doing differently?
He actually smiled at me, opened the door as
we went outside to have a coffee.
It will only get better.
What was this ripple that caused your dad to
be like this?
```

Oh no, it is much worse than the word implies, Nicole thought.

```
I will tell you when I see you.
```

Nicole didn't want her mother to know about the Hag until she had gotten rid of it.

```
And I will send pictures of Orra.
```

A knock on the door startled her.

```
I have to go, my dinner is here. Love you,
and will talk soon.
```

She tapped out of her palm computer as Shanazz came in with a trolley. 'Room service,' she said cheerfully. 'We have all the Frail movies for your screen.' She pointed to a blank space on the wall. 'There are also movies from other Magic worlds, if you're interested.'

It sounded fantastic. 'I would be interested in the other Magic channels.'

'It will be on your palm computer. You will get a list of all the applications that are available on the device.' Shanazz lifted the cloches to reveal her dinner. 'I hear you're having a night to yourself. I don't mind them either.' She winked at Nicole. Shanazz was wearing a black evening dress that floated around her, showing bare arms and no shoes. Her long red hair was out and at all angles, messy and thick.

'You going out?' Nicole asked.

'Why would you think that? This meal is full of croze.' Shanazz left with a wave.

All dressed up and nowhere to go, Nicole thought as she eyed the food.

On the plates were a delicious-looking burger, fries, a chocolate smoothie, and a bowl of ice cream, with a cupcake on the side.

She picked up the burger, took a bite and closed her eyes. This was incredible. The juices caused an immediate jolt to her taste buds. *They should incorporate this in Raisa's bakery – they would sell like hot cakes.*

28

Nicole awoke to the sound of that dim familiar music and rubbed her eyes. Where had she heard it? The bed was incredibly soft, the sheets delicate, and the pillows feather. She sat up and looked at her lounge area where a collection of the books that assist the Marnie with their Magic were set up. Each day the library got bigger as the busy Belba added areas she needed to understand. Jinn had said that all Marnie received the library during their younger years, which consisted of hardbacks with gold jackets, some small, others encyclopedia large. Last night, she had read through one about colours and their meaning and healing of blocks to further her knowledge from the class she attended.

This time with Jinn's pink, they would get rid of the Hag, she thought. She got out of bed and went into her wardrobe. Clothes lined the shelves, and she chose a pair of jeans, a red shirt and a pair of sneakers. At the last minute, she popped on a cap.

A soft knock on the door sounded and Rook came in.

'Hi, Rook.' Nicole smiled and opened her blinds with her palm. She could get used to this.

'Good morning. Would you like a silk lesson before

your trip? It will come in handy with Marnie not knowing your thoughts 24/7.'

They sat opposite each other. Rook wore casual shorts and a blue top. He had one leg crossed over the other, his arms splayed on the back of the couch. His Hallr Crystal glistened with maroon; Nicole couldn't get over how bright it was.

'So, how are you doing? You go through the colour manual?'

'I learnt the basics in class with the Savant and Marnie, like white, orange, and blue are the first colours to come into the Crystal and they need to be brightened so they go directly to the Magic cells.'

'Yes, and then once they do that, more colours can come in and the strong ones will go out to your aura and produce Voltz.'

'Yup, and then that is the circle of Magic production?'

'You might have one hundred colours and they will each take a turn to make Voltz. But it is your job to make sure they can grow by rubbing out the greys. Without greys they become strong.'

'Only the strong colours get sent to my aura?'

He nodded.

'I would love a silk lesson.'

'Great. Close your eyes and picture a piece of silk, the size of a handkerchief, any colour. When you begin this process, Magic attaches itself to the piece of material and becomes a thought inhibitor; the more you concentrate, the more effective it will be. Once you have created this in your mind, you can retrieve it to block others from telemuting your thoughts. Once it becomes a working silk, you attach it to a thought, and it will take over. You can place a silk and leave it to do the work.'

'Sounds too easy.'

'Because it is. Once you get going, it will become second nature.'

Nicole stood up and walked from one end of the room to another. While she felt a surge of calm and focus on what she needed to achieve, the process still was daunting. The mood elevator the Belba had given her and the tiny Gloine bubble from Nava were doing their job; she could physically feel them working, eliminating the negatives and highlighting the positives of her already acquired magical skills, telling her how to use them to her advantage.

'You want to stay another night?' Rook asked.

'Maybe two. It was great to learn things at my own pace.'

'There is a book there' – he pointed to the shelf – 'on silking, so go over that. I will tell the Marnie. Is there anything else you specifically want to learn?'

'I know the Prefects told me about my aura, but are there books on that as well?'

'There are books on every subject.' Rook crossed his legs. 'They are found on the palm computer as well, but I know it's lovely to hold a book.'

'The Magic will drag strong colours out into the aura for Voltz building and will send them back in once completed,' Nicole confirmed.

'That is great, Nicole.' Rook stood up to leave.

'This means that auras are powerful tools. Not just for Voltz, but they are a strong Magical presence. That's why mine developed the purple dart.'

Rook smiled. 'Magic folk can have auras, and many do. They are a symbol of their enchantment and they do relate to their powers, however small. But they cannot build on these powers. Only us Dellamana can do this with Voltz, and you will too, Nicole. Darts are rare when a Dellamana or Stoneycraft reach their potential, then they can use them whenever they want.'

'But even without my Crystal for twelve years? I could not build up a colour stack?'

'Every Marnie is born with a base number of Voltz. True, they are not fully formed – that is why we call them splashes. So, too, you would have had a splash. As this has never happened before we don't know how many, but we now know you did have a few lingering there. Waiting to be built upon.'

Nicole thought this interesting, but she was still thinking about how better to control her dart – or, in Dellamana terms, a splash – of Voltz. 'My aura must have played a part for them to have got there in the first place. I believe the dart is the key to getting rid of the Hag – that extra punch of Magic.' Nicole walked over to the bookshelf and ran her finger over the books. 'Do you have any information on the Night Hag?'

'I can get it from the Vault and send it to your palm computer.'

'Sounds good. Oh, and can you send some facts about the Sylph while you are at it?'

'Will do.' Rook left the room, closing the door softly.

29

Three days later and feeling more equipped than ever, Nicole decided to jump to the kitchen on her own after messaging her mother saying that she was coming back home later that day. She managed a slight lift but fell back down. Holding onto her Crystal, she concentrated hard on the kitchen and away she went, up into the red and yellow sparkles that made up the sky.

Shanazz was already organising breakfast on one kitchen bench. Other kitchen benches around the room had a Belba doing the same thing.

'Do you cook for everyone in Orra?' Nicole asked as she approached the cute Belba in the green overalls.

'Oh, when we do that, we use the replenishment ovens – they replicate everything in bulk. Mostly we cook for the Prefects and Dellamana who request it. But we do all the baking of cakes, smoothies, and nectar bars.'

'Wow,' Nicole said. 'That's a lot.'

'It keeps us busy, but not all Belba are bakers. Like the Dellamana, we all have our areas that we choose to work in.'

Frowning, Nicole asked, 'Rolte is so far away. How do you get it all there? In the Zisis?'

'Actually, yes, we do. There is a Zisis station over there.' Shanazz pointed to the other side of the kitchens and there it was – she hadn't noticed it. 'That is a private Zisis. That one goes straight to Rolte.'

Nicole wondered why they couldn't teleport it.

'You can't teleport or jump with food because it jumbles it and turns it into a mashed mess.'

'Did you just telemute?' Nicole asked, surprised.

'No, I knew what you were thinking by the look on your face.' Shanazz laughed and placed a huge smoothie and muffin in front of her.

'That got croze in it?' Nicole couldn't take her mind off the amazing food she had had for the last three nights. The croze made everything taste inconceivably good.

'You liked it?' Shanazz grinned. 'Knew it!' She slammed both hands on the counter.

'That's an understatement.' Nicole attacked the meal, and her taste buds roared into life again.

Ten minutes later, Rook, Dinkletons, Jinn, and Strom arrived via a jump.

'Today's the day,' Jinn said impatiently.

'Man, that is soooo good.' Nicole finished off her muffin. 'Thank you, Shanazz.'

Nicole could tell they were all impatient. Strom was pacing; Dinkletons tail swished; Rook leaned against the kitchen counter, his fingers tapping against the bench.

'You all ready?' Dinkletons asked as he moved close to her.

'Yes, I feel more prepared now,' Nicole said, thinking it was worth it even if she had to make her mother wait a little longer. She now had more knowledge and a plan of what to do.

'Shall we get started, or do you want another night to relax?' Jinn asked, frowning.

Nicole smiled. 'Yes, I am ready.' She knew Jinn wasn't mad, just excited.

'First, you guys deal with the Night Hag, and then we will have to talk to your mother to pull out more memories. You do the talking, and I will do my thing,' Dinkletons said. He brushed his tail around Nicole's waist, a standard move of his. Every time he did it, she got a strong jolt of confidence. She felt she could accomplish anything with him by her side. Then she looked at the two Marnie, who were full of excitement to come to the Frail Realm.

'What is your thing?'

'I will telemute into your mother's thoughts to get answers,' Dinkletons said. 'You might pick up a thing or two, so don't freak out.'

Nicole squeezed her eyes tight then opened them. 'Was that a joke or are you serious?'

'The Moon Garden visit has given you the boost for doing this difficult wedge. I wish you the best. How did you do with the information I sent you?' Rook said.

'It was so good, Rook, I learned heaps about the Hag. I read that she will leave a tattoo on my mother, in a circle or daisy wheel. It's awful to think she sits on my mother's legs all night.'

'Yes, and did you see they originate in the rolling hills of the Frail deserts?' Rook asked.

'They're used to their freedom and not being stuck in a ripple. But they're one of hundreds that have the weakness of being able to be dragged into one. They spend all day running down the dunes, but at least they're doing their work in keeping the rodent numbers down.'

'Does it make you feel sorry for it?' Rook asked.

'No way! I want it gone.'

'Rebo me if you need to,' Rook said and squeezed her hand.

She looked to her three companions. 'Let's do this.'

'Don't forget to use the mood elevator,' Shanazz said as they left.

30

They were in the wedge, shaped like an arc, blue in the middle and white around the edges. 'This must be what it feels like to be in a tidal wave,' Nicole said, putting her hands out to the sides. This wedge elicited a different feeling than the last one. It was like the wave was rushing around them while they stayed still. Nicole couldn't focus on it – she felt dizzy. She clutched Dinkletons' paw tightly.

Jinn and Strom stood up and mimicked surfing. They were going with the flow of the water, skimming the wave and racing through the middle of it. Their faces glowed with excitement, and their white hair stood on end from the force.

'What will you do?' Nicole asked Dinkletons to distract her from the wave. She could feel wind and a sprinkle of blue water on her face, which made it feel real.

'One small idea from your mother and I'm able to track its pathway to a larger thought underneath. This is advanced telemuting only Stoneycraft can do. So, when your mother has a faint memory, I will be able to see the detail and track it.'

It was hard for her to think within the explosion of

the wedge and the Marnie noise, but she tried. 'I want to know how I became a Sape.'

That got the attention of the Marnie. 'Awesome, let's talk to your mother!' they yelled.

A few sharp turns and three long drops and they had arrived, this time in her backyard, hidden by a group of trees. She knew and was grateful Dinkletons could navigate with pinpoint accuracy to any spot in any realm. It would be an awful feeling being in the wedge not knowing where you would land – at least with Dinkletons present she didn't have that to worry about. Nicole shuddered; she hated the G-force of the long drops. But then the dreaded distortions set in.

'So, when you go to other Magic worlds, there is no distortion?' Nicole asked.

'Only here in the Frail Realm,' Dinkletons replied. 'The air attacks our body and stretches our insides like elastic.'

Nicole felt her throat close, making it hard to breathe. The pain in her head was terrible. Even her eyes and lips ached. Wedging might be a privilege, but it was agonising.

'Take a few deep breaths and hold your Crystal,' Dinkletons said.

The Marnie hid behind a bush and were watching with great curiosity a lady and her children next door. They were pointing, whispering, and giggling. Steam covered them.

'Their blocks still happen here?' Nicole asked Dinkletons.

'Oh, yes,' Dinkletons said. 'I will keep a close eye on them, so don't worry.'

'What is she doing?' Jinn asked, pointing at the woman next door. 'She seems to be attaching clothes on a wire. Who would do that?'

'It's bizarre, scary even,' Strom said, watching the children play with a ball attached to a pole, batting it to each other. 'What is the use of that activity?'

The Marnie distortions lasted a few moments – only dirty, blonde hair remained. It dimmed their Magical shine, allowing them to fit in.

Dinkletons was looking through the trees next to where the Marnie were fascinated by the Frail next door. 'Come here. Take a look at this Rogue – there's a big difference to the lovely Sylph.'

What Nicole saw made her jolt with surprise. Their house backed onto a walkway and there she saw a tall, skinny thing. He looked like a tall man on stilts, a beanpole, together with extra-long limbs and huge feet and hands. His head was smooth, white, and bald, an unfriendly ghost. She looked past him and saw large numbers of the same being and other weird creatures. They were all mixed in with people who were out riding bikes, walking, running along the path, pushing prams. A so-called normal day, but abnormal now to Nicole. None of them had any idea what monsters were among them. She felt tears overflow. She wiped them away and a pain in her side gave way to grief. *This is how we live and how I used to live, without knowledge.* It wasn't fair that people didn't know what was going on around them.

To her horror, one of the creatures jerked his head up and looked straight at her. His eyes were black holes in his white head, and he had long, pointed, gelatinous ears. Nicole hid.

'They are Waife, and they are trespassing. They tend to move in large groups. See the others there? They are the Waife cousin, the Scatterwhite, and look practically identical,' Dinkletons said.

They all looked the same to Nicole.

'They have the same frame and colouring, but instead of black eyes, a Scatterwhite has pinprick, white dots, hence the name. Even though Frail cannot see them, if they get too close, as these fellows are doing, they can send shivers down spines. They are mean and thrive on energy caused by vibrations they sweat, and this causes Frail to be scared for no reason,' Dinkletons said.

'How are they permitted to be here, so close to humans?' Nicole whispered, peering out and biting her nails.

'They are not allowed here.' Strom poked his head over Nicole's shoulder. 'Prefects should have already banished them.'

'Do not worry. He will not harm you; he will be scared of you,' Dinkletons said. He was watching the Marnie reaction to the Waife. Their eyes were wide, and their fingers were on fire. They shook them out, leaving threads of smoke.

'Do they go in our houses, these Waife?'

'No. Because of their height, they would have to bend their bodies, and this is something they cannot do,' Dinkletons said,

'They cannot bend at all?' Nicole squinted at the Waife's long, straight back.

'Stiff as posts,' Dinkletons said with a grin.

'So, what are they doing here?' she whispered.

'This realm gives them space. They live in tented communities in their realm that span long distances. Coming here they can be outside. The sun here is mild in comparison to theirs. They can stretch their bodies. I'm going to evict them all. You will have to do similar in the future.' Dinkletons leaned in and bumped Nicole's shoulder. 'This means learning which Rogue are bad and which are important for the health of the Frail Realm.'

Dinkletons breathed some pink steam into his paw and threw it towards the path.

The Waife, alerted to their impending exit, started running in all directions but kept falling over. Finally, all that was left of them was a tea-towel sized rag, which was sucked into the soil. All traces of them were gone.

The sanctioned Rogue, who had stopped what they were doing to see the Waife banished, clapped their hands.

Dinkletons clapped his paws together.

'Where did they go?' Nicole looked all over the place.

'Waife disposal.'

Nicole, Jinn, and Strom laughed. Strom rolled on the ground. Nicole thought he was overdoing it again. Something about the Frail Realm made him silly and giggly. *Why did I let them come? They make me nervous.*

She turned around to face the Marnie. By the looks on their glum faces, they had telemuted her thought. She hadn't silked; she had too much to think about.

'How am I supposed to remove these things?' she asked, now worried.

'You won't be doing it very often, but it is a skill you need to have. You will use a mixture of your aura and colour to weave a banishing ball. Rook will teach you this. You're signed up for his class and we will not have you return home unprepared. These Waife and Scatterwhite would have only arrived just now. It was good you got to see them.'

'Come on then – let's get this over with,' Nicole said as she saw her mother come out onto the back deck with her coffee.

'Jinn, you need to concentrate on what you are here for. This is a good test for you. All three pink colours will be used, so concentrate. We have to get rid of the Night Hag,' Dinkletons said.

Dinkletons, Strom, and Jinn ran out from the trees and into the open.

'Wait for me,' Nicole whispered, knowing the words would be lost in the wind. She saw Jinn meet her mother first.

'Why do they have to naughty all the time?' Nicole gaped at them and ran fast to join them. But at the same time, she knew they were just being Marnie, playful and curious about every single thing they did not yet know.

Abby jolted when she saw the group and silently watched them approach.

'Hi, I am Jinn, another Marnie.'

'I didn't realise there would be more of you coming,' her mother said. Nicole felt far better that she had given her mother a heads-up via a Rebo to her cell.

Abby looked at Jinn and then at Nicole and her face visibly paled. 'Oh, you are the same as my daughter?'

'That's right, although she is not as powerful as a Marnie.' Steam came from her feet as she sat next to Abby who leaned away.

Nicole went around the table to hug her mother. The Hag hissed but stayed firmly in place. Nicole could see the tattoo on the back of Abby's neck, two separate circles.

'Good girl. I'm glad you're here,' her mother said.

Nicole sat down and tried to ignore the Hag that was moving from one shoulder to another. The Hag looked heavy; no wonder her mother was exhausted by lunchtime. Nicole held her mother's hand.

'You have to tell me what happened at Lena's. Dree rang to ask what was going on.'

'I explained the relationship curse to her.'

'I can't believe you two had a conversation – neither can Dree.'

'It was because I had Dinkletons there to smooth the way,' Nicole said.

'Dree said Jaya was acting hyperactive after you left because of you.' She pointed at Strom across the table.

'Guilty as charged,' Strom said, and Jinn elbowed him.

'Well, you know Strom is a Marnie, remember – a Magic with charisma that can't be found in Frail. It's not surprising that happened,' Dinkletons said.

Strom stuck out his chest. 'I only have eyes for one person.'

'Stop it, Strom,' Jinn said, frowning.

Nicole noticed her mother look from Strom to her. 'Nicole is far too young to have a boyfriend, especially one from another world.'

'Too late,' Strom said, grinning.

The embarrassment was unreal – what was he doing? Nicole wiped her eyes and decided to ignore him. She could hear her mother's thoughts about how she knew this day would come, but not this soon and not with this kid. The Hag smiled. It had two sets of teeth, one in front and one behind on both the top and bottom of its mouth. Nicole wished she had a tennis racket to belt the Hag as far away as possible.

A tennis racket would not remove her, Dinkletons telemuted.

'You said you are removing something from me?' Nicole's mother asked, her voice shaky.

'That's right,' Nicole said. Nicole looked at the veins that ran up the back of her mother's hand. Nicole could feel her fear, hear it in her head; she was so vulnerable. 'Let's start.'

Jinn, Strom, and Nicole put their Crystals together and placed their hands around them.

'Oh, you are doing that thing again,' Abby said.

'It's a strong dose of healing,' Jinn said and nodded at Nicole to continue.

'What do I need healing for?' Her mother jerked back.

'You know how you have nightmares? Well, that,' Strom said.

'You did that before.' Nicole noticed her mother's hands were trembling.

'It worked on Dad but not you. That is why I brought Jinn.'

The three squeezed each other's hands and concentrated

hard. They looked from one to the other. There were three auras now with Jinn's pink one. They all collided together, rolled around, and shot the colour straight into the Hag. Nicole could see her mother's red neck and shoulders from where the Hag leant on her all day.

Why is it called a Night Hag when it is there all the time?

It is at night the Hag gets her energy off your mother because she is still. During the day she hangs around like a parasite, Dinkletons telemuted.

They all watched the Hag vanish. It closed its eyes, peaceful now that it was going to be released.

'That is some crazy stuff,' Strom said.

'It sure was,' Jinn said. 'That Hag did not want to be here.'

Her mother rubbed her neck. 'I feel better already.'

'You wouldn't believe what an ugly Rogue you had hanging off your body,' Strom said.

Abby said, 'My throat and feet feel less closed over; I feel like I can breathe.'

'That's because you had a seven-foot, skinny Hag dribbling all over you,' Jinn said.

'What do you mean? That sounds dreadful!' Her mother shook her head.

Nicole decided that now was a good time to use the mood elevator.

Dinkletons said to the Marnie, 'You two go wait over there.'

When Strom and Jinn were gone, but not without making a fuss with groans and moans, Nicole studied her mother. The Hag was still gone, thank goodness.

'I've been wondering about when you were pregnant with me and what went wrong. I know something did.' Nicole's voice sounded assertive, but inside she was a mess of nerves.

Abby put her arms around herself at this unexpected

question. *Where did that come from?* Nicole heard her mother think.

'Well, you were premature but perfect. My doctor was stunned because you surprised us and arrived two months early, giving your father and me a fright. You were the size and weight of a full-term baby.'

Dinkletons replied, 'Because of Magic you did not need the normal incubation time of normal Frail. You grew at a fast rate.'

Nicole noted that her mother's face drained of colour as Dinkletons spoke.

'Has something unexplainable ever happened to you?' Nicole asked. If she jogged her mother's memory, the thoughts would come. Abby didn't even have to open her mouth because Dinkletons would be able to track her thoughts. To Nicole, it seemed to be an invasion of her privacy, and she felt bad for doing it.

Abby's sharp intake of breath surprised Nicole. Her mother covered her ears and held her head as if it were too heavy.

'Are you alright?' Nicole could hear whispers of her mother's thoughts and pieced them together as they came through. The tips of her fingers burned at what she heard.

Nicole connected her mum's thoughts. She was remembering the day she and Dree wanted to surprise their mother that they were pregnant and due only months apart. She could feel her mum's elation at this prospect, the excitement of the news of two baby girls.

All that changed in an instant when her Abby's mother fell to the floor, eyes wide and unseeing. Abby was smashed by a tremendous physical pain and a guttural scream that brought her to her knees. Nicole could hear it, feel it and it was the most awful thing that she had ever heard in her life. The last thing Nicole telemuted was both Dree and her mum screaming in unison and the terrible confusion on the unanswered questions on what had really occurred.

She looked at Dinkletons and swallowed a hard lump. It was hard to hold in her tears. Telemuting her mother felt so awful, but the horror of what she learned upset Nicole. Abby and Aunt Dree had watched their mother die in front of them. Both still suffered every day; both grieved with anguish and could not move on.

31

'Oh dear, we have trouble,' Dinkletons said and jumped off the bench.

Nicole thought he was talking about her and what they had learnt from her mother just now. But she saw where Dinkletons was headed, she took off after him.

'Nicole, where are you – oh no,' Abby said, standing up.

Dinkletons launched himself over the fence into the neighbour's yard and raced up the huge tree to where the Marnie and the neighbour's boys were.

'How did they get over there so fast?' But Nicole knew they had jumped.

Nicole couldn't believe her eyes. The Marnie and the boys were almost at the top of the tree. Their mother was screaming and stumbling on her feet as she looked up; at the same time, she was stealing looks at her new garden. The grass was green and covered the area, whereas before was nonexistent and a small garden formed underneath her lounge window.

'How on earth did they get the time to do this?' Nicole asked.

Nicole could hear Dinkletons telemuting the Marnie. *Come down at once.*

The boys were yelling with delight at the height. Soon they clambered down and joined their mother.

Nicole watched her neighbour, Kylie, gather her boys, their faces bright with excitement.

'What have you got to say for yourselves?' Nicole asked as she approached the Marnie at the base of the tree.

'We couldn't help it! They looked so bored playing with that bat and ball, and we had to show them what real fun is,' Strom said, now looking suitably sheepish.

'I have no idea how they got that far up the tree, and what have you done to my yard?' Kylie asked.

'The garden is amazing. It was crappy before,' one of the boys said.

'I don't understand.' Kylie tapped her hand against her lips. She was looking at Dinkletons.

'They have special skills,' Nicole said, looking at the shrubs and small ferns in the area the Marnie had built. Even in the nugget game, it took ages to be able to get a flower or a blade of grass here.

It is because they are here and able to do it, like you were able to build gardens. A Magic in a non-Magic place has the ability to do this, Dinkletons telemuted.

'Well, that's obvious.' Nicole looked over at Kylie and could tell she wasn't angry but mystified.

In the distance, sirens rang out.

'I called the fire brigade to get the children down,' Kylie said and ushered her boys to go inside. They reluctantly waved to the Marnie.

'Bye, Jinn and Strom. Promise you will come back again – that was cracking!' one boy yelled.

'Aw, not fair,' said the other, who was being carried into the house by his mother. 'That was so much fun.'

'Kylie, I will explain all this later. But now we have to go.'

'Oh, I will hold you to that, Miss Nicole,' Kylie said, looking around at her new garden.

'You need to water and love that garden,' Jinn said as they went through a side opening into Nicole's yard.

32

Nicole and Dinkletons went straight to the Arx in Orra. The Marnie were sent to their Savant for a 'discussion' on their behaviour, but before that, in the Fire Garden, Nicole had told them, 'I don't think you did any harm, but if you come again, you must promise not to go off like that again. I'll have to explain it to Kylie and the boys now; they'll be always asking about you.'

'We were justified to come along. How long ago was it that two Marnie and a Sape had the exact same shade of pink? Like, never,' Jinn said. 'I should've come in the first place.'

Nicole twisted her mouth. 'I know it was great to get rid of the Night Hag. But that is not the point.'

'It was all your idea, Strom,' Jinn snapped.

'We won't be allowed out again,' Strom said. 'It's not like we did any harm.'

'Maybe it won't be so bad?' Nicole soothed.

'Maybe it will,' Strom said.

'That's enough. Off you go,' Dinkletons said as they stood in the foyer.

In the Arx, the Prefects eyed Nicole as she stood before them. Rook shot her a warm smile. Shanazz and

Zosmine had brought food – cupcakes, pies, and mugs of smoothies.

Nicole heaved a sigh. This wedging caused Nicole aches and pains across her body, but the worst was her raw throat, it was like swallowing razor blades. She would never understand the process of moving from one realm to another and how their bodies disfigured. But the nasty distortions did not last long in the Magic world as their bodies were put back together with Orra's Magic. The nectar bars helped quench their desperate thirst – Nicole was on her third one.

The Arx was an eerie place, Nicole thought, as she looked at things she didn't notice the first time she was there. To each side of the room, in front of pretty, silk curtains for walls, there were two long wooden shelves and on them Nicole saw old clocks that kept different times, drawings, coins, cups of all shapes, and many boxes.

'They are illusion instruments Thisbe have found. We are getting them ready for the Vault storage,' Rook said, seeing her taking in the objects.

'Those boxes cannot be examined 'til they get there because we do not know what is inside them. They can be very dangerous,' Jivan added.

'Do you work in the Vault, Rook?' Nicole asked.

'I do, I love it there. Dex used to work with me,' Rook said.

At the end of the shelves, the Prefects sat in their leather seats. The outside was only a few steps away with a massive drop into a vast gorge that went down so far Nicole couldn't see the bottom. The only nice things about it were the waterfalls that fell from the sides. Nicole's feet went numb, and she stepped away.

Zosmine waddled over and took her to a seat. She sat and devoured a pie and two cupcakes that were to die for. Nicole was still dizzy at the thought of her mother's experience. She noticed all eyes in the room were on her.

'Take your time, Nicole,' Jivan said.

'But don't you all know already?' Nicole asked them, her voice rushed.

Everyone in the room nodded. 'Dinkletons relayed it all already. It is excellent that your skills are coming to the surface, but along with these, you will have some burdens. But once you have healed Ripples, things will get better,' Jivan said.

'It is your news to tell, Nicole. You explain to us what you have learnt and we can come up behind you and eliminate any issues,' Shanazz said.

'Yes, and use some mood elevator – it will be terribly helpful,' Zosmine said.

Nicole dabbed the mood elevator to her neck. It was surprising how fast the awful pounding in her chest was replaced with stillness and not dread. 'Wow, that works fast.'

'It is designed to be speedy,' Zosmine said as he shared a happy glance.

'You became Magic the day.' Jivan nodded.

'But your mother witnessed her own mother die,' Jivan said as he nodded, staring intensely at Nicole.

'But why didn't she ever tell me?' Nicole's face crumpled.

33

Nicole went to her Orra bedroom and thought about Raisa and the image her mother let her see and by her own invasion of her mother's thoughts. Nicole felt like a thief, stealing away precious memories.

If Raisa was only responsible for her Magic side, then there must be more to the story. Nicole sat up and dried her face. After a soft knock on her door, Dinkletons came in, his huge paws silent on the floor, long whiskers directly sideways, a puff of aura around him.

Nicole pulled herself to the edge of the bed, got up, and walked over to her lounge area. Dinkletons followed.

'So, Raisa made me Magic. This happened at the same time as my nana died. So that means I need to identify each ripple and go fix them. If we are to be free of Ripples, I need to get Raisa's Illuminance. That will make sure there will be no more Rogue pulled in the future.' She ran her hands through her hair.

'Your molecules have been damaged and need to be free of the Tangle,' Dinkletons said.

'I was able to get rid of the Knocker and the Hag with help. Can't we do the same thing with the Tangle?'

Dinkletons turned his big body around. 'Those Ripples

were serious on your parents and Lena, but the Tangle is on another level. Not only does it require the Gloine prescription but your own input, as you hold them in deep inside your body.'

'Only I can do it. I get that. Time to deal with the Tangle. So, what do you suggest?'

Dinkletons put his nose close to hers. 'We need to go back to the original site of the Tangle.'

'We just did that, didn't we?' Nicole glared at him.

He nodded. 'Only in a telemute. This allowed us to "hear" the thought but a telewedge will allow us to "see" what is happening.'

Nicole shook her head. *No way.*

'We don't need to go back physically. I can interpret the memory from here, I just need that link. I can take you back into the memory and we will see what happened. How Raisa performed the Spark, what happened at that moment to cause the Tangle.'

Nicole stared at him with a blank look. 'Why didn't we do this at first? Save all this running around, all this back and forth?'

'Well, we know now when you became Magic, so this is the next step,' Dinkletons answered. 'I can only do it when two people are thinking the same thought about that day. This gives me a tunnel to travel down the memory.'

'That will be my mother and Dree.' Nicole stopped walking and stood in front of Dinkletons, who was still looking very comfortable. 'How do we know when they are doing that?'

'The Prefects have informed me that your mother is upset, and they can do a prompt to get her to call Dree and talk about it. Then we know for sure they are both thinking about that same thing.'

'I don't know. This is so intense.' Nicole paced.

'We can leave it for now if you want to get mentally prepared, but time is important.'

Wide-eyed, Nicole cracked her knuckles. 'Let's just do it now and get it over with.'

Dinkletons pointed his paw in the direction of the door. It closed shut. 'We don't want to be interrupted by Marnie. I will Rebo the Prefects and tell them to go ahead. You have to be still, Nicole. Lay over there.' Dinkletons stood on the couch, his great body taking up half the space.

Nicole did as she was told; she got herself comfortable.

'We are ready to go. Don't open your eyes.'

Nicole's vision turned pink. They were in her nana's lounge inside Dinkletons' telewedge. Nicole tried hard not to move, but the memory was so clear. Her nana was steps away. She looked young. Her straight, dark brown hair reached her shoulders, and she was wearing jeans and a T-shirt on her slim body. She was talking to Raisa, demanding to know why she was in her house.

The lounge was small but cosy, with a floral pattern lounge suite, fresh flowers, and a sideboard with tea set collections – loads of them. She didn't know that about her nana. Next to the lounge was a very formal living area with six chairs. She had knick-knacks all over a second unit, and Nicole's eye was drawn to a long set of wooden camels.

Raisa had not yet lost all her powers. Raisa's stance was hard, and it was obvious she was caught in a moment she didn't want to be in. With no wings, she looked small, defeated. Her chin trembled as she looked around for a way out.

Nicole watched her mother and Dree come into the room and stop short when they saw Raisa. She could see a glimpse of her cousin Jaya in the kitchen, then she moved out of sight.

Raisa was waving her arms around. The Spark, in the shape of an orb, flew from her and raced around like a bee, checking everyone out. This looked harmless and when it landed on people it did so in a soft manner.

Then Nicole saw a creature hiding behind the sofa. He fumbled and ducked back behind the couch trying to get closer to Raisa by crawling on his hands and knees. A bolt bounced off him. Nicole noticed it was only a small flash. It looked sharp, and with the way it moved, she could see how it would damage people. It was round and black with red, sharp blades protruding all around. Nicole knew that this was the Tangle – the beginning of her problems.

Nicole could see Raisa's Spark and the Tangle merge. They swirled, interweaving, becoming faster as each one tried to take over. And now it headed straight at her nana.

'That is enough; we have the information we need,' Dinkletons said, bringing her back from Nana's house to her bedroom in Orra.

Nicole opened her eyes and cried loudly. Dinkletons jumped over beside her. 'Ahh, no, don't do that. It will hurt your Magic molecules.'

'What was that thing?' Nicole asked, sitting up.

'That, Nicole, was a Rustic.'

'As in where Raisa's Illuminance is?'

He nodded, his eyes both open now and focused on her. 'The Tangle is a Toxic fungus brought from the Rustic Realm, a mould that is harmful to Frail.'

'Not Kyacin?'

'No, he brought it to do harm. He did it deliberately.'

'That Tangle killed my nana!' Nicole banged her fists on the couch.

34

Later that night, they were back in her room. Dinkletons had shooed away the Marnie that had accompanied Nicole back from dinner. She was grateful for the silence.

'Raisa wasn't responsible for my nana's death, was she?'

'No. We have no idea why the Rustic was there. Rustic are forbidden from entering Frail houses like most Rogue. The only thing is Raisa didn't tell anyone about being in the house. I believe she silked it so she could not dwell on it.'

'Why would she do such a thing?' Nicole asked.

'She was weak and scared. In doing that, she lost control of the knowledge that could have prevented you from being lost to us. If she had told Dex, they could have reported it.'

'Maybe the Rustic followed Raisa to my nana's house that day? And he was involved in her stolen Illuminance in the first place?'

'I believe he followed her with the intent of using the fungi. Fungi with Magic is toxic. It is the root of the Tangle, what it is made of. He must have known about you. Prefects are unable to pinpoint where your Thisbe went,' Dinkletons said.

She looked over to where Dinkletons was looking out at the red and yellow sparkles of space. 'Tell me about when Raisa lost her Illuminance.'

'Historically, Marnie were allowed one excursion to the Frail Realm, and it has been an activity of the Dellamana for centuries. Marnie learnt a lot from watching Frail and Rogue in their natural setting. They got to see Rogue who were allowed to stay for a limited time in the Frail Realm and the reasons behind this rule. They learnt how certain Rogue can affect the air and cause allergies, how other Rogue are good for the environment. Bringing the Hallr Crystal without wearing the cloud-stepping boots is a well-known and followed ban. They protect Crystals from theft by warning Rogue not to come near the Marnie. They give out painful zaps to any Rogue coming within a short distance, and these can last days and are most unpleasant, we have been told. Raisa for whatever reason failed to follow this simple rule.'

'What happened?' Nicole leant forward.

'The Savant that was with the group said everything was going as planned and they had covered most of the trip when they came across four Sylph. The Marnie were so excited to see a sanctioned Rogue and they interacted, sat together, and discussed their work.

'At first, the Savant didn't think anything about it, but he noticed that Raisa went from being overactive and hard to keep quiet to very still.'

Nicole listened hard to Dinkletons and stayed speechless, trying to remember every detail.

'Raisa was acting to appear indifferent about what had happened to her, but she knew. A few Marnie say they saw a Rogue that had been lingering nearby observing them draw out her Illuminance. They were so shaken up they returned to Orra immediately. The Frail Realm is not the place to resolve Magical errors.

'Prefects worked it out that it was a Rustic, and for a short time after this, they were able to pinpoint that the Illuminance had gone to the Rustic Realm, but then the source went blank. We don't know what the Rustic have done with it over the years,' Dinkletons said. 'But we do know the Tangle was manufactured; when Nava had you tested, she found you full of fungi. Without Raisa's Spark, it couldn't do anything.'

'The Illuminance is the collection of all the colours. So how did a Rogue with less power than a Marnie manage to draw it out of the Hallr Crystal?' The thought froze in her head. How awful that must have been for Raisa, despite her sloppiness at guarding what should have been a treasured gem. Nicole knew that she would take the very best care of her own Crystal.

'Most Marnie are not reckless in regard to their Crystal; it is a rarity.' Dinkletons was nonchalant.

'You've told me that Orra is one of the most powerful of Magic worlds. Why can't we order the Rustic to give the Illuminance back?'

'Well, that is due to the Kyacin.'

Dinkletons watched her. She could tell he knew what she was thinking.

'I can't help think that I am the missing link to Raisa's Illuminance.'

Dinkletons ears perked up.

'Imagine the possibilities if Raisa got her Illuminance back! She could take the Tangle off, which would heal my Magic cells and then I wouldn't make any more Ripples.'

'Yes, but you would have to go through a lot to get it.'

'I don't have a choice.'

35

'How's your head?' Dinkletons asked when they had wedged around the corner from her house, now back in Frail Realm.

'Not too bad, thanks to your dart.'

As they made their way down the familiar road, she saw her old world from a different perspective. It was dreamlike. This was her neighbourhood, her place, and now she felt disconnected from it.

'Ahem.' Dinkletons flicked her with his tail.

Dinkletons raced up a steep driveway, and Nicole ran to catch up. They walked around the back and stood at the bottom of the stairs that led to a deck. Raisa and Dex sat on the deck, in conversation. Raisa had been mid-sentence when she saw them. She was surprised to see the girl, who looked fearless, with steeliness etched on her face.

'What are you doing here?' Raisa asked, a flush of red forming in her neck and cheeks.

Nicole and Dinkletons climbed the steps. Nicole was overwhelmed by Raisa, who was vastly different to the girl in the telewedge, with her thin body, enormous wings, untidy hair, and red-rimmed eyes.

Dinkletons whispered to her, 'Silk, Nicole.'

In a strong voice, Nicole said, 'I don't know where to start.'

'Try telling us why you are here?' Dex asked, his eyes boring into hers.

'I'm going to get your Illuminance back.' Her voice was letting her down. She locked eyes with Raisa.

Dex groaned loudly and put his head in his arms.

'You didn't kill my grandmother,' Nicole blurted out.

Raisa's face tightened. 'What did you say?'

'Wait a minute – how do you know this?' Dex asked and then his eyes widened at Dinkletons. 'You did a telewedge?'

Raisa's mind was racing. Could it really be true? She never knew what had happened to Lily. 'She died?'

'She did but it was not your fault,' Dinkletons said. 'But you did silk it and hide the whole situation, which should have been reported to Rolte.'

Raisa was openly crying now from relief. All these years she had been worried sick about what happened to Lily. 'Oh my god, I am so sorry.'

'You weren't the only one trespassing in Nana's house that day. There was a Rustic,' Dinkletons said.

Raisa stood up and her stool went crashing to the ground. 'Are you sure? I didn't see a Rustic.'

'Yes,' Dinkletons said. 'It was hiding.'

'I saw it myself, behind the sofa. You let go of a Spark, and at exactly the same time, the Rustic let go of a Toxic fungi that became the Tangle. They joined together before hitting my nana.' Nicole noticed Raisa's face had crumpled.

'What are the odds of that happening at the same time?' Raisa asked. She could not believe the mess she had gotten them into. She was a coward for silking such an important event.

'A Rustic that knew what he was doing,' Dinkletons mumbled. 'The Tangle came from the Rustic.'

'If I can get your Illuminance back, we can get rid of the Tangle for good,' Nicole said.

'That sounds unbelievable.' Raisa tried to keep calm.

'I've been watching them every single day since I got here. Trying to work out a way to get Raisa's Illuminance, but it's no good. You can't talk to a Rustic; they are infuriatingly uncooperative. In the whole time I've been here, I have not managed to get one to utter a word to me,' Dex said.

'Dex has information from other Rogue that associate with Rustic, but that, too, is limited,' Raisa said. 'Rogue of a certain type stick together, like the Scatterwhite and Waife. They are loyal when they want to be.'

'You have Tracers?' Dex asked Dinkletons.

'I have them.' Nicole showed him the marble-size, shiny black stones that Nava had given her.

'We need Dex to locate a Rustic for me. I have seen one, but I wouldn't be confident in recognising another,' Nicole said. 'When you locate one, I will put a Tracer in its pocket and hopefully the other Tracer will kick in and follow its companion stone. That's the rough plan – it's all I have.'

Dex leant back in his chair. 'Not an easy thing to do. But I can point you in a Rustic direction,' Dex said.

'Can you do me a favour? Get me a good one, a nice one.'

'None of them are nice.' Dex gave her a side-on glance.

'Dex has made a Tracer,' Raisa said.

'Very impressive, let me see it,' Dinkletons said.

Dex fished the stone out of his pocket and handed it over to Dinkletons. 'Not bad at all, Dex. I feel small vibrations. Here, Nicole, you take that along with you.'

'I've only just finished it. There are forty-five layers there. I would be surprised if it activated considering it was created without being in the Magic world.'

'You never know what it will do, especially since the

creator is Magic,' Dinkletons said. 'Prefects knew you were making a Tracer.'

Nicole turned the yellow stone over in her hand. It didn't look like forty-five layers. It was very small and half the size of the black Tracers. 'How did you make it?'

Dex stared out the window. 'Zosmine sent me star dust and Mikkel, a rare dust, via Orra birds. Together they produce a chemical reaction with ice. Orra bees sent fragments of blue garnet, the gemstone.'

'You never told me you got all that from Zosmine.' Raisa shot him a look.

Dex gave Raisa a lift of the shoulder. 'You would have hit the roof.'

'Those items have the potential to have inner fire,' Dinkletons said. 'Good choice.'

'Then what do you do with this stuff?' Nicole asked.

'At first, it was trial and error on which components go first. For a while, they didn't do anything. Then I added heat to the process and then slowly built up each layer, then they started to bond. It was amazing to see, but it took years.'

'There is Kyacin to consider,' Raisa said as she noticed the colours rotating through Nicole's Crystal.

'Which only affects the Magic molecules? I have some resistance as I'm Frail as well.'

'Consider you are successful and get to the Rustic Realm and you do find my Illuminance, they might have more Tangles there that they can use against you.' Despite wanting Nicole to go through with this trip, she was worried.

Nicole rubbed her eyes. She hadn't thought of this. She groaned and told Raisa what she'd told Dinkletons earlier. 'I have no choice.'

36

They headed to a shopping center Dex said Rustic often frequented, wandering around looking in shops, mingling with other Rogue and Frail. Nicole was surprised to find this was true – they were everywhere.

'What are they?' Nicole pointed to a group of small, winged things whose features were not far from Frails. They were oblivious to them and chatted confidently with each other. They were as tall as Nicole's knee.

'They are Abbot; they gain Magic points when they give out good vibes and check on children around the age of twelve,' Dex said. 'Ugly little mites, aren't they?'

'More like kooky looking,' Nicole said.

Seeing all these Rogue, sanctioned or not, was weird. At this moment, they were the least of her problems. There were so many Rogues lurking, but Nicole had no time to ask about who they were and what they did. They chatted in foreign languages and laughed as they went past them, not a care in the world, it seemed to Nicole. These were sanctioned Rogue who didn't feel threatened by high Magic as they were allowed to be in the Frail Realm.

'What are they all doing here?' Nicole's hands were trembling so hard that she had trouble steadying them.

'They love being around Frail. This is a common, everyday scene,' Dex said. Nicole fumbled along. Her neck hurt from turning her head back and forth so often, and her mouth stayed permanently open.

'Come here, Nicole.' Raisa put her arm around her and squeezed. A thick shawl covered her wings.

'My wings are being good; they have a mind of their own most of the time,' Raisa said, close to her ear.

'Rustics come to the surface often and drift for days. Once, I followed what I thought to be a Rustic – turned out to be a Squib that looks similar. It almost bit my finger off. Rustic are evasive, and each time they look different from their realm shift. This makes them hard to pinpoint. If they feel eyes on them, they take off to the nearest Propylaeum,' Dex said to no one in particular.

They left the building and went out the front where all the restaurants were located. They left the building and went out the front where all the restaurants were located. They stood before a burger place, tavern, fish and chip shops, and a café with umbrellas covering outdoor tables.

'Wait, there's one right over there,' Dex said, pointing to a group from an aged care facility getting out of a minivan, parked a few feet away. 'This is amazing and faster than I thought.'

The Rustic's clothes were shabby and looked too small for him. He had a baseball cap, and a growth of stubble covered his face. He was young, too. Nicole thought he was about thirty-five years old, and he wasn't bad looking, which she had not been expecting. After all, he lived miles beneath the earth and in poisonous air.

Nicole felt her nerves reach into her throat that closed over. 'But you said they are hard to identify, how do you know it is one?'

'A Rustic can stand out; you need to know what you are looking for. The vapour of orange breath is distinctly

Rustic,' Dex said excitedly. 'I have seen this one many times. He always looks the same, so he must be important in his world.

'That breath is from their environment in the Rustic Realm. they bring it with them,' Dex said. 'They normally come in pairs. This one is on his own, which means he is a regular traveller. This is good for us as he will be more confident and not so suspicious. But we need to act fast.'

'I thought you said they look different every time they come here?' Nicole said.

'Not this one.'

'Oh no.' Nicole stared at the Rustic and took a closer look at it.

'What's the matter?' Dex asked.

'It is the same one that was at your nana's house,' Dinkletons said.

'He's part of all of this,' Nicole said.

'You will have to be careful,' Dex said.

'I don't like this.' Raisa shook her head.

'I have to be careful, anyway. At least we know about that particular Rustic's involvement before I go.'

'Where are your Tracers?' Dinkletons asked. 'Now you know they are linked. Once you place one in his pocket the other will be zoned into following it.'

'I have them here.' She showed him the two black ones and Dex's single yellow one, which was not as smooth as the Orra stones. The edges on his were rough like pumice. All three gave Nicole comfort, and she hoped they would help her.

'Once in the Rustic Realm, they will guide you,' Dinkletons said. Nicole crouched down to pat him. Again, she was off to an alien world, and this one would not be so nice. She clutched her Crystal and silently asked it to help her.

'He is about to leave,' Dex said.

'How do you know?' Nicole asked in a shaky voice. She felt like running.

'Just before realm shifting, they increase their breath, and this changes the colour to black to get energy for the trip. See how his breath is shooting a long way in front now?'

The black mist was sword-like, long with a pointed edge. It was different from his previous breathing, which had been orange and controlled, and she noticed the Rustic seemed manic and wasn't walking straight.

'Oh gosh, are you sure?' Nicole closed her hand over the Tracers now in her pocket. She was terrified she would lose them.

Dex nodded. Nicole could see that he was worried because he avoided looking at her.

Dinkletons said, 'Rolte will be able to monitor you via the Tracer you have and your Gloine. That must be invisible; Nava would not want to lose such an exemplary piece of technology.'

'I know. She did explain it, but it's all a blur. I'm glad to have it with me and my Crystal.'

'I will be waiting for you. Good luck.'

Nicole's bottom lip quivered, but she could not let herself cry and experience the pain that went with it. She could not cope with that right now. She took a breath and started to walk towards the Rustic before she could chicken out. He was about three steps ahead of her but was weaving from side to side. *This will make it trickier to get the Tracer into his pocket.*

He had on a grey-hooded track top with gaping pockets. Nicole wiped her sweaty hands down her legs. It was a hot day, but the Rustic was rugged up. Dex had told her they do not feel temperatures, that the Toxic Realm damaged their inner gauges for feeling hot or cold.

She was now walking directly behind him; his black

breath darted way ahead and smelled sickly sweet. The Rustic was making a weird vibrating sound in his throat. He continued his dizzying swaying from left to right. Nicole was wondering how she would manage to get the Tracer in his pocket, when she saw her opportunity. He manoeuvered towards her as she came up behind him and let the Tracer fall out of her hands into the depths of his pocket.

It seemed too easy. Relieved, she turned to look at her support team. Dex and Raisa waved and Dinkletons flicked his tail.

37

It didn't take long for the separated stone to start singing and the one in her hand pulsated like a phone on silent.

Nicole was now being moved, not like a wedge, more like being on the end of a rope that was pulling her. She was unstable on her feet and had no idea of the direction she was going. It started with a slow pull and built momentum. Then she was running, every second step airborne. She tried to avoid the annoyed people who were leaping out of her way.

What could she do? Apologise and say she was going to another world? The Gloine was moving her at a growing pace.

He was out of her sight now, racing ahead. The only thing linking them was this invisible thread that joined the Tracers and dragged her into the unknown. Nicole shrieked, as the Rustic turned his head. Did he just see her?

At this point, she couldn't do anything if he had seen her. She was whipping past the last restaurant and saw people pointing at her as murmurs came from diners. She flew past a taxi rank, and two couples leapt out of her way. A bus narrowly missed her as it left the terminus. Nicole couldn't help but scream when she saw where she was heading – to the main road filled with cars driving fast. She was going to be killed. She screamed again, wanting to stop this whole thing, but she was at the mercy of the Rustic and the Tracers.

Just as she was entering the busy road, she was projected into darkness. Her arms and legs were flying, and the air was knocked out of her. She was free-falling into darkness, engulfing her, pulling her into the gloom. When she was able, she took a rushed breath that hurt her throat. The cold air hit her full on, and she was freezing. It was the most frightened she had ever been. Wedging was easy compared to this.

Finally, the darkness cleared, and she abruptly landed. Her bottom lip shook uncontrollably, and she rubbed her arms in an attempt to keep warm, but it was no good. Her movements were cautious and slow. She had landed in an industrial area, filled with containers and sheds. Nicole looked all around her and saw no one. Compacted, sticky dirt pulled at her shoes, covering them with a black substance. It had a sickly smell.

Nicole twirled around. She was in the Rustic Realm, and she had never felt so utterly alone. Nava allowed the Gloine to follow her, but she had been reluctant, considering the polluted air. In the end she made it invisible to Rustic. Nava agreed they needed the Gloine to transmit information from Nicole about her environment and help her with Magic medication.

She trembled and moaned out loud. First, she crouched down to take a minute to herself after such a horrible shape-shift and arriving in a place she could easily call hell. Nicole pulled herself up and started to walk, but every step was heavy, and she knew that at any minute she would be spotted. She pushed herself along and could hardly see due to the orange smog. Her feet squelched as she moved – more strings of gunk pulled at her shoes. A lacework of grime now building in quantity stuck to every part of her that wasn't covered. She pulled at her sleeves and pants. The muck was everywhere, staining her skin.

'Please let the Tracer do its job,' she said to herself over and over as she held onto her Crystal for dear life. This had to work, but she had misgivings. What if she failed? She would always have this Tangle attached to her, which would forever send Ripples out to her family and everyone else around her. She would continue to infect Frails with Rogue like the Knocker and Night Hag. *Stop it! Manifest good things. This has to work.*

Nicole stopped and wiped her cheeks. She felt the grime on her face. It gloved her hands and was pushed solid under her fingernails. The only thing she could do was let the Tracers do their job.

38

Dinkletons had told Nicole the Tracers would send information about her activity to Rolte, which was a comfort, because in spirit she felt their presence. For the past hour, she had been stuck in the maze of shipping containers, sheds, and outbuildings. It was a dreary, depressing place; Nicole wanted out.

If someone had come along, spotted her, there would be no escape. The walls were high, sound-barrier type structures and were made of the same substance as the ground, which looked wet and sticky. Within the confinement of the area, the smell grew stronger.

She came to an open space out of the container area and away from the barren path with high walls. She didn't feel so claustrophobic. It was a small consolation. Nicole wiped at tears and her body ached with fear. She looked ahead and saw a street bumper to bumper with cars that looked like golf carts with doors. She froze. She could not see inside the cars, as the windows were blacked out, like pitch black. The individuals on the street did not look like real living people, but of course they were living somethings. They made awkward robot movements, arms striding like soldiers, heads suddenly jerking from left to right. On the outside of their bodies, it was obvious to Nicole that they adored colour and the brighter the better. All together, walking along the sidewalk, their neon brightness was outrageous and gaudy. Everybody clashed to the highest level there could be. As a group, they were a blended, blazing fashion mistake. They had wrinkly skin and high hairlines, which the women of their kind obviously put a lot of time into. All had the same pointed sharp chins and thick veiny necks.

Come on. Keep going, she told herself sternly. She could feel the Tracer in her pocket gently pulling her.

The first thing Nicole noticed was the silence; no one spoke, the cars moved without noise, doors closed without bangs. It was eerie and scary. It was a town that looked animated, out of a cartoon. Every building was labelled with 'Osiris' written in bold.

Rustic were walking in front of buildings that to her didn't seem real, then she saw a group go into one of the shops. She was right beside them; they would've been able to see her. They didn't seem too bothered about her presence.

Up close, she got a clearer view of these individuals. They were all short of stature, all coming up to just below Nicole's shoulders. Nicole considered their bright but smart clothes created a contrast to their dreary surroundings. They were cute, with untamed, wiry hair in all colours. They all wore thick glasses. Their movements were exaggerated, almost to the point that made Nicole cringe thinking it must hurt them to move like that. Their heads were far too small for their bodies, making their shoulders seem large and bulky. Nicole pulled her hoodie up over her head, adjusted the glasses that Nava had given her to protect her from the toxic air and also the added bonus, as Nicole had found out, from their blinding clothes.

Nicole kept her head down, focused on the sticky surface of the ground, and tried hard to breathe through her mouth. Her Crystal was warm to touch. With great effort and going against everything she wanted to do, she walked, the Tracer pulling her. The orange dullness continued to be the only light source. The buildings had no windows, and each had only one door. Nicole had no idea why, but they still were unconcerned about her. She turned into one of the doors, which opened automatically, and she allowed herself to be pulled forward. It seemed the Tracers were on a quest to shorten the distance between them.

'Can I help you?' asked a high-pitched voice.

Nicole went numb but tried to clear her throat without noise.

She turned and faced the Rustic who had spoken to her. She had pink hair sprouting everywhere. Her nose was flat against her cheeks, and she had spooky, red-pinky eyes with no whites and no eyebrows above them. Her hands were large with four long fingers, each loaded with rings. She stood up, displaying a lovely peach dress gathered prettily in bunches that looked like expensive satin, along with her gold-framed glasses that were tied around her head with a chain. Nicole wondered how they got their clothes. Did they make their own? And how did food get down here? So far, she saw nothing growing out of the ground.

Nicole saw a sign and was surprised it was written in English. It read: 'Osiris Developments – Taking Rustic Technology into the Future'. She realised she had seen the name Osiris everywhere on buildings. Was Osiris the real name of this realm?

'Um, hello,' Nicole managed.

'You Ida?'

The voice was funny, like when she had played with

helium balloons and her voice came out high-pitched. It was like how a mouse would talk, if it could. The words blended into each other in a baby-like babble. When Nicole did not respond, she continued, 'Take a seat. Volox won't be long.' Nicole worked out a couple of the words to get by.

She sat on a metal bench and glanced around cautiously. The room was also cartoon-like, with bright walls. Surrounding the desk were fake flowers. She felt sweat dripping down her back. Nava had warned her that the temperature would not be what she was used to, and it was likely to fluctuate from hot to cold. Was she hot or just plain terrified?

She was dismayed when she saw the girl come from behind her desk wearing high heels. Her hips jerked back and forth, her legs unbending in the way she had seen the people outside move. But this one was coming over to her. She would now have to deal with this. Getting the Tracer meant having to communicate and deal with strangers. Besides any help she was getting from her Crystal and Rolte, who were screening her constant movements, she felt terrified. Time seemed to slow down at this moment. Nicole tried to avoid eye contact with the girl.

'I am Mim, Volex's assistant.'

Mim placed a small cup and a slice of cake that didn't look bad down next to Nicole. She'd been warned not to consume anything, no matter how hungry she was. Right now, she was starving. She hoped Mim wouldn't talk again. She didn't know why, but she felt like she could laugh but at the same time be scared witless.

The place was musty with thick, grainy air that got caught in her throat. Her eyes hurt, despite the thick lenses Nava had given her to protect them. The glasses felt awkward.

Mim had only just left when a male arrived at her side.

Nicole had been too distracted watching the girl leave to notice him creep up on her. He raised an arm towards her, startling her. She noticed his hair was standing on end and looked so ridiculous that she felt like she was in the middle of a comedy show. A nervous giggle bubbled, and she curbed it.

He stood there watching. She felt alarmed at this scrutiny. 'Ida, come through,' he said, as he guided her hand. She resisted the urge to pull away. His fingers were puffy and the rings on his fingers looked tight. She followed him into a dingy office. *No wonder they all need glasses, you can't see clearly anywhere.*

The room had a large desk, fake plants, and fruit in bowls. One side had an array of photos of Volox with other Rustic, all taken in the Frail Realm. Nicole considered that their distortion went the other way. On the surface of the Frail Realm, the Rustics looked almost human, but down here their appearance was straight out of a comic book, with colourful characters and buildings that didn't look real.

Nicole focused on this new Rustic called Volox. He was the same height as her, she noticed as he sat down. Brown eyes glared at her. His skin was smooth, and he had a nice mouth. He was dressed smartly in an apple-green suit. To Nicole, he looked pleased with himself as he juggled a device in his palm. It was a pyramid shape with symbols she had seen outside.

'It is the latest model. This phone can range for meters, so now I can call my neighbours without having to walk there.'

They have some technology, she thought, *but this brand new phone looks like it has the range of a kid's walkie-talkie.*

'We are excited to be chosen by your company to distribute this ground-breaking technology. Just think of Rustic being able to go to the Frail Realm without the current restrictions, of how long we can stay and realm-shifting pain. My next trip will be fantastic. No more breath that tears my throat. Not to mention the pain associated with the increased gravity. The freedom is going to change the lives of all of us down here.' He poked a small fob in her direction. He signalled for her to pick it up. With a shaking hand, she did so, and she was sure he had seen her tremble.

The Tracer moved in her pocket. She looked around and spotted a jacket draped over a chair. He had just taken it off. It looked nothing like the top worn by the Rustic she followed into this place. She looked at one of the photos on his desk. For a second, she couldn't swallow. It was him! In her world, lying on a beach, dressed in the same shabby clothes that he'd been wearing when she followed him in here. The Tracers had found each other, being a pair again, their forces together as they should be.

'Everything alright, my dear? You look unwell.' Volox asked, sitting back comfortably in his swish chair.

Nicole couldn't answer; she was filled with dread. *What does he see when he looks at me? I must have some cover, or I would look Frail to them.* She trembled and finally swallowed the hard lump in her throat that had been there since she arrived.

'We want to sign the contract as fast as possible,' he said as he picked up a thick file on his desk and pushed it towards her. 'Oh, are you cold? Let me just go and adjust the temperature.' Nicole kept still and clenched her teeth as he touched her hand. She did her best not to pull away.

Unbelievably, he got up and shuffled awkwardly out of the room. They thought she was someone else! She wasn't cold but burning hot. She had to act and *now*.

She tried the pocket of the jacket; her hands were shaking so badly she could hardly control them. In the next pocket, she felt the smooth Tracer. It was warm on her skin. The Tracers were now together in her pocket and the relief was consuming. As she made her way back to sit down, she spotted her reflection in the mirror, just for a couple of seconds, before she tripped over a table, sending the contents crashing to the ground. She saw an overlay of a Rustic and her blurry self underneath. Nicole thought it must be like another form of gravity that caused them to wedge and distort. Here, visitors took on a Rustic exterior. That was such good news.

For a moment she was dazed at what had happened. 'What an idiot,' she said to herself. This she did not need. She got up and started to fix the mess when she heard voices behind the door. Nicole bit the inside of her lip and waited.

39

Volox and Mim stood in the doorway.

'I'm so sorry.' Nicole scrambled to get up onto her feet. But the two Rustics surprised her and waddled to her aid then stopped. Long fingers pointed to her hand. Nicole felt the rest of her skin go clammy with fear. She looked down at her hand where the thick metal of the tray had cut her skin. It had the colour of golden maroon, the Frail red and the Dellamana gold mixed together to make Sape blood. Nicole realised that she had never accidentally scraped her knee or anything before now. She saw spots appear in front of her eyes and she hoped she wouldn't faint.

After seeing how slowly they moved, Nicole knew she had to get out of this place, and fast. 'I must go. I'm sorry for the mess.' She moved past the dazed Rustic. They turned their heads as she went out the door, their open mouths matching their wide eyes.

If Volox remembered that she had his fob, he was not concerned about it now. Nicole raced through the foyer and out the door. Rustic were all around her, but she wasn't too worried because of her Rustic façade. She looked behind her to make sure they hadn't come after her. She looked at her hand and saw the wound had healed.

Nicole closed her eyes for a moment as nausea ran from her stomach and into her throat, and to her horror, she vomited. A couple standing nearby used angry, slapping hands and hissed the word 'quarantine' at her.

The Tracers were pulling her down blocks of streets, each with a colour theme. Volox and Mim hadn't tried to come after her, which was good and bad. She came into a place filled with blue houses, which snaked as far back as she could see. No gardens or any type of vegetation grew in this smoggy area. She opened her palm to check that the fob was still there.

She looked around frantically. In the middle of the row of identical houses, she found herself at a red door the Tracers had brought her to. She knew that once she had the Tracers back together, they would focus on leading her to the Illuminance.

It was the Tracers' job to identify where the Illuminance was in the Rustic Realm. But once located, it was going to be up to her to retrieve it and get out with it safely. But how was she going to get out? Did she have to go to where she arrived, at the container site? She didn't have a clue how to get back there. She would put her attention on getting the Illuminance first – one problem at a time.

Her legs nearly gave way as the Tracers rang a high-pitched squeal; she was jerked forward so hard she banged fully into the door, which sprang open upon contact. Nicole stood frozen to the spot, trying to contain her terror. Her breath came in sharp, constant gasps. She adjusted her glasses that had fallen sideways and dug into her nose.

She was standing in front of one big room. Florescent light filled the space. She was surprised to see a modern television on the wall, with a decent lounge filled with pillows and a blanket. One whole side of the room was shelves, filling every available spot, making it an organised chaos. In the middle of the room was a black, granite kitchen bench with matching cabinetry – very classy. The bench was crammed with more books and fake flowers. The room had a proper wooden floor. On the other side of the kitchen was a dining area. A table with two chairs was set with unlit candles.

Nicole looked to the left of the eating area and noted two doors. *Maybe a bedroom and bathroom*, she considered. Her breathing was getting under control thanks to her Crystal, which was warm on her neck. She also had faith in the Gloine that was beside her, only visible to her, that Nava and her team were keeping an eye on her, adding medication when needed.

The Tracers were in action mode, chiming and moving in her pocket, working towards finding Raisa's lost Illuminance. Nicole felt she was doing well considering her location. She knew the Tracers were trying to help, but the sensation of being pulled and pushed was difficult. The decision now was not up to her; her body was a puppet with the Tracers in charge.

Nicole was drawn to a carving on the far wall. Wooden animals, elephants, lions, and monkeys, all in 3D, individually designed. The animals seemed to be jumping from the wall. In between two of these, she saw a clear ring box. Her Crystal and the Tracers were telling her that this was the Illuminance. The Tracers were making such a racket that if anyone was home, she would be found. Nicole gulped and was so relieved she nearly collapsed.

'I have been waiting for you,' said a voice behind her, causing Nicole to jump.

40

Nicole turned around slowly and was shaken to see who the voice belonged to; while it was loud it wasn't squeaky, like Mim's and Volox's.

'You have?' Nicole gasped.

He came close. He wore a black tank top that didn't cover his orange-tinged belly. His skin had taken on his environment colour. He wore shorts that fell just above two weird-looking bones for kneecaps. He had dumpy, hairy legs. His black hair travelled well down his back and ended in a knot bigger than her fist; she couldn't imagine how hard it would be to get all the visible lumps out. By the looks of it, it had never seen a brush.

'Oh yes, yes, very much so. You are here for the treasure, am I correct?' He indicated the box. He had an astonished look on his face. 'Well, I haven't seen it glow in a very long time.'

'This Illuminance doesn't belong here and must be returned to the rightful owner,' Nicole said. While her voice sounded level, inside she was trembling.

'Ownership can change.' His breath reached her. Bile rose in Nicole's throat.

'This has no use to you anymore,' she said, trying to

ignore the odour that surrounded him. It was like nothing she had ever encountered, and so horrible it was starting to turn her stomach.

'Oh, you are wrong there.' Smoky colours escaped from the box. Dinkletons had told her it might light up with faded colours after linking with her Crystal and Magic molecules.

'It has recognised me,' Nicole said. A ring of hope ignited within Nicole. She had found the Illuminance through all the odds of coming to this place.

'You mean it recognised your Hallr Crystal. Now, why would you own such a thing?' He narrowed his eyes, but the full force of his question scared her.

'That is none of your business,' Nicole said. But she was feeling out of her depth. Her voice cracked with emotion. Her body felt tired and hollow. *I can't do this*, she thought. *It's too much.*

'Raisa was an arrogant Dellamana who brought an unprotected Crystal into the Frail Realm. Gross stupidity. She deserved what she got.' He wiped his dripping nose with the back of his hand.

'You don't know the full story.' Nicole wrung her hands.

'You don't either.' His mouth twisted.

Nicole had to change tack, suck it up, show no fear. 'I'm not talking about when she first lost it, and you know that it was stolen from a vulnerable Marnie. I'm talking about the second encounter, at my nana's house.'

The Rustic gave her the side-eye. 'Well, I have no idea about that. What were we supposed to do? Gift wrap it and send it back?'

Now she was sure the Rustic knew more than he was telling her. 'That would have landed you in Dellamana good books if you had. Ever consider that?'

The Rustic shrugged.

'Can you tell me what happened when it got here, the first time?'

'All I can tell you is that it arrived via a Rustic from the top. It was a phenomenon.'

'Volox, you mean?' Nicole didn't know for sure, but it was worth a shot.

The Rustic coughed. 'Well, he is very high up in the council here. Often goes to the Frail Realm. He runs most of everything here. Where we live, how we live. He builds houses and organises most of the food. He has an army of Rustic that work for him.'

'Where do you get your food and clothes?'

'They come from pirate Rogue; they sell all sorts of produce. Then there are others who come to build or deliver household items like televisions. They come and go all the time. We don't like them, but we have to outsource everything we need to be able live here. We even get ice cream delivered.'

'So, if Volox is high up, why do you have the Illuminance?'

'I work for him. I do what he says otherwise I don't eat.'

'Volox was there. He caused all of this.'

'Well, good for you. I don't think Raisa should get away scot-free either.' The Rustic smiled but it didn't reach his gloomy eyes. 'There is more to you besides having a Crystal. This is getting interesting. How would you have seen such an event? You need to be honest now, if you want the treasure.'

The Tracers, now that she needed them to guide her, were silent. She considered grabbing the box and taking off as fast as she could.

'I don't waste my time worrying about Raisa. I'm angry with her.'

'Why?' Nicole frowned.

'Because of her, I am stuck in this house all day,

minding a useless piece of junk. Well, it was useless until you showed up.'

'I'll take it off your hands and you'll be free to do what you want.'

'Humph. I will never be free. I am a servant here. Who are you? You are not from Orra, or the fumes would have got you. You have adopted the Rustic edge from the realm shift, but everyone gets that. I can see you're Frail underneath.'

Nicole looked around for a mirror so that she could see her situation. *The edge must be wearing off, just like wedge distortions do.*

'You will find no mirrors here if that is what you are searching for. You look like a dim, smudgy Frail.'

Nicole felt adrenaline race through her. Things were getting out of hand. She was losing her cover.

'Who are you?' he asked as he burped.

'That does not matter,' she said as she put her hand over her nose.

'You want the container, so it does,' he shouted.

Nicole covered her ears from his loud scratchy voice.

'If I don't shout, you would not hear me. I cannot whisper. Better than sounding like squeaky birds.'

Nicole ground her teeth, feeling irritable at this stupid excuse for yelling. 'Okay, I need to get the Illuminance back to remove a Toxic fungi called a Tangle that has infected me; the Prefects know I am here.' She hoped that would scare him.

'I am not scared of those pretentious idiots,' he said with a sneer. 'They have the cushiest job known to Magic. And it might surprise you that we get Helix messages from time to time. So even low-level Magic count, for what it's worth, which is zilch.'

This surprised Nicole. 'So you know about them and Orra?'

'Every Rogue knows them, you ignoramus. All Magic know about all Magic. Just like all you humans know about humans.'

Nicole noted he did not refer to humans as Frail as the Dellamana did.

'Humans are held in very tight care of the Dellamana, as you must be now learning.'

Nicole's senses were heightened to hearing other sounds, maybe of someone hearing his shouting and coming to see what was going on.

'We might be low Rogue, but we aren't stupid,' he went on. 'Prefects can't intervene here in the Toxic Realm, and to me, that is unforgivable. If they could, life would be better here. Everything the Illuminance offers the Magics would be doubled here. Imagine that. How great would that be? It would not hurt them to gift us some power. Having even one Dellamana Illuminance gave us huge progress in many areas. We used to walk with pain, we had no taste buds, and no idea on fashion to make us happy. But Rustic grew greedy and didn't ration it well and it soon was all used up. Now I can't taste my tin creamed corn.'

'You should have considered giving the Illuminance back then. Maybe they could have helped you.'

The Rustic glared at her. Nicole realised arguing with him was not getting her out of here.

He saw her eyeing the Illuminance. 'Beware. A million units of Kyacin cover the area. Even a Frail would not be safe going near it.'

Nicole shuffled her feet. She had been daydreaming at the Illuminance, feeling her body shudder and breathing to a near panic attack at the enormity of what she had to do. *What if the toxin harmed her?*

'There is one option I have been working towards,' he said, as he fiddled with his hands, the fingertips gnarled, as if they hadn't grown fully.

Nicole balled her fists. 'Why was it your job to mind the Illuminance?'

He shrugged again.

'Sounds like you have been used. Once Rustic knows the Illuminance was activated again by me being here, you won't stand a chance. You will be pushed aside.'

'You are catching up with me,' he said, tapping his head. 'That is why you will take me with you.'

Her face strained. 'What?'

'The three of us – you, me, and the treasure – go together!' he exclaimed.

Nicole looked around. 'Can you please not yell?'

'That is the deal. Take it or leave it.'

'Take you where? Frail Realm?'

'Now, why would I want to go there?' He wrinkled his nose at her suggestion.

'I thought all Rustic go there.'

'As you can see, I am a deformed Rustic, not a whole one. A Halfrus they call me.'

Nicole thought this made sense. He looked different to the others. Volox and Mim were educated; this Halfrus didn't come across the same and his looks were unfortunate.

Intrigued, she asked, 'How did you become like this?'

'During the incubation, but who cares? Let's get back to our trip!' he bellowed.

Nicole covered her ears, her head bursting with the noise the Rustic was making. A headache pounded at the back of her neck. 'What is this incubation?'

'Rustic don't grow in mothers' wombs like Frail.' His face scrunched as if he'd inhaled a bad smell. 'We are developed in pods. It's the only growth that exists here. Developing inside hundreds of oily cocoons allows us to grow into adults. Once we are formed, we are expelled from the pod. Some die in the process of being expelled.

Then there is me: a deformed Rustic who was claimed and used for the sole purpose of slavery. Not an experience I would recommend.'

'You're grown?' Her skin crawled as she realised the purpose of the containers she'd seen upon arrival in this land.

'Yes, from seeds. Some take, others don't. You could call me a weed.'

'It sounds awful.' Her voice wobbled and she took a step back.

'It's better than being harvested from inside a belly. That is so repulsive.' Halfrus screwed his face up.

Nicole deepened her tone and bared her teeth. 'Your way has no mother or father, and no love that goes with that.'

'Rustic or Halfrus do not know the meaning of the emotion. It does not exist here.'

Nicole considered this other awful situation the Halfrus lived with. She couldn't imagine it.

'Let's get back to what's important here. I don't have any desire to go to the Frail Realm. I grew to hate the "normal" Rustics' trips and their stories about the top. How much better they felt when they returned and the food they ate. Something I would never experience. So, it is better to hate than to crave, in my humble mind.'

'I have to go to the Frail Realm first. That is where my friends are waiting for me.'

'I can't go there; the sun would burn me to a crisp.' His voice was devoid of emotion.

'I don't understand where you want me to take you.'

'Orra, stupid.'

Nicole gaped at him. 'How do you think you are going to get in there?'

'You're a little slow, aren't ya?'

'Look, I had trouble getting here on my own. Even

with the Illuminance, I'm not sure your trip would be any easier.'

'I will take my chances.'

Nicole saw by the set of his mouth that he was serious. 'Why would you want to go to Orra?' Even if she could take him there, the Prefects would not be happy. He was poisonous. Besides, she wasn't sure she could physically take an extra creature, anyway. She'd been told that if she got the Illuminance, she would be able to wedge and not have to travel back in a realm shift and she knew there was a big difference between the two. She never wanted to experience a realm shift ever again.

'You see this place?' Halfrus asked, waving his arm around. 'A dreary existence I have never fit into. I am miserable. I want to be transformed into the creature I was supposed to be.'

'I can see how you would hate being here. Must be lonely. But what does being transformed have to do with any of this?' Nicole asked, interested in his answer.

'I am not of any species,' he said. 'I want them to remove this deformity. All I have ever wanted was to be my true self. There are no other Halfrus like me. I know the Prefects are the only ones in the Magic groups who can do this. When I was charged with looking after the treasure, I thought, you never know. It gave me hope. I have been waiting forever.'

This struck a chord with her. He said he wanted to be his true self, and that was exactly her dream. The years of waiting for the Thisbe to come back had left her feeling at odds with the world.

'How do you know anything about this process?'

'I'm a Halfrus, not a halfwit,' he spat.

Nicole thought about what he said. She didn't come in on a wedge; it was a realm shift. So she could now wedge back. Bringing him back would be the last choice, but if it meant securing the Illuminance, was it worth a shot?

'You know, Volox checks in with me every day,' Halfrus yelled, tapping his foot. 'You don't want to end up in our quarantine. I would not be able to help you.'

If he had wanted to scare her to death, he'd succeeded. She remembered the Rustic in the street when she was sick mentioning quarantine like it was prison. Nicole thought that there might not be a Kyacin sheet covering Raisa's Illuminance. It could be just a ploy.

She reached for the Illuminance.

'That's a big mistake, you silly girl.' She heard him run off and return with a bucket just in time for her to be sick.

As she blacked out, she saw him up close as he caught her. His hair smelled sweet but unpleasantly so, and the feel of his orange skin felt cold on her arms. His body was solid, like Volox's hand had been, hard as a brick. His small, brown eyes had no lashes or brows. His nose was flat and his nostrils flared, but it was his breath that swept over her senses making her feel rigid, and she thought she could feel every hair on her arm. As she lost consciousness, she thought that now she was in the hands of this Halfrus, anything could happen.

41

Nicole became aware of silence as she came to and blinked a few times before her eyes focused. She found herself on a couch, covered with a blanket, but she was freezing.

'Well, there you are.' Halfrus was sitting next to her. How did she get there? He didn't look strong enough to lift her. 'Do you feel better? I thought I'd lost you and that would have been bothersome. You're my only way out of here.'

'I do feel better.' She sat up.

The Halfrus sat with one leg folded over another. He leaned forward and pointed to her hand. 'The main cure was that strange stone.'

Nicole opened her hand expecting to find one or both Tracers, but instead it was Dex's yellow stone. The stone had made an impression where she had been holding on to it. Nicole rubbed her sore eyes. 'But how did it do it?'

'When you blacked out, I put you over here.' He pointed to the couch. 'I watched over you for hours; you were deep in your unconscious state. That is what the Kyacin does: plunges you down to almost death. You hovered there for a long time. I wasn't sure if you would ever wake. Then I heard a sound from your pocket. I found the yellow stone, which sounded like a drum. It healed you.'

Nicole kept looking at the stone, blinking slowly, realising the enormity of what had just occurred. Dex's stone, made in the Frail Realm with the supplies from Orra and his own Magic, could heal the Kyacin on someone that was infected.

'It is important you go now. And that means me as well!' Halfrus cried.

Shivering, Nicole pulled herself up to stand, still with the blanket over her.

'Why can't you realm shift? Other Rustic can.' Even that could help her – if he could just accomplish a small shift, it would help with the wedge.

'I told you, I am Halfrus. Zilch. Zero skills. What you see is what you get. *Comprendo?*'

'How do you expect me to take you back?'

'Same way you were going to get back. Just this time, you have more luggage.'

'I can't guarantee your safety.'

Halfrus made a show of rolling his eyes.

Nicole threw her arms in the air. She had no choice but to take him. Otherwise, she couldn't see a way of procuring the Illuminance without him. Nicole put her hand out to let him know he had won that argument. She watched him click both thumbs. The Kyacin sheet slid sideways, just like opening a window. It went from a thin clear glass look to a thick cloudy cover the size of a small coffee table, which rolled neatly to the side. 'Go ahead.'

She didn't wait; she reached in careful to not touch the Kyacin. She felt herself unbalanced on her feet and rocked backwards. A wave of light-headedness hit her when she put her hand around Raisa's precious Illuminance.

Nicole held Raisa's Illuminance in the small box in her hand. The colours evaporated. The box dissolved away and all that was left was an orb of blurry colours. She took a smooth piece of cloth, that Nava had given her, from her pocket, wrapped it carefully around the Illuminance and secured it in her deepest pocket, zipping it up for good measure.

For the first time since she had been in the Rustic Realm, Nicole smiled. Everyone in Orra would be proud. She would make her family and herself safe by removing the Tangle. Raisa would have the heart of her Illuminance back in her Crystal where it belonged. That was if she could get out of here without this annoying Halfrus.

A thought hit her. Maybe she could ditch him now that she had what she came for? But before she could think it through clearly, she turned around to look at him.

He was shaking his head, slowly, with his jaw closed tight. In his open hand were both of her Tracers, her only guidance home.

'Insurance,' he said.

42

Nicole ran through the wedging instructions in her head. She had no trouble recalling the steps that had been relayed to her. It was all very well in theory, but now she had to do it for real. The Tracer had got her here. How was she to return without that extra pull?

The Halfrus was staring at her with his hands on his hips. 'Come on, why don't you?'

'I need the Tracers.'

'I will keep one and you can have this one.' He handed her the black, shiny rock, which she stored in her pocket with Dex's stone.

The Tracers rumbled, now separated. Dex's beat like a drum. It was the first time she had heard it. And it made her gasp. Her hands shook, nearly uncontrollably. It sounded menacing.

'Do you know that your cover is now faded? I can see what you look like.'

The time was up: she needed to work out how to leave. She decided to try incorporating this wedge with a jump. She had her three Tracers, Crystal and her Magic. Not to forget, Raisa's dusty three colours added to her Illuminance to give her that extra oomph. She had to somehow harness all of this together to wedge up and out of this place.

Her Crystal vibrated. Nicole held her hand out to the Rustic crooked one. It felt like a block of ice. Then she held his other hand, so they were both linked. She closed her eyes; he closed his eyes also. She could hear the Tracer in the Halfrus' pocket shriek. All three stones were loud now; they were not in tune, just three separate noises.

'Keep your eyes closed,' Nicole said as they glided slowly out the open door. She had to get out of here now. Instead of going straight up, they went in a slow, sideways, and upward motion. Halfrus had his eyes tightly shut, his mouth contorted in panic. They moved through the orange mist. As they went higher, the fog thickened, but they were still not very high off the ground.

Nicole was not scared of being seen but rather how slowly it was all happening. Normally wedges shot you fast. Not this time. It was like they had all the time in the world for gliding and sightseeing. Nicole noted her surroundings. At least they were away from the ground. The tension holding Nicole's body taut dissipated.

She was still holding onto the Halfrus' hand, and she could see snow forming around them. An orange vapour swirled and attached itself to them, leaving a black, lacework pattern thick all over their bodies. They were not too far away from the ground, about six feet.

Suddenly the Halfrus let go of her hand. It took a moment for Nicole to realise that he was dropping towards the ground. Her Tracer and its mate howled.

She watched him wave his limbs around, his legs wide apart. He dropped like a stone.

His screaming was unbelievable. For someone who wanted out of this world, he really was drawing attention to himself. Nicole then realised the Tracer the Halfrus had was not helping him. It should have started dragging him back towards the Tracer Nicole had in her pocket.

She could ditch the Halfrus, but something held her back.

Now there were dozens of Rustic making their way towards the screaming Halfrus. He had no chance. Something within her screamed at her to go as she took in the commotion. They were dragging him to his feet, his arms pinned behind him as one Rustic punched Halfrus in the stomach.

43

Nicole made a decision. She had to save the Halfrus. He had saved her, technically. Plus, he had one of the Tracers. Nicole turned her wedge back to the toxic ground, focusing her thoughts to keep the fear from taking over. It was the very last thing she wanted to do. She baulked as she glided back to where Volox stood. He wore a bright pink suit and red tie. *Who said pink and red didn't go*, she thought as her skin tingled with sweat. She landed without any problem just a few feet away from Volox. Behind him were about fifty Rustics standing in perfect line formation with determined and solemn looks on their faces. Nicole thought they were far from being threatening, with their yellow dungarees, blue beanies and identical brown thick glasses.

'Well now, what have we got here? You are not very good at acting,' Volox said as he approached.

Nicole had difficulty in responding.

'You are a Frail,' Volox accused, but she saw his body tense.

Nicole steadied herself.

'But you do not bleed red,' Volox added.

'I have Dellamana blood.' Nicole saw them all retreat a couple of steps.

'Well, come straight to the point, why don't you?' Volox stepped closer, leering at her.

'Let the Halfrus come with me,' Nicole said. 'Nothing good will come of this if you don't allow us to leave. Besides, he is of no use to you now.'

'Halfrus is rubbish; it is not what I care about,' Volox said. 'Kick him.'

The captors kicked Halfrus, and he let out a yelp.

'I will not give you back the Illuminance.'

'That is no use to me either. Not now, in any case.'

Nicole rolled her lips together; they were hard and dry. She knew he was lying because the Illuminance still held value with its three murky colours.

'The colours are only there because you ignited them.'

That made sense as to why he was letting her take it.

'You take your friend here.' Volox held onto the Tracer that had been in Halfrus' pocket.

Nicole twisted her hands together. 'That it?'

'No, that's not it! Are you crazy? I want your word you will gift us Voltz, just enough so we can go to the surface without pain. Enjoy food and walk without any pain.'

'You and I both know who owns that Tracer stone.'

Volox threw his harms up in the air. 'I. Don't. Give. A. Rats.'

'I can talk to the Prefects when I return to see if something can be done to help you with your issues. It must be horrible for you.' Nicole thought showing some awareness would be a better way to avoid a stalemate.

'Aw, I think I have a tear. Do you think I am stupid? Look, whatever, non-human girl. I am keeping this Tracer.' He held his arm out towards Nicole with his fist tightly closed. The other Tracer in Nicole's pocket rang a continuous hum.

'You do realise that it is not worth anything without its other Tracer?'

'Exactly. The Dellamana will want it back for that exact purpose.'

Nicole Looked at the Halfrus, who was still being held tightly by two yellow dungaree Rustics.

'And knowing the Prefects, they will surely want it back.' Volox sniggered in his high-pitched voice. Nicole found it hard to take any of this seriously. The whole lot of them were more like toys that children would play with rather than a race that lived way underground.

Adrenaline swept through her, the sudden shot of electric energy gave her what she needed in the moment. Nicole stood solidly and confidently moved closer to Volox.

'You give me Halfrus, and I will check with the Prefects if you can keep the Tracer for a temporary time. Once I am back in Orra, I can discuss your plight with them.'

Volox had a look of longing so intense, Nicole could almost feel his desperation. She knew then they would be able to come to a truce. She did not have to get an answer. She sent a Rebo to Rook.

While they waited, Nicole asked Volox, 'Do you ever eat food that is not in cans?'

'Oh yes, the pirates bring loads of vegetables and fruit. But they are always mouldy. Luckily, we cannot taste rotten food.'

Nicole gaped. 'Yuck. So, you have never enjoyed eating?'

'Before the Illuminance came here, we did not know what we were missing. When it was at its best, the Illuminance helped prevent our food spoiling, our back pain improved, and our eyes stopped stinging. But having had that time where our taste buds worked, even with the crappy tin food, it was bliss for us. It has made us miserable ever since that wore off and we were plunged back to where we started.'

'Come on, let Halfrus go,' Nicole said as she watched

the Rustics still kick and slap the poor guy. The Halfrus screamed continually, which was not surprising since that was all he did. But Nicole felt sorry for him even though she was angry that she had been tricked into bringing him. By now she should be back giving Raisa her Illuminance, which she was so looking forward to doing, Her body was tense as she saw how big this beating of the Halfrus was. He had whitish green stuff coming out of his eyes and ears.

The Rustics were mean to their underdogs, for sure, which did not make them a nice group. Nicole was now regretting feeling any empathy for them at all. They were just a greedy, brainless race, especially since they wanted something from the Dellamana. Nicole thought that they would have been on their best behaviour. Why would Rolte okay Voltz power to these idiots? Nicole knew for sure she would be careful with how they would use them.

Nicole's palm lit up with Rooks response.

```
Let them keep the Tracer for now. Get out of
there.
```

Nicole lifted her palm and showed Volox. She pointed a finger at Volox and, before he could say anything, Nicole said, with flattened lips and a deep voice, 'If one of you so much as touch Halfrus again, the deal will be off. We have other options.'

Halfrus was immediately released, but he crawled and groaned in pain, making sure everyone knew he was suffering. Nicole could see the skin of his legs had been beaten off. His face was not much better, swollen and covered with the gross shiny greenish substance that Nicole guessed was their blood. Nicole ran to help him, pointed at a couple of the Rustics to assist. Their hesitant steps and muttering between themselves showed their lack of desire to help.

'It's okay, we are going now,' Nicole said to the bawling Halfrus. 'Get yourself together, we have to get out of here.'

Within a second, they were flying high, through the atmosphere of the Toxic Realm. Halfrus was sobbing as she held his cold hands.

44

Raisa noticed that Dinkletons was lying on his back, his front and back paws splayed. It was getting dark now, and she heard something out back. Raisa had showered and changed into a sun dress that let her wings out. Dex was lying on the couch with his eyes closed; Raisa knew he wasn't sleeping. On the table nearby sat an uneaten plate of sandwiches that were curling at the edges and a glass of juice that had a layer of skin forming over it from melted ice.

'What was that?'

Dinkletons jumped onto his feet. His ears flopped listlessly, still in distortion mode.

Nicole stood at the bottom of the garden. Raisa could just make out that she had someone with her. They all rushed outside to meet her.

'Hello,' Halfrus said.

Raisa looked at what she thought must be a Rustic, but he was obviously not. She had never seen anything like him before. He was misshapen, hair a black mess, flaring nostrils, mouth full of rusty teeth hanging wide open.

'I had to bring this Halfrus,' Nicole said as she looked at Dinkletons.

'It's okay. I'm just happy you are here.' Dinkletons voice was calm as he studied the extra guest. 'What is your story?' he asked Halfrus.

'I let her have the Illuminance,' Halfrus said. 'You have me to thank.'

'You have my Illuminance?' Raisa bit her lip.

'Ahh, the famous Raisa,' Halfrus said. 'And her brother, the martyr, who gave up Orra to take care of his sister. A touching story.'

'What are you?' Raisa couldn't help herself.

'I am Halfrus, not Rustic, but I live in that world.'

'Your Illuminance was locked in a carving with Kyacin sheeting,' Nicole said.

Raisa touched her shoulder. 'Tell us you didn't touch it?'

'Of course she did,' Halfrus said. 'Otherwise, we would have been here hours ago, but I am glad now as it's dark, and I won't get burnt by the sun.'

'I did get sick for a while.' She looked at Dex. 'Your Tracer healed me.'

'It sure did. I thought she was a goner,' Halfrus said.

Raisa noticed Dex had gone pale. 'It has healing properties?' he stammered.

'This is wonderful,' Raisa said and hugged her brother.

'I believe it was the Mikkel that combined with the garnet that did the job, but it is your success, Dex, one that will be a great tool in the future,' Dinkletons said.

'Since I developed it here in the Frail Realm, it must have taken on some of the resistance to the toxins.' Dex beamed. 'I never dreamed it could have this potential.'

'I am so grateful for it. Our Tracers couldn't help me when I was under the Kyacin.'

'Which means that she was bordering on death. She nearly went into the big leap,' Halfrus said.

'You have toxins. And look at that sticky stuff all over

you. We must go now,' Dinkletons said. 'We can discuss this later.'

Nicole noticed her Gloine bubble was visible now. 'Nava will be giving me some medicine via the Gloine. Wait, just a moment. I want to give Raisa her Illuminance.'

'Nicole, you were away for far too long. You are not well,' Dinkletons said, shaking his head.

'Please, stop.' Nicole raised her voice.

Dinkletons, Raisa, Dex, and the Halfrus all became quiet.

Nicole nodded. She looked at Raisa. 'I want to give you this.' Nicole took the package, unwrapped the silk cloth and handed her the small, coloured orb. It was the size of a marble and the Marnie first colours were swirling in the formation that it was supposed to.

Wide-eyed, with tears, Raisa took it gently back into her care. Once the Illuminance made contact with her Crystal, it seemed to get sucked in. Her ring that was white stone before now had a colour swirling around trying to settle back in.

Raisa threw her arms around Nicole. 'I will never be able to thank you.'

'Just take away this Tangle.'

Dex also joined the group hug.

'How touching. Now, get onto me. I am in a hurry,' Halfrus said.

'Halfrus believes that he is not in the right form and wants the Prefects to transform him into what he is supposed to look like. He wants them to get rid of the deformity.'

'Nicole, just so you know, I am a girl,' Halfrus interrupted. 'But not such a pretty one, right?'

Nicole looked at her and laughed. 'Okay, Miss Halfrus.'

'What makes you so sure the Prefects can transform you?' Dex quizzed.

'I am not so sure – I just have a feeling. I'm prepared to give it a go. Besides I was the only living weed in Osiris – all they others die at birth. I always wondered why I was so lucky to have lived,' Halfrus said, nursing the obvious grudge of her pathetic life.

'You're mad to think that Prefects would let you in just like that,' Raisa said, thinking the whole thing was preposterous.

'Ah, I anticipated a sorry state of affairs.' She shook her head and opened her buttoned pocket to reveal a sick Thisbe tied to her pocket with tiny chains inside a plastic cylinder. 'Double insurance.'

45

Nicole felt the air drain away from the group. Everyone froze. How had the Thisbe withstood the beating that the Halfrus had? The Thisbe had his hands tied in front of his body. Dinkletons moved closer to the Thisbe, sniffing. Raisa cried at the sight. Dex's face contorted in fury. 'How dare you chain him like that! Get him out of that bottle.'

'Err, get your facts right. I didn't put him in this situation,' Halfrus said. 'Nicole, didn't you notice I was face down when the Rustic yellow pants were giving me a hiding?'

That was it – Nicole's body was ready to spring onto the Halfrus when Dex held her back.

The Thisbe whimpered and squinted his dull eyes. Nicole noted it was like a cloud covering his face, which was tinged with orange and contorted in pain. He was almost naked, wearing only undershorts. His straw hair was in knotted tufts.

The Thisbe squinted at Nicole. 'I was ambushed when I came out of your house, Nicole, when you were a baby,' he stuttered. 'That time I met you.'

'You're Hamish?'

'And you are the lost Sape. I knew your powers were strong when I met you.' Hamish managed a small smile.

Raisa was still crying at the sight of this magnificent Magic in such a terrible state.

'Volox has been involved all along,' Nicole said.

Hamish whimpered and managed a nod. 'It was him. He took me to make sure Prefects didn't know about you.'

'Nicole stayed hidden. That meant his Tangle could grow and take control over her Magic,' Dinkletons said.

They all huddled around Hamish. 'Don't touch me! These chains are Kyacin poison.'

'He was in a container out the back of my house. It held him captive by Toxic fumes; he wasn't able to move a muscle. We became friends,' Halfrus said.

Raisa narrowed her eyes. 'It would have taken a huge amount to catch a Thisbe, and they are extremely resistant to all ammunitions in most worlds.'

'Most is the operative word, Miss Famous-for-losing-her-Illuminance,' Halfrus said.

'What is it the Rustic want?' Dex asked.

'They want Voltz for their realm to help with their day-to-day living. They still have the other Tracer.'

'More like survival,' Halfrus sneered. 'Even though I am not one of them, I do feel that their situation could be greatly improved. I saw myself how the Illuminance assisted them and that is why they want more of that kind of Magic.'

'Can you please give him to me? Please, Halfrus, he is very sick.' Nicole could hardly look at the poor Thisbe.

'Ah ah ah. Not 'til we get to Orra.'

'How dare you! Prefects will never give you Voltz,' Dex said.

Halfrus rocked back and forth. 'I'm doing you a favour by bringing him back. Besides Rustic has the Tracer.'

'That is not the way you do business with Rolte,' Raisa said, her voice shaking.

Dinkletons motioned Nicole to move away for a private conversation. 'It's a miracle the Halfrus has brought Hamish back to us,' Nicole said once they were away from the group, out of earshot. 'I've let Rook know about the Thisbe.'

'Do they know that there is a Tracer left in the Toxic Realm?'

Nicole nodded, her face and neck red. She looked at her palm. 'I have word from Rook that the Halfrus is deformed by toxins. She is not contagious, and the damage is internal. He says not to worry about the Tracer.'

Nicole pulled out the black Tracer and placed it on the flat ground. Without its pair, it was humming and spinning wildly and was almost invisible as it rotated. 'What's wrong with it?'

'It's been infected. It must have been the one that we put into Volox's pocket.'

'Volox didn't have it for very long,' Nicole said.

'A Tracer is not meant to be held by anyone but Dellamana or those with Voltz Magic, like my clan has. It can easily be damaged,' Dinkletons said in a firm voice.

Nicole's mouth fell open. 'It hasn't been infected by the toxic fumes of the Rustic Realm, has it? That will mean the Tracer left behind will get infected as well.' Nicole thought of the fungi that was everywhere in the Rustic Realm. It was on the ground, in the air, and in their funny little bodies. It affected their limbs and eyes and restricted their movements. They couldn't shape-shift anywhere they liked because whatever Magic they had in the first place had been destroyed.

She looked down at the black rock that was rotating so fast she couldn't see its outline. 'It's going berserk.'

'We have no choice but to take it back to Orra,' Dinkletons said, and they joined the others.

Raisa couldn't stop looking at her Crystal. The colours

were warming her hand, giving her energy she knew would help her get rid of her Frail illness. But still, her muscles felt tight at the unknown, until she overheard what Dinkletons said.

'We're all going?' Raisa asked.

'Just like one big happy family,' Halfrus said.

46

Nicole wedged in to Orra with Raisa, Dex, Dinkletons, Halfrus, and Hamish, who whimpered in pain the whole way. Dex's jaw was hard and unflinching the whole journey back.

'That was far better than the first trip,' Halfrus said, frowning when they landed. 'Why couldn't you have done it that way?' He threw a look at Nicole.

'Dinkletons is an expert at wedging.' Nicole couldn't help but smile at the memory of her wedging with Halfrus, who had been terrified.

As they went through the Fire Garden, Nicole asked Dinkletons, 'What now?'

'We are going straight to the Arx to see the Prefects.'

Nicole knew he was serious by the set of his chin. He'd gotten rid of his distortion before the others; his coat glowed and glided with him as he moved. It looked like he had taken a tonic. Since they left the Frail Realm, Raisa had cried happy tears and Dex had a permanent smile on his face. Nicole made eye contact with Dex, and she could see the pride he had in her and his joy at being successful with his Tracer.

Nicole wondered what would happen to them. Raisa

would be punished; she had silked that day at her nana's. Would Thisbe recover his health? And Halfrus – Nicole wondered how things would work out for her.

'You glad to be back?' Nicole asked Raisa, who looked nervous.

'I haven't got time for that – I have work to do,' Raisa said. 'I've started the process to remove the Tangle.'

The wedgers moved from the Fire Garden and into the Foyer. This time, Nicole walked the tunnel of fire without even noticing. She was deep in her own head. She knew this had to be finished before she could go home.

Nicole saw Rook step out of the crowd and approach her with a hug. 'We need to get the majority of the Tangle removed; the process can be continued when you are at home.'

'But how can that happen? Don't Raisa and I need to be together?'

Rook turned to Raisa. 'You went against the rules of Magic, first by taking your Illuminance to the Frail Realm without the protection of cloud-stepping boots. Then you went inside the Hale house and put that family at risk, and then what did you do? You put a silk around it so you could not be found out.'

Raisa went to speak, and Rook held his hand up. Raisa hung her head. Dex closed his eyes and flinched. Nicole felt sorry for them.

'Your Tracer saved Nicole. We want you to start designing them here,' Rook said to Dex.

Rook now focused on Raisa. Nicole was holding her breath.

'You will go back to the life in the Frail Realm,' Rook said.

'Nooo!' Raisa cried. Dex put his arm around her.

Nicole couldn't believe it; she opened her mouth to protest.

Rook shook his head. 'I haven't finished. You will go back for a year, on your own, and continue with your baking business. You can stand on your own two feet. Learn to make good decisions. If you do well, you then will be allowed back into Orra.'

Raisa swayed on her feet, seemingly lightheaded. What did she expect? Nicole wondered. 'Certainly not a hero's welcome.'

'You will have your three colours of your Illuminance, and I will be back soon. I can come and help you,' Nicole said.

Raisa looked at Nicole with a wobbly smile. Relief flooded her face.

'1320 are expecting Hamish. Dex and Raisa come with us,' Rook said.

'No bother, I am here to get him. We can't waste any more time on pleasantries. We must get to work on Hamish's medication prescription.' Nava said, all business. Her white hair was pulled back from her face, her green eyes flaring. 'Hand the Thisbe over.'

Rook whispered to Nicole, 'I have never seen Nava angry. It is not a Dellamana trait.'

Halfrus seemed taken aback by the force of Nava's mood and fumbled with the chains that held Hamish in place. Finally, the chains fell away. Halfrus went to open her mouth, and Nava said, 'Don't you speak.' She took the Thisbe and carefully wrapped him in a silk shawl. There was silence in the foyer as everyone watched them leave.

47

Dinkletons and Rook accompanied Nicole and Halfrus to the Arx where Jivan, Mahala, and a few other Prefects were waiting. Last to enter the room were Dex and Raisa, who looked around the room they hadn't been in for years. They saw many Magical artefacts that had been seized and were in the process of examination prior to being sent to the Vault.

Raisa eyed the shelves; the overflow of relics that had been seized from different Realms by Thisbe. She recognised a death mask; it was made up of many gemstones and was a dangerous item for Rogue who used it for changing their appearance. They used it in deceptive ways to fool and steal Magic. Prefects would have been happy to have that secured here and not out being misused.

Raisa looked to Dex and met his eyes. She could sense he was conflicted about her returning to the Frail Realm. Dex was about to speak when she said, 'Don't you dare worry about me. You have done enough. I am grateful. But from now on, I stand on my own two feet.'

Dex stopped and shook both her hands. She saw he had trouble containing his joy at being back in Orra and seeing the Prefects.

Once everyone was settled on seats scattered around in a circle, Zosmine and Shanazz handed out smoothies to everyone but Halfrus.

Halfrus muttered, 'Great hospitality.'

'We allowed you into Orra because you are not contagious,' Jivan said.

'It didn't have anything to do with a little Thisbe?' Halfrus grinned.

Jivan frowned.

Halfrus looked at Dinkletons, who was staring. 'I am baffling you.'

'I have used my portal eye to look deeply below the surface of your body,' Dinkletons said.

'I suppose that is not a pretty sight.' Halfrus' voice echoed off the walls.

'What is happening with Hamish?' Nicole interrupted, to the annoyance of the Halfrus.

'Who cares? This is about me now!' Halfrus said.

'Hush,' Mahala snapped at Halfrus. 'Nicole, Hamish is in good hands and will receive Magic intervention now. You must go as well. Dinkletons will you take you down to 1320.'

'What about the fob?' Nicole was concerned about why Volox let her leave with it. She fished it out of her pocket.

Jivan stepped forward to look, but he did not dare touch it. 'Well, it won't be up to any good. Let Nava take a look.'

On her way out, Nicole stopped in front of Halfrus. 'I hope you get what you came for. Thank you for bringing Hamish, regardless of the way you did it.'

Halfrus made a face and an unpleasant sound erupted from her throat.

Dinkletons flicked his tail on Nicole's leg and guided her out the door.

48

Raisa couldn't take her eyes off Dinkletons as he left with Nicole. Now his distortions had worn off, she'd forgotten just how hypnotic Stoneycraft were. How truly beautiful the Magic was that beamed from the inside of their bodies to the outside, reaching out and gifting all around them with energy. She had also forgotten the light of Orra and the dazzling auras they all owned. She hoped one day to get some of that back. She noticed Dex was already improving in the colour on his necklace and his purple aura was now visible.

'Dex and Raisa, we welcome you back home, even though for you, Raisa, it's temporary. But a year is not long. You have to be grateful for the Sape and her courage; without that you would still be in the Frail Realm permanently,' Jivan said.

'We are indebted to her, Jivan,' Dex replied, sitting forward in his seat.

'Raisa, we need you to be separated from Nicole. We can't have the prescription mixing up between you while you are here. As your Magic molecules are identical, they can be interchangeable. We don't want her catching the Frail diseases you have. She has never been sick, so we want to keep it that way.'

'I understand.' Raisa, who had been standing while being spoken to, slid back down in her chair. Dex grinned at her, which made her feel instantly better. She returned his smile.

'You can stay for this, Dex, as you understand Rustic better than all of us. We may need you,' Jivan said.

Raisa sat still; they hadn't asked her to leave. She was preparing herself for the likelihood of retuning soon to the house and business they had created. But they wouldn't let her go without her removing most of the Tangle from Nicole, so she had some time. Being back in the Frail Realm without Dex would be hard. But with her healing done and her three colours expanding, she would cope better than she had done the last time.

Mahala swept out of her seat and walked towards the Halfrus. Her white gown floated on the floor. The Hallr Crystal ring dazzled sapphire blue. Her white hair was plaited, interwoven flawlessly with golden threads. As she approached, the Halfrus made a funny squeak and steadied herself. 'We have decided to allow a transformation.'

Halfrus opened her mouth, but before she could speak, Mahala held her hand up. 'We are grateful that you have returned our Thisbe. However, we do not appreciate you bringing any form of Kyacin into our world. You will explain its properties to our lab.'

The Halfrus shook her head. 'I don't have the foggiest clue. Don't ask me.'

'I reckon that would be the truth. She would not have been privy to that information,' Dex added.

'I wasn't able to get the chains off him. Volox always had the key.'

Jivan pursed his lips. 'That may be true. You did have the foresight to bring him back.'

'That is right. I didn't want Hamish to suffer anymore. And when Nicole arrived, I saw our opportunity to get out.'

Mahala pointed at her. 'You might not end up looking as you do, but you may end up as a normal Rustic. You know what that will mean?'

Halfrus shook her head.

'It means that you return to the Rustic Realm,' Mahala said.

'Oh, I hope for a far better outcome than that,' Halfrus screeched.

Raisa noticed everyone in the room looked surprised at the noise.

'During this process, I ask you to talk softly.' Mahala waited for a response.

'Okay,' Halfrus whispered.

'Just find a sound in between,' said Jivan, from the side chair.

Raisa couldn't help but smile.

'And tell me, what result are you hoping for?' Mahala asked, her painted eyebrows shooting up her face.

'Depends what the transformation reveals. Without the deformity, who knows? I might be allowed entry into a variety of worlds.' Halfrus had her voice level now.

Raisa could see Mahala was getting impatient as she walked back to her seat, her heels clicking on the floor.

Jivan waved to five Prefects all in blue robes, all with their computers round their necks and Hallr Crystals as rings. They moved away from the edges of the room and placed a white robe around the Halfrus.

'This will absorb the deformity if there is one,' a Prefect said.

They were a colourful sight as they formed a circle, and in a few seconds, the red and yellow glitter from their coats formed a loop around the Halfrus.

Raisa had never seen a transformation, but she knew all about the theory of it. It was very exciting to witness; it was so dramatic. The Prefects were hardly visible now, lost in the sparkles.

'Bring the sparkle down and move slowly away from the subject, please.' Jivan stood up.

Raisa watched the glitter float back into the Prefects' robes in perfect line formation and moved away from the Halfrus.

'Thank you, Prefects, for your assistance in this. You may return to Rolte.'

Raisa watched the five Prefects bow and leave, but not before they all looked towards her and Dex. Little smiles on their old faces made the solid day more perfect.

Jivan and Mahala walked towards the girl that now stood in front of them. She was neither Halfrus nor Rustic. She lifted her head to show eerie, black eyes.

Halfrus lifted her hands from her robe and looked at her perfect hand, normal without the three fingers and stubby thumb. She ran to the side of the room where there was a floor to ceiling mirror. Raisa watched the girl look at herself in shock. Staring back at her was a dark-headed girl with thick, curly long hair. It dropped over her shoulders like she had just walked out of the hairdresser. She was a pretty thing with lovely features and skin. She started to jump up and down with sheer joy.

'Why, thank you muchly!' Halfrus said. 'I am not a Halfrus. I shall be called J'beal.'

49

Nicole was sitting on a ball seat with her feet up and her arms wrapped around her restless legs. She had been in 1320 for ages now not doing much, but she knew the tests Nava was doing were extensive and would include her entire body.

'Here you go.' Nava released the Gloine that now hovered beside her head. 'This is a complicated prescription. I will visit you in your room from now on. You must stay there until the toxins are fully removed.'

'How will it work?'

'Similar to the first Gloine that had a Magical medicine programmed to work on your tired Magic cells. This time the medicine is more pharmaceutical in nature, like antibiotics to remove toxins.'

'But I'm not taking pills?'

'No need – your Gloine works in conjunction with your aura, and it gives you the doses you require every two hours.'

Nicole understood the reasons, but to be confined to her room when so much was going on was annoying. She wondered what was happening to Hamish.

'Can you tell me how Dex and Raisa are going?' Nicole

jumped from the ball and followed Nava to a glass bench in the middle of the room.

'They are getting their prescriptions. I hear Dex is talking to Rook about his Tracer. It's getting a new name,' Nava said, her fingers flying over the desk panel.

'Well, it's not really a Tracer, is it?'

'Not at all. It can work alone,' Nava said.

'I'm so pleased for him. He gave up a lot for his sister – now it's his turn to shine.'

'He went to the Frail Realm with strong Magic as he had a good dose of saffron, so he is well.'

'You know they had a bakery business that was doing well?' Nicole asked.

'Yes, I heard that, and that Raisa is to go back there. Okay, Nicole, you are all set. You understand what is happening?' Nava asked, sitting down beside her.

'One side of the Gloine has a prescription working on Frail cells still infected by the Tangle,' Nicole said.

'And the other side of the Gloine?'

'Has antibiotics for the Toxic infection to the Magic cells from both the Tangle and Osiris.' *This is so confusing, but I think I'm getting it.*

'You are, indeed. The toxins from Osiris attached themselves only to the Magic cells; your Frail cells were resistant to the poison. For both medicines to work, you must rest. It won't be effective if you're running around Orra with Marnie. The impatience is a Marnie trait. I know it will be very overwhelming for you.' Nava took Nicole's face in her hands and kissed her on both cheeks. 'I am so proud of you.'

Nicole blinked slowly at the affection Nava gave her. 'That means a lot.'

'Of course.' Nava turned swiftly back to her desk. 'Just a few more moments and I can let you go.'

'What happened to Hamish?'

'He is in a state of rest. He is not conscious. It is better to treat him this way for his comfort. But try not to worry: Thisbe are strong little Magic.'

'I can't wait to see him. How did Volox catch him?'

'Volox had enough ammunition to stun him, and Hamish has residues of that in his body, even after all those years. The shots that wounded him were from another world. We have no idea how Volox got hold of them. He lay permanently paralysed the whole time while being in the Rustic Realm due to the toxic fumes.' Nava avoided eye contact.

'Poor little guy.'

'Volox will not get away with this.' Nava was rotating the Rustic fob in her hand, peering into it.

'Volox wants Voltz in return for letting us leave.'

'We would never allow pure Voltz to go to such a realm. They have never been trustworthy on the surface of Frail Realm; they gossip and cause trouble within other Rogue groups.'

'But I told him that we would.' Nicole leaned forward. Somehow, she wanted to help those poor Rustic, not specifically Volox.

'That is why he let you leave with the fob. He was hoping for the best.'

'Do you think there is something inside it?' Nicole pointed to the fob.

'I am working on it. It has a lock mechanism, too advanced for Rustic. I don't believe it was made there. They have acquired it.'

'I was going to ditch it, but I forgot.'

Nava placed the fob under a screen and was studying it.

'Why don't you put it in the Vault and not try to open it?' To Nicole, it looked like a flat guitar pic.

'We have to examine what is inside. I believe it is full of poison.'

It was obvious to Nicole that Nava had finished with her. She quietly left the lab, alone with her updated Gloine.

50

'Hello, Nicole,' Rook said, standing behind her as she came out of 1320.

'I thought I was alone.' Nicole jumped.

'You can't be with all the healing going on. You are lucky you can go to your room and not stay in the Lab hospital,' Rook said.

Dinkletons stood at Rook's side, flicking his tail from side to side like he was agitated. 'Come on, let's get you back.'

The three walked along the wide corridor and boarded a Zizis for a quick trip to the end of another hallway a long way from 1320.

'What was it like?' Rook asked.

'It was horrible from the moment in the shopping centre to arriving back at Raisa's house.'

'Was the realm shift hard?' Dinkletons asked.

'It was icy and pitch black, but the worst of it all was the speed I was travelling at. There were no dips and turns. It was straight down. I will never complain about wedges again,' Nicole said seriously.

'What about when you arrived in that container area?' Dinkletons asked.

'Yup, the place had high walls and in between there were hundreds of these steel containers, very similar to the ones we can get in the Frail Realm.'

'The whole time you were gone, Rolte had never been busier. You should have seen the information pouring in about you and your surroundings,' Rook said.'

'How did that work?'

'We got the information from the Tracers about the surroundings. It sends data to your palm computer, and the technology team was able to download it to Rolte,' Rook said.

'You still had the sticky substance on you when you arrived back. Initial results show that it is important for the Rustic growth outside the containers – they require it to stay alive,' Dinkletons said.

'Is it like food?' Nicole asked.

'No, it is more like air,' Dinkletons said. 'For Frail, it's food, and for you, it is your Magic molecules. We all have something that we need in order to stay alive.'

'So interesting now I am out of there,' Nicole said in a quiet voice.

'You handled yourself way beyond what we thought you would,' Rook said, placing an arm around her shoulders.

Nicole smiled at the praise.

'Your Frail cells prevented any worse harm to you. That and Dex's Tracer,' Rook said.

'Our race is not so weak after all.' Nicole stopped to thrust her chin out to them.

'Frail blood is the key,' Dinkletons said.

'So, being called Frail is a misjudgement, I feel. You know that word means weak?' Nicole took a deep breath.

'Frail are central to the universal puzzle. Their blood cells make them far from weak.'

51

Nicole was chatting to Rook and Dinkletons as they made their way through the hallway, flanked by the same glass doors as 1320. She looked in to see other technicians in white coats, working, sitting on balls, and tapping at computers. Each door was numbered. When they were going past 1401, Nicole saw the Belba, Shanazz, Zosmine, and a girl making their way towards them.

The girl towered over the Belba who were on each side of her. She was covered by a sheet. Her hair was brown and recently brushed. Her face was small with nice features. Nicole noted that she looked nothing like a Dellamana or herself.

The Belba became clumsy, tripping on their feet, and looking around. Nicole had learnt that they were easy to read; when they were curious or worried, they wore their emotions on the outside.

But Nicole felt the sudden tension. 'I haven't seen you around.'

'I have only just got here, and I'm off to get some tests done,' the girl replied.

Nicole's ears pricked and she studied the girl.

'You must go then. You going to 1320?' Rook asked Shanazz.

'Yes, she will be there for a while. She has to stay hospitalised,' Shanazz said as she tried to guide the girl away.

'Wait a minute! Is that you, Halfrus?' Nicole stepped forward to get a good look at her, but the girl in front of her was nothing like the creature she brought back.

'My name is J'beal, and yes, this is the new me. I am not well, they tell me. But I feel better than I have in my whole life. Anything was better than what I had.'

Nicole looked at J'beal. Her eyes were the darkest she had ever seen. Her lips were pink like she had gloss on them.

J'beal laughed at Nicole's surprise.

'Wow, this is epic,' Nicole said.

'Indeed, I am super pleased. By the way, I can see your tonsils.'

Nicole closed her gaping mouth.

'The Prefects don't know exactly where I fit in. But the good news is that I don't have to go back to Osiris. Don't you think I am gorgeous?'

'Dinkletons, what are her options? Is she Frail?'

Dinkletons flicked his tail and the Belba slouched. Nicole noticed again her tense companions. 'I don't get it? What's wrong?'

'I am here now, and I can stay for a little while, not get shoved off like I thought I would. The Jivan chap said I was a glitch in the system, and that toxin build-up is high, which is no surprise to me, considering where I came from. You understand more than anyone here,' J'beal said to Nicole.

'I sure do.' Nicole felt nauseous at the memory of the Rustic Realm.

'It was the pits. I reckon the worst world in all the realms,' J'beal said.

'Come on, we have to get J'beal to the Lab,' Zosmine said in quick breaths.

'Why are you all so nervous?' Even Dinkletons didn't look impressed. He was tapping his paw on the ground.

'We can't have you mixing with J'beal. You have your prescription, and she doesn't,' Rook said, giving Nicole a little push.

'Just wait a moment.' Nicole held her arm out.

'What is a little toxic garbage between friends, right?' J'beal grinned, showing brown teeth.

'So, you will stay in Orra?'

J'beal nodded. 'I'm going to enjoy it while I can. Orra is more beautiful than I could have ever imagined.'

Nicole smiled and tried to reach out, but Zosmine intercepted her hand and gently pushed it back.

'I'm sorry for tricking you all. I'm glad Hamish made it back in one piece.' J'beal gave Zosmine a side-eye. 'I felt sorry for him.'

'You were right to ask to be transformed,' Nicole said.

'Even though I was positive I could be something better, I was still nervous. What if I had been wrong and was supposed to be a Rustic in the first place? Volox would have locked me in quarantine for life. By the way, what's happening with the Tracer?'

'Last I heard is it was deactivated. Then Nava was just going to wedge it back.' Nicole folded her arms. 'I am not sure about what they have decided about helping them.'

Nava came storming around the corner, a furious look on her face. 'What is this holdup?' She grabbed J'beal by her arm and led her away.

52

Nicole was confined to her room to rest, but she had no time to be bored. She had Nava, Marnie, Dinkletons, and other Dellamana visiting her. Nava was there to monitor her progress. She said that the Gloine prescription would encourage Nicole's Frail cells to add more volume to overcome the Kyacin attached to her Magic cells, like glue remover.

'I've been watching the statistics on my palm computer; it's a fascinating process. The Frail cells protect the Magic ones. Nava showed me in the Lab how the cells do it. The Frail cell enlarges with the prescription and then the excess bursts into the infected Magic cells and dissolves the Kyacin,' Rook said, on one of his many visits with Dinkletons.

'When that burst occurs, some of the Frail cells are taken into the Magic ones, and that is where the healing begins. Nava has been telling me, too,' Nicole said. 'Another reason we should not be called Frail.'

Rook and Dinkletons grinned.

'You will be pleased to know that Dex is a reinstated Dellamana and is creating his Tracer with his technique. But it won't be called a Tracer, as it does not have the same components and focus as the original Tracers. He's finished transcribing all the information about how Rustic act in the Frail Realm,' Rook said.

'What will it be called?'

'Dex has called it "Mikkel".'

'Ah, I love that. Did Rolte put a hold on Rogue in Frail Realm?' Nicole asked.

They dipped their heads. 'Only sanctioned Rogue will remain. That will give you time to find your feet.'

'What happened with sending Voltz to the Rustic Realm?'

Rook shook his head. 'We did send an elixir. That way they all benefit.'

Nicole believed that was fair. 'Volox was keen on being able to get to the Frail surface easily.'

'No way, not after what he did. His interfering has put him in the Prefect's bad books. Taking down a Thisbe – well, he is lucky he can't get to the surface. There is a warrant out for him,' Rook said and folded his arms. 'Taking Raisa's Illuminance was one thing, but what he did to Hamish is unforgivable.'

'Like Magic police?' Nicole asked, wide-eyed.

'As soon as he shows his face, he will be sent to prison for his part in Hamish's kidnapping and suffering.'

'I'm gathering it's a place for bad Magic?'

'Oh, yes. Can you imagine how horrible that place is and how difficult it is to keep order? Angry Magic are not easy,' Rook said.

Nicole shivered. It would only be a matter of time before Volox found himself there. He could not stay away from the Frail Realm.

'What elixir did you send?' Nicole asked.

'First, we had to sort out Volox. He was running Osiris like a self-appointed king, and that was because he had the Illuminance and Hamish. He kept most of the power for himself. Did everything he said, but only got small amounts of the Illuminance. Power made him mean and that made the rest of them so envious they became a race paralysed by hopelessness and longing.'

Nicole remembered the yellow dungaree Rustic and the beating Halfrus got that had been so unnecessary.

'So the elixir has been modified for Osiris by Nava, and her team in lab 1320 are sending it in stages.'

'What about the orange mist and sticky ground?'

'They will only receive medications to treat the symptoms of that environment. We can't take it out on the general population of Rustic what Volox had done. We can't change the world they live in, but we can offer a special medication, given out fairly to each individual Rustic.'

Nicole smiled and felt that the Rustic were fortunate. Hopefully it would make them less gloomy.

Shanazz and Zosmine came and brought delicious food and drinks and stayed long hours, explaining all the products Nicole would find in her room back home.

'Everything will be waiting for you,' Shanazz said. 'There will be clothes, shampoos, soaps, perfumes all made by Belba.'

'We have a surprise for you,' Zosmine said, with a wide grin.

'It is a Belba recipe,' Shanazz gushed.

Nicole dropped her mouth open. 'But I thought they were only for Orra?'

Shanazz waved a hand at her. 'You will have to grow your own food to make it exceptional. Now, with your skills you will be able to grow a few Orra veggies, like croze. You should never be deprived of this delicacy.'

Nicole hugged them, her eyes gleaming. 'Thank you, guys. I am going to miss you.'

'Nicole, don't forget your mood elevator,' Shanazz said.

53

'You're going home soon. I just know it.' Jinn jumped high on Nicole's bed and did two perfect somersaults, landing on her back in a very dramatic display.

Nicole smiled and put the book she was reading about treasures in the Vault down to focus on Jinn. 'You know we will always be friends, right? You can contact me on my palm computer, and we can do a visual every day.'

'You promise?' Jinn sat up, steam pouring out of her ears.

'How could I possibly lie to you, Jinn? You would know.' Nicole smiled.

'When will you be allowed back?' Jinn crossed her arms.

'They haven't told me, but soon, I hope. Don't light up on my bed, Jinn.' Nicole noticed tiny red sparks flying from the ends of her fingers.

Jinn jumped off the bed and shook her hands. Slowly, the sparks faded.

'Will you visual call me, also?' Strom rocked as he sat in a chair opposite the bed.

'I will not forget you, Strom.' Her face burnt, but she didn't care. Everyone knew they had a crush on each other; Marnie teased them relentlessly, Belba just smiled.

Jinn jumped from the other side of the room next to Nicole on the couch. 'I hate jealousy, it sucks.'

'Gosh, Jinn, that was lazy – you could have just walked the ten steps.' Strom shook his head.

'What happened to the fob?' Nicole asked for the millionth time.

Their faces told Nicole they hadn't even heard about it. 'Oh, we always miss out on the best news. You have to tell us now,' Jinn burst out.

'I didn't think it was a secret.' Nicole looked over to Dinkletons.

'It was chock-a-block full of Toxic fungi, but also had information of daily life, Rogue that visit, information on the containers. The information was written by a group close to Volox. They had one chance to get a message to Orra, to help them live a less painful life.'

'Now they have the Magic to restore them,' Nicole said.

'Volox is no longer bossing every Rustic around. He no longer has the power to. The elixir is spread to everyone. Nava has that control.'

'How do you know that?'

'Rogue have loose tongues.'

'We won't breathe a word, will we, Jinn?' Strom said.

Jinn zipped her mouth.

'I love the Frail Realm and I hope to be able to visit you there, once they forget about what happened with your neighbours.' Blue steam erupted from Strom's feet. Nicole watched it fly high until it reached the roof.

'We will be in touch,' Jinn said.

They got up and group-hugged. She felt Strom's soft kiss on her cheek. It was the loveliest feeling ever.

54

When Mahala and Jivan turned up in her room, she and Dinkletons knew that the time had come for her to go home. They shooed Strom and Jinn out, with much steam and verbal protests. Nicole laughed. Their rudeness was so bad it was funny.

Once seated, Mahala asked, 'How are you feeling?'

'I feel amazing; my colours are coming in slowly now and are settling. I have twenty-five steady colours that are growing more of my aura and Voltz.'

'Raisa has been bringing down the Tangle, and this will continue to reduce, together with the prescription on your Gloine.'

'How has she been able to do that? I haven't seen her?'

'She started the process immediately in the foyer when you arrived back from Frail Realm. Her colours sent vibes to your Voltz and, in turn, sent them to heal your Magic molecules. Her colours are the only thing that can dismantle the Tangle,' Mahala said.

'No wonder I'm feeling great.'

'Rook has been giving you lots of instruction on how to deal with Rogue, we heard,' Jivan said.

'I have a ton of things to learn.'

'You are aware of the ones that are the main cause of Frail issues – that's important,' Mahala said.

'Oh, yes, I know them.' Nicole thought of the hundreds she had already been made aware of. 'Scatterwhite and their cousins Waife from the Tent Realm, Puck, and those others in my kitchen better not return.'

'Absonsams were the ones in your house,' Jivan said. 'They are messy little beasts.'

'How is Raisa doing?'

'She's out of hospital and resting in her room. She has three solid colours in her Crystal and the plan is she will be back in the Frail Realm soon. She can continue removing the rest of the Tangle there.'

'I've spoken to her via my palm computer, and we are going to meet up.'

'Yes, we heard that you might,' Jivan said. 'You will be a great support for her.'

'Since I won't need too much sleep and need to work off the energy, I'm planning to help out as much as I can.'

'Excellent idea. Now, are you up for some news?' Mahala asked, shuffling back in her chair.

'You know that everyone present at the time of the Spark absorbed some Magic from Raisa?' Jivan asked.

Nicole bobbed her head in understanding.

'Jaya was in the kitchen and recorded an eight and a half percent Magic molecule grade. It is enough for her to be gifted; it has made her into a fine artist. Your mother and Aunt Dree were too old to absorb any,' Jivan said.

'Why does their age affect it?' Nicole asked.

'They have stopped growing, so it's like a closed door.'

'That is why she was able to absorb the purple arrow, as she has Magic molecules.' Mahala's voice was barely audible.

'Because Aunt Dree was pregnant with Lena and was in the room.' Nicole sat forward. 'And more Magical molecules went to the unborn, just like me.'

'Now, before you ask, Rolte is still investigating Lena,' Dinkletons said.

'But she has higher Magic than Jaya?' Nicole asked.

Mahala nodded. 'When we are certain of the numbers, we will send you a Rebo. A Thisbe has been assigned to her.'

'And me? Do I have a Thisbe as well?' Nicole smiled.

'When Hamish is well, he wants to be with you,' Jivan said.

'Thank you so much. I will treasure him.'

'Your first jobs are to help Raisa and nurture Lena,' Jivan said.

'Will I be allowed to come back to Orra?'

'You are Frail as well, and your parents need you, and you need them,' Jivan said.

'Yeah, I realise that.' Nicole looked down at her hands.

'Now you have a new life to focus on. We suggest you do just that. Know that anytime, Nicole, you can wedge in,' Jivan said. 'This is your Magic home. But use your hand computer and send us a Rebo first.'

'I've promised Jinn and Strom one every day.' Nicole smiled. 'It's great to be able to send messages from realm to realm.'

'You can telemute to us Prefects any business that comes up with Rogue,' Jivan said.

'How are my parents doing without the Rogue?' Nicole thought of the Hag and Knocker, her mind going to the worst-case scenario.

'We would like you to look after them and provide healing. They have deep wounds.'

'I thought Rolte was doing that,' Nicole said.

'Not anymore.' Jivan smiled. 'That's your job now.'

55

'Thank you for everything. I'm going to miss you both so much,' Nicole said. Her mouth quivered.

'You have come a long way. We are proud of you,' Rook said.

'We will not say goodbye,' Dinkletons said. 'We don't need to.'

'Will you go back to Vail?'

'I will make sure you are settled first, but yes, I will make a trip back home to see my family.'

Nicole, Dinkletons, and Rook wedged back to the Frail Realm. The wide portal streamed with colour, framed by the pink space of Orra. Nicole held onto the beautiful gold bag the Belba had sewed for her. Inside was a copy of the Vault book. It was only the size of her fingernail, but once it came out of the bag, it became large and heavy, with thick colours and gorgeous calligraphic writing. Nicole already treasured it.

'We will not be far away, Nicole,' Rook said. He took her hand and kissed it before they climbed high into the wedge and over a giant waterfall. Then she was dropped out of the wedge, landing on her feet outside her house, alone, without Rook or Dinkletons beside her. They had returned to Orra on the same wedge. The loss of them swept over her, but then her mother came out and rushed her inside.

Her dad, seeing her distortion, went into a panic. 'Oh, Nicole, darling, come sit.' He collected a blanket and placed it over her. He got down on his knees and held her aching hands. Nicole could tell that her father's Ripples had been removed; no longer could she see an angry face, and his normally pinched expression was replaced with soothing concern.

Her mother had her hands resting on her legs. 'Tell us what to do.'

'It will pass in a few minutes.'

Nicole waited for her wedge distortion to pass and thought of her new self from a Magical perspective. A Sape living in the Frail Realm would be an asset to Orra. Only sanctioned Rogue remained and Rolte had put a nine-month time ban for the rest. They hadn't let her know when she might return to Orra. Her Magical side already longed for it, but her Frail side was happy to be with her parents again.

'That is incredible,' she heard her dad say.

Her parents were wide-eyed as they watched the distortions disappear. They sat in an unnatural stillness, too afraid to move.

'How do you feel now?' her mother asked.

'I am Magical; I feel wonderful. I'm in charge of myself now, confident in what I must do. I don't want you to worry about me anymore. Lena and I will be friends, now that the relationship curse has been removed. Our family gatherings will make you guys happy from now on.'

They all laughed and hugged. She went up to her room after her parents, shattered from all the news, had gone to bed, cheerful for the future.

At first glance, her room looked to be the way she left

it. Her bed was unmade from her nap, clothes strewn after she had discarded them for Sara's party. Falling out of her dance bag, a water bottle, hair tie and towel lay on the ground. Her purple curtains were half-open. A half-full glass of water sat on her nightstand. The room was small, had only enough room for her bed and desk, and a built-in wardrobe on her left.

When she held her Crystal in the way Shanazz had instructed and looked through it, the room transformed into the same one she occupied in Orra, complete with wardrobe and inside/outside bathroom. It had the lounge room and the study piled high with dozens of books that had golden binding. The light coming from the figure-eight lamps were sent from Orra. When she let her Crystal go, the room didn't go back to its original form. How would others see it?

She walked over to her window and opened the curtains fully. Outside she saw Rogue who had been allowed to stay, the ones that did the Frail Realm and its people good. Now they moved with strong postures, knowing they did not have to deal with the interference of destructive Rogue. Nicole felt good for them; they also needed the break, not just Frail. Imagine if Orra was not there to manage all that survived in the Frail Realm? Nicole could not help wondering what the world would look like.

Out of nowhere, the air conditioner turned on. Before she could throw something at it, she heard a familiar tune. It was the same Magic music she heard in the hallways of Orra. On some level, they had always been with her.

She couldn't wait for tomorrow. She was meeting Lena, and when Raisa arrived, she would visit her. She jumped on her bed and opened up the nugget game.

ABOUT THE AUTHOR

Debbie Hofstetter is a proud mother and grandmother. She is never happier than when she is among family and sharing her love of stories with readers. *The Lost Sape* is her first novel with Shawline Publishing.

Shawline Publishing Group Pty Ltd

www.shawlinepublishing.com.au

SHAWLINE
PUBLISHING
GROUP